CU00781623

CONOR CREGAN
CHRISSIE

POOLBEG

A Paperback Original
First published 1992 by
Poolbeg Press Ltd
Knocksedan House,
Swords, Co Dublin, Ireland

© Conor Cregan, 1992

The moral right of the author has been asserted.

Poolbeg Press receives assistance from
The Arts Council / An Chomhairle Ealaíon, Ireland.

ISBN 1 85371 170 5

Cover photography by Gillian Buckley
Cover design by Pomphrey Associates
Set by Richard Parfrey in ITC Stone Serif 10/15
Printed by Cox & Wyman, Reading, Berks.

Conor Cregan was born in Dublin in 1962 and attended University College Dublin, where he graduated in History. He subsequently worked as a journalist in England and Australia. *Chrissie* is his first novel.

For Kay

PART I

THE WASTE LAND

CHAPTER ONE

When Chrissie Halloran was in first year at UCD, her father deserted the family. Joe Halloran had left Dublin and gone to London in the Fifties, made money as a sub-contractor there and married a nurse from Dundalk. Chrissie was born in London. In the Sixties, the Hallorans came back to Dublin and bought a house on Rathfarnham Road. I'm from that end of Rathfarnham and it's possible I played rugby against Chrissie's brother, Billy, when I was at Mary's and he was at Terenure, but I didn't know the family and I don't know anyone who did. In the early Eighties, Joe Halloran's sub-contracting business went bust. That was about a year before Chrissie went to college. They had to sell their house and go and live with Chrissie's grandfather in Dundalk, and Kay Halloran went back to work as a nurse. Billy was in the bank by then, and he stayed in Dublin. Joe Halloran suffered a mild breakdown after the collapse of his business and became depressive. He did some carpentry work around Dundalk when he could but he spent most of his time out walking. One day he walked off and didn't come back. There was a card from San Francisco but nothing after that.

In second year at college, Chrissie shared a house in Ballinteer with two girls in my class, Clare O'Reilly and Lisa Bryant. We were doing history, and Chrissie was doing languages. Clare was from Howth, and I'd been hanging around her since the middle of first year without anything happening between us. I can't say why nothing happened, except that maybe we were too shy. Clare liked to be around people and that could have been a factor too, though I can remember plenty of times when we were alone. She was beautiful in a classic way: golden hair swept back to her shoulders, golden-brown skin and green eyes. It was in the eyes though that she lost out to Chrissie. Chrissie's were sea-blue and warm, and on their own they were enough to make you fall in love with her. Chrissie didn't dress as well as Clare did, but bad clothes looked as good on Chrissie as good ones looked on Clare. She had this tatty combat jacket with torn sleeves which really used to throw me. Her hair was brown with a hint of red, which came out to dominate whenever the sun was shining, and her face was a happy face even though Chrissie wasn't much of a happy girl. Clare's face rarely looked happy, even when she was smiling and looking really beautiful. I tried hard not to compare the two of them in beauty;

there was no point.

Lisa was a little cherub from Cork, who spoke with an American accent because she'd lived in Virginia for about ten years. She had a crush on me, and I played along enough to make sure that if I got no one else I could always have her. Don't think I didn't like her, I did. But there were better, and it was all a matter of getting the best you could. Lisa was a reserve option.

Chrissie was big into Dramsoc at college, and one of the first times I saw her was playing Polly Garter in *Under Milk Wood*. It was a crap production. She was the best thing in it. But then I'm biased. She was going out with Charlie Shaw then. Charlie was doing law: a designer socialist who wore collarless shirts, braces and drab woollen trousers to pretend he was some kind of working-class hero. He got his socialism from magazines and wine bottles and wasn't interested in any causes that weren't at least a thousand miles away. He'd been to school with me, though we hadn't been very close, and we'd played freshman rugby together in first year. I think the only reason he was still hanging around with us was that he'd been to school with me and maybe I felt a kind of loyalty to him because of that. I'd really begun to tire of him. We'd exhausted all our school and rugby stories—though that never stopped Charlie repeating them—and apart from my passing interest in the L&H and his passion for its cliquish Dublin 4 politics, we didn't have too much in common. I put up with him because it was easier than getting rid of him. And I wanted Chrissie.

One Friday morning, we were sitting in the belly of the Belfield restaurant with Tony Bruton, another history head who worked on the same college magazine as me. Tony couldn't stand Charlie, and Charlie couldn't stand Tony, but that didn't matter to Tony as much as not being liked mattered to Charlie. Charlie was going on again about rugby at school, and I was sitting beside Clare and staring at Chrissie. Tony kept interrupting Charlie with sarcastic digs every few minutes. The rest of us were listening or pretending to listen because none of us had yet reached the stage where we would openly tell anyone else to shut up. Even Tony. His digs were the nearest any of us got. Anyway, Charlie was getting surplus mileage out of the celibates who'd herded us around any chance they got, to try and mould us into a cup-winning side. We never won anything, but that didn't stop them channelling their energy into rugby with the same zeal they channelled it into their faith. *I must take and give my pass at speed*. That was the first commandment, the greatest commandment. Driven into me with the chain of a bicycle lock on a

Wednesday afternoon when I'd been unlucky enough to be caught in breach of it. And I'd accepted it as my just punishment for having failed in my duty. Only at college did I begin to question it and by then it was only good as a funny anecdote.

I was staring deep into Chrissie's eyes and she was staring back. You know in moments like that when you're not sure if the other person feels the same or if you're just imagining it? Well there was nothing like that with Chrissie. I was sure. And when Clare got up to get more coffee, Chrissie winked at me and I winked back and we both smiled big broad smiles. Lisa saw it and her eyes opened wide and she moved her jaw back and forth, which only happened if Lisa was nervous. Chrissie winked at Lisa too. I threw my eyes down and picked up my cup and moved it about in my hand to take away the thin layer of skin which had formed on top. It was cold when I drank it. I held the cold coffee in my mouth and the cup to my lips so I wouldn't have to look up. Charlie asked me to confirm something but I wasn't listening. I nodded, and he went on without questioning me again, until he had to go to a tutorial. Tony threw his eyes up to heaven when Charlie was going and sighed loudly enough for Charlie to hear. I was looking at Chrissie again and wondering.

Chrissie must have dumped Charlie quietly before

the exams because I didn't hear anything about it till she'd gone to Geneva for the summer and I'd gone to America. I got a letter from Clare while I was working in the basement of a steakhouse in New York, telling me she was having a great time in this pizza place in Frankfurt and that she was thinking about skipping a year to stay on. And maybe she'd come over to the States if she had the money. The information about Charlie and Chrissie came at the end of the letter. One line. Chrissie haunted me for the summer. I went through an endless series of outcomes, all of them crass. And I came back from America early. Clare didn't stay in Frankfurt and Charlie was a bigger dick than when we'd left.

Our group began to loosen in third year. It never broke up completely but we didn't hang around each other as much. Chrissie moved out of Ballinteer and into a bedsit in Rathmines. Lisa slipped off my reserve list with a Commerce student beside the lake during the Fresher's Ball. I was in the bar at the time. Tony came in and told me. I must admit to some sadness. I ordered a whiskey chaser for my pint and pushed my way into a corner. I half expected Chrissie to come over, or Clare. Neither of them did. I slagged Lisa about her Commerce student for weeks after.

In the end, I kissed Chrissie out of frustration. It was somebody's party. I don't remember whose. After

Chrissie'd ditched Charlie, I guess I thought she'd come straight for me. We were still exchanging looks, long looks but nothing else. I was turning over inside. And I suppose I felt she owed me for Clare.

Thinking about that kiss always makes me feel good. It was a slow kiss, built up to over months, and we were alone in the room with Simply Red. The house was one of those redbrick jobs in Ranelagh, and the fire in the room didn't make much difference unless you were beside it. When the party was over, I asked her to bed, and she thought about it before refusing. We lay beside the fire all night under an old sleeping bag.

Ten days later, on a freezing night when the frost silvered the ground, we went out to dinner in town. We went back to her bedsit for coffee after and made love. I kept thinking we hadn't used anything and maybe she'd get pregnant. I didn't say that to her. I told myself it'd be okay. She might be on the pill or something like that. It took some of the romance away, but I suppose that's what happens when you begin to think clearly again. She told me it was her first time and I was glad because it was my first time too. I thought maybe she'd done something with Charlie but I didn't say that either. I was in love with her and I didn't want anything to spoil it. I told her I was in love with her, right after, when we were still breathless, and she said she loved me. It was a good feeling, being in love. I thought about how cold it was outside, and how warm it was in her bedsit, in her small bed, in love.

CHAPTER TWO

I t was a real time of came and wents. All the speed of a silent movie. Third year, exams, people. Flickering images on a screen. Caught in the shadowland between Eliot's idea and reality. Work— or the lack of it—was the catalyst and most people were going to go to London looking for it, because London wasn't too far away and Thatcher's empire was booming. That's what they told us.

Life seemed to be passing through the fingers like water, all insubstantial. A great empty hologram. We were all looking to hang on to something. When I think about it now it was a selfish time. And friendship didn't mean as much as it should. Everyone for themselves. Lifeboat mentality. None of us ever said it like that, but that's how it was. The Me Generation let loose on a country that couldn't cope with it: a red giant become white dwarf, heading for black hole.

We used to joke about having the best-qualified dole queue in the world. Real middle-class joke, that. Because we didn't really believe things were as bad as they were. And there was always somewhere abroad.

Designer emigration. Very fashionable. Most of us had families with just enough money to hide what was happening: we were only going to work abroad for a while, for experience, a big adventure, like going away to work for the summer. We'd be back, when we wanted and on our own terms. And if someone left college because they couldn't afford it any more—and they did—they were conveniently forgotten. A kind of conspiracy. If you keep quiet, it'll go away. Secrecy is easy in a secret conspiratorial whatever you say say nothing country. Fact was, we were first-worlders with first-world expectations living in a third-world shanty about to pay for a few years of a bright shining lie of economic prosperity. Bit of a shock finding out the bleeder was bleeding again. Being told we had to go. Like the others. That cheated feeling. So alone. Go on, get lost, you're sinking us.

Clare fired off applications to anything anywhere she could think of. She got nothing back and threw a wobbler in the bar one night because of it: she was high on something, and we got her out before she did any damage. Plans were pretty vague, like most of the people concerned, and they changed by the day. Lisa was going to the States, then China to teach English, then Florence because she liked the idea of living in Florence, then London to get some money together to do all of the above. It was damn hard to believe there was nothing for us at home.

And some of us were going to have to be dragged screaming. Jesus!

Why? For myself, I guess I was afraid. And proud. They often go hand in hand. Scared of losing what I knew. Fucked if I was going to be pushed around. Disinherited. I'd a pretty inflated impression of myself. Having Chrissie inflated it even more.

Charlie Shaw used to sit and watch Chrissie and me from the far end of the restaurant, at one of the window tables. From where we sat, at the wall opposite the stairs, he could have been a reflection in the glass. Charlie and I didn't meet much then, except for Fridays in Theatre L when I bothered to go to the L&H. He always made a point of sitting beside me, and I didn't mind that because I had Chrissie and I liked what that did to him and he hated it. Tony wrote a send-up of him in our magazine, and Charlie got narked over it and said he'd sue if Tony didn't apologise. That lessened his standing further. Tony refused to apologise, and Charlie didn't do anything about it, which was typical of Charlie. He had a complexion which went bright red when he was saying something he didn't mean. He was always red when he talked about suing Tony. Tony didn't give a shit anyway. He'd probably have loved the publicity. He liked to be known in college, and if I'm honest, that was one of the reasons I liked being around him. One of them. Maybe it helped me feel important. He was even cockier than me—there was a touch of coat-tail conceit in me—and by the time the cherry blossoms had spilled their petals all over the ground between the Arts block and the restaurant, we'd decided we were going to set up a news agency, start freelancing and expose everything there was to expose in Dublin. Better than going to London or somewhere else. Pathetic really, but we were cocky, like I said, and I didn't want to be another statistic. If things had been fine, I'd probably have pissed off immediately. That's me. Tony'd already done some work for *The Phoenix*, and that made us pretty confident. He did one great bit on Charlie because Charlie's dad was a pretty high-powered lawyer with a load of Fianna Fáil connections: Charlie used to tell everyone he'd once sold a fresher two oxo cubes as hash in the Belfield bar. Tony just told it like Charlie said. Charlie went ape over that. He knew it was Tony but he couldn't prove it.

The only one of us who shut up completely about after college was Chrissie. And I didn't bother talking to her about it. I didn't talk about anything like that with Chrissie. I didn't want it to end with her, not with everything else ending. I wanted her to stay with me, and I figured that if we talked about it, she might say something I didn't want to hear. So I avoided it. And she seemed to like it that way. I was happy to hear her say she loved me and to lie in bed with her. I'd think of something when the time came. Sometimes, in bed, I'd talk about what Tony and I had in mind, and she'd be enthusiastic about it. That helped. I didn't really want to question why she was, I was just glad of it.

Chrissie gave up studying early on and went heavy into acting. She paid for it with a third but by the time she found that out it didn't matter to her. She went through phases: around January, in the snow, it was *Dr Zhivago*. She tried to look like Julie Christie. She even dyed her hair blonde, but it looked so shit she wore a hat until she could get it all out. Then it was Liz Taylor in *Who's Afraid of Virginia Woolf*. And that was a real pain. Then it was Meryl Streep—and that really stuck: trying to talk with that Polish accent Streep used in *Sophie's Choice* and sounding more like Streep in *Out of Africa*. *I hod a farm in Awfrika*. She got a job in the Royal Marine as a waitress and used to pretend to the guests that she was from Poland, telling them she'd escaped during the martial law of 1981, leaving behind her family, married a German, then divorced him after he'd beaten her, and come to Ireland. And they believed her, or wanted to believe her, because even if you didn't believe Chrissie, you wanted to believe her.

The day after finals finished in September, Tony found an office in D'Olier Street. It wasn't much. We had two chipboard tables, a couple of portable typewriters, a radio and an old black phone. Tony put up a few posters on the bare walls to brighten the place up. It didn't work. We had a gas heater we turned on for half an hour every two hours when it was cold. If it wasn't cold enough to warrant the heater, we wore coats and mittens. He got hold of two girls from Trinity to help with the rent, Cathy and Anne. I can't say I ever got to know them much. Anne was the better of the two, and she had a sense of humour Cathy didn't. Tony hit it off with Anne. There might have been something going between them for a while. I never asked. I wasn't interested. We sent around letters and made phone calls to newspapers and magazines. Everyone was polite but that was about it. I don't know why we expected more. Like the whole world owed us something. For something we'd done or were going to do. Fuck.

Chrissie got involved in a theatre group with some of her Dramsoc friends who weren't my friends. So with me trying to get going in journalism and her doing that, we didn't have so much time together. I'd call into her place at night, especially when I'd had a bad day, and we'd sit up in bed doing lines from a play or watching a video on a machine she'd borrowed from this RTE fellow who was mad about her. She was into the old black and whites from the Thirties and Forties: Bette Davis, Joan Crawford, Barbara Stanwyck. She got heavy into *Random Harvest*. Ronald Coleman and Greer Garson. It did something to her. It was the kind of film Chrissie could have done without seeing. She said it was a fabulous idea, losing your memory and becoming someone else, just for a while, to lead another life, completely different from your own. She'd often disguise herself and go out on the street to see if anyone she knew would recognise her. Complete disguise. She'd put on different accents and ask directions. And back in her bedsit, she'd throw off the disguise and tell me she was a bitch, that she didn't care for anyone, that she didn't need the stage, that the whole world was her stage and everyone her audience and she had a star's contempt for it all and hated herself for it. That would usually end in tears with me holding her, wondering if what she was saying was how she felt or just another act.

"I love you, Liam," she'd say. "You know that. I'm just having a crisis. Chrissie crisis. I need to get noticed. You do too. You understand?"

Then she'd say something from one of those black-and-white films and burst out laughing.

Lisa was the first of our lot to leave. For London. On a Wednesday. We all got pissed in the Belfield bar the night before. I was too busy to get very worked up over her going. Like I said, it was a selfish time, and I was infected as much as anyone else. Lisa got all emotional and kept whispering in my ear how much she cared about me, which made me uncomfortable because I didn't care anything for her any more and I didn't want anyone else to hear her. She was off my menu if you like and didn't count much except as an acquaintance. That was pretty rotten. I regret it now.

I suppose I should have seen the Charlie thing coming. The way he was. But I wasn't looking out for it, and you don't see what you're not looking for till it's right up on you, and then it's too late. Dublin was almost always dark in my memory of those first weeks out of college, battleship-grey skies, drizzle in showers, miserable depressed streets. In the way childhood's all bright sunshine. Maybe that blurred my vision. Maybe, but I doubt it. Mostly it was that I didn't care about Charlie. And some of me resented him for having his dad's law practice to go into. A head start on the rest of us once he could scrape into Blackhall Place. And that meant something. There was a desperate urgency in life then. Mortality presented itself like the crack of a starter's gun. We were out and running, the clock ticking.

It was October and I hadn't seen him for maybe a month. I wasn't counting. My mind was full of Chrissie. I'd gone over to her place the day before, and she wouldn't let me in. And there was no key over her bedsit door the way there usually was. I'd sat outside for an hour, occasionally knocking at the door and calling her name in a subdued voice to avoid having the whole thing broadcast to everyone else in the building. I could hear *La Traviata* playing inside. That's how I knew she was there. Placido Domingo. It was low but I could still hear it.

Charlie caught me going through Stephen's Green, coming from a short chat about nothing at the *Sunday Tribune*. He must have planned it. He was standing on the stone bridge over the lake, throwing pieces of hamburger bun at the ducks. My eyes were sore and I only realised it was him when he turned and faced me.

"Liam!"

He looked slightly unsure when I stopped. His black hair was tossed, and he was stooping, a bit wasted. Charlie was bigger than me, broad and fit, but he looked smaller in that raincoat.

"Didn't see you there," I said. "What you up to?"

"Just in town."

"Right. Swotting?"

"Going to lunch?"

I thought about saying no, but he looked shit. The coat was stained and creased.

"Yeah. I can't stay long though. I've got to get back to the office. I thought you'd be buried in your books again."

"I amn't doing a tap."

People said that all the time. Usually the brainy ones. It was kind of a stock phrase, a catch-all introduction to small talk, and I didn't take much notice of it. Charlie wasn't brilliant, but he was better than me. We both got two ones, but his was better. Law. More points, you see. And I resented that, too. His false modesty bit annoyed me.

"You'll waltz through," I said. "Think of the poor bastards like me who have to work. Or take the boat."

"I'd have liked to have done something like that."

That was crap. In school he'd told everyone before the Inter that he was going to do law. He was always going into his dad's practice.

"And miss out on all that's waiting for you?"

"I was thinking of dropping out."

I stopped under the Dublin Fusilier arch, beside a punk with pink streaks in her spikes of hair and chequered patches in her leather pants. She had a skinny face and a pale boyish mouth. I looked at her a couple of times and then I stared right into Charlie's eyes. They were hollow, somehow drained, like a lake in drought.

"Don't be a fool. You've come this far. You can drop out when you're qualified. It'd be bloody stupid to do it now."

"Do you think I'm a fool?"

"No."

He put his hand on my shoulder.

"Do you think I'm a fool?"

The punk turned on the ghetto-blaster she had beside her.

I crossed the road without waiting for the lights, and Charlie followed me. We stopped at the other side.

"Do you?" he demanded.

"What do you want, Charlie? It's not Chrissie?"

"Do you love her?"

"What do you think?"

"She loves you."

"How do you know?"

"She told me."

"I didn't know you were talking."

Three kids came up to us from Grafton Street and shoved their hands up at us. The smallest didn't even reach my waist. They were dirty and wearing tracksuits and polyester jackets. I shook my head and walked down South King Street towards the Gaiety. I was as much a doorstep socialist as Charlie. Charlie pushed through them after me. They followed us and kept moving around us, still asking.

"Give us a few shillings."

Charlie told the biggest one, who was all freckles, to go away. They continued their routine, the pathetic monotonous give us a few shillings speech.

"Would you fuck off!" Charlie said.

The middle fellow put his hand up to my face. His eyes were crooked, his hands were thin, too long, and the veins stood out. The skin around the nails was chewed.

"Give us a few shillings."

I looked at Charlie, and we turned around and walked on.

"Fucking jammy cunts!" the biggest yelled.

Charlie turned around and lashed out at them with his foot. They retreated in a line.

"Now fuck off, you little shits!" he roared.

He was going after them when I grabbed him and pulled him back. His face was red.

"Leave them, they're only kids."

"Knackers. Shits. Check your pockets."

I did.

I didn't really care about the kids. I didn't want Charlie getting us into something we couldn't handle. He might have if I hadn't pulled him back.

We left them to their curses.

We had lunch in a small coffee shop near The Old Stand. The menu was chalked up on blackboards. The girl behind the counter wore a shiny synthetic uniform which was see-through if the light caught it a certain way. Her expanded belly pushed hard against the front of the uniform and pulled it tight against her wide fat buttocks. She filled our rolls with her bare hands and then washed her hands in a steel sink before ladling our mushroom soup into bowls. She had a vulgar engagement ring, and her arms were covered in thin black hairs.

Our table was small and varnished, and covered, except for the corners, with a red table-cloth. There was an imitation flower in a fragile vase in the centre of the table.

"I thought maybe I'd hitch around Europe or something," Charlie said.

"You're not still going on about dropping out. Look, if you want to do something like that, why don't you hitch to Capetown or Sydney, or somewhere like that. Europe's too easy. You have to have a little danger."

"You don't think I'm serious."

"I don't bloody care."

"You hitched around Europe."

"That was in first year. That was the time to do it.

I met this fellow from Birmingham going to Cape-town. Rob. Can't remember his second name. Doesn't matter. I suppose he's made it by now. Or he's dead."

"I had to work for Dad when you were doing that."

"No one forced you."

"Sure!"

"My heart bleeds for you."

"You don't give a shit, do you?"

"Too much on my mind. Any scandal? We're looking for business."

"Screw Bruton."

"Talk to Colette Lynch about that."

"Screw Colette."

"Too far away now. Look, what the hell do you want?"

"Just talking. Haven't seen you for a while. We're allowed talk, aren't we?"

"What about? Chrissie?"

"Whatever."

"You can be a trying little shit when you like, Charlie. Do you know that?"

"Look who's talking."

"Ask me a straight question, and I'll give you a straight answer."

"Do you love her?"

"Yes."

"That's pretty smug, pretty satisfied."

"It's the truth. I don't know what the fuck I'm telling you for."

"She just took me to dinner."

His eyes searched mine for a response.

"What do you want me to say?" I asked.

"Do you think you're cool?"

"No. I'm getting pretty pissed off at all this."

"She took me to dinner. That was it."

"And?"

"Doesn't it show you anything?"

"You're full of it, Charlie. It's none of your business. Thanks for your concern, if that's what it is. Is it?"

"Don't take the piss."

"What do you expect?"

"Can I ask you a question?"

"If it's not stupid."

"Have you screwed her?"

I wanted to have a go at him, but me being me, it wasn't the time or the place.

"Jesus, Charlie, you're being a real prick. I'm going back to work. Go annoy someone else. Give me some gossip if you have any."

"I was really into her."

"What are you telling me for?"

"So you'll know."

"Better to have loved and lost."

"That's a shitty thing to say."

"Talk shit and you get shit back. I'm going."

"Don't. I need to talk."

"Why me? You're fucking around, Charlie. Chrissie and me, well, you know, that's it."

"She's a pricktease, Liam. A pricktease. Know what I mean?"

"Fuck off!"

"Sorry!"

I stood up and wiped my mouth with a paper napkin.

"She is, though."

I tossed the napkin at him.

"I said, fuck off, Charlie."

He put his hand on my arm. Two men near us cast furtive glances at us and then returned to their conversation.

"Why don't you go off and get pissed, Charlie," I said. "Go and get completely out of your head. Then you'll forget all about it. I've got to get back to work. We're not all going into daddy's office. I have to work for a living, and it isn't easy."

I moved to the door, and he almost tripped over one of the small varnished stools around the small varnished tables in the coffee shop. The girl with the see-through uniform grinned.

Charlie caught up with me at Switzers. He swung me around.

"Listen, Liam, I'm sorry about what I said. I got carried away. We'll forget it. I'll see you at Clare's. You and Chrissie going? You are going?"

"Maybe."

We were going. Clare was flying to London in the morning. We were going.

"I've got to go, Charlie. I'll see you. And don't drop out. The world turns. Have that drink. I'll see you."

I didn't wait for him to say anything more.

CHAPTER THREE

I wasn't going back to work. I made my way up Grafton Street, through the human cholesterol of early afternoon. Charlie must have known where I was going. I didn't care. My reflection changed with each shop window, all different shapes of me. At the top of Grafton Street, I stopped looking at myself and turned my eyes to a couple standing in the middle of the street, holding one another around the waist, and I had a need to be held by Chrissie, and loved.

I walked over to Harcourt Street, with Charlie at the back of my mind and Chrissie at the front. The sun broke through the clouds when I was halfway up Harcourt Street, and the colours of the day changed from Charlie colours to Chrissie colours. I was happier. I hoped it would stay that way and she'd let me in this time. When I was inside, Charlie could have the day.

Chrissie wasn't in. Or if she was she wasn't letting me in again. Maybe she was at work. I couldn't remember. I hadn't seen her in four days. No, six. There might be a key over her door. I just had to find someone to let me in the main door. I rang three bells and waited. A young man, unshaven, opened the door. He was barefoot, and his shirt was open and hanging out. I wondered if I'd disturbed him at anything, or maybe he was only sleeping. His face looked swollen, and his eyebrows met in the middle.

"Sorry," I said. "Just want to see if someone's in."

He'd already turned his back on me and was going through an open door to my right, scratching his head. There was a black-and-white poster of Sting on a cupboard inside the door. I didn't see anything else before he shut the door. There were letters and cards scattered all over the hallway, so I crouched down and took a look to see if there was anything for Chrissie. Maybe a postcard I could read. I wouldn't open her letters then, but I'd read a postcard if there was one lying around. There was nothing. I went to the door of her bedsit and reached up to the frame. The key was there this time.

The bed was the best place to sit in her bedsit. It took up most of the space. I poured some water in a pot and boiled it for coffee on her stove. The stove served as a heater too. It was pretty good at heating the bedsit in winter. It didn't need to be heated in the summer, except maybe some nights. Chrissie had her books and folders on a small table at the end of the bed. There was a mirror too, and it had a hand-

cream stain on it and a crack running down one side
of it. And there was a basket of dried flowers. She had
dried flowers all over the place. There were some
pinned to the walls and others in jamjars on the
wardrobe. They looked fine but they left a terrible
mess when the petals started to come off. Sometimes
we woke up covered in petals. Along one wall, in
between the flowers, she had sketches and water-
colours of birds. She was a really good artist. She'd
done sketches of me but they were on top of the
wardrobe.

The water was splashing over the side of the pot
and spitting on the element. I watched the bubbles
try, furiously, to climb over the edge, but they never
managed. The odd splashes which made it out were
vaporised by the element. I took the water off and
turned off the stove. The coffee was in a small press
over the stove, and the sugar was beside it, in paper
sachets taken from restaurants and coffee shops. Her
cups and plates were from the Belfield restaurant.
She used to empty whole trays of the stuff into a big
leather bag she always carried, and walk out. She
took far more than she needed. Every time she did it,
I'd shit myself, thinking we'd be caught.

I reached under the sink for the small carton of
milk she kept there. She had no fridge, and that was
the coolest place in the bedsit. Sometimes it wasn't

cool enough, or she had a carton there too long. I put my nose to the carton and sniffed. I shook it around and looked inside. It seemed fine. I poured a drop into my coffee. It didn't coagulate. I poured some more, and it mixed, white streaks in the black, then brown, then milky brown. I stirred it with a spoon which lay in the sink and took a book of poetry from the table.

Three books later my cup was half empty and I was stuck on Gerard Manley Hopkins. I heard the main door open and slam shut, then the sound of rushing feet and bicycle wheels.

Chrissie.

She stuck the bicycle under the stairs, probably scratching the white paint and splintering the wood. There were loads of scratches under the stairs where she kept her bicycle. It didn't matter much, the paintwork was shoddy. Her key clicked twice in the door of the bedsit, and she pushed the door open wide and thrust herself in. She stopped dead when she saw me.

"Hello, you," she said.

She always greeted me like that if we met and she wasn't ready. She shifted nervously for a few seconds and closed the door without looking behind her.

"How long have you been here?"

"About half an hour."

She took her long woollen cardigan off, threw it on the bed, knelt down beside me and kissed me. Her kiss tasted good, and I took her face in my hands and held it tight. Her face was cold, and it made the kiss better touching her cold face.

"I've been up the mountains," she said, breaking away from me. "I was going to call into your office. I thought you'd be out."

"I was. Where'd you go?"

"Glencree."

"No work?"

"Day off."

"Well for some."

"I deserved it."

"Did you?"

"What's that supposed to mean?"

"Nothing. Why wouldn't you let me in yesterday?"

She shrugged.

"It hurt."

"Sorry."

She put on a Greta Garbo voice.

"I vant to be alone."

"I needed you."

"Just drop it, Liam."

Her tone was harsh. I obeyed.

"Glencree was beautiful," she said. "I walked around the German cemetery. It's very peaceful."

"I saw Charlie at lunch," I said.

"What for?"

"He came up to me in Stephen's Green."

"You still friends with him?"

"Not really. You?"

"Jesus, no. Is he coming tonight?"

"Yeah."

"I haven't seen Charlie in yonks. He sent me a birthday present. And a stupid card."

"You never said."

"Should I have? It was a book. Yeats. I'll show you if you like."

I put my hands around her waist and she pushed me off. Charlie's pricktease. No. He was a dick. Why listen to his shit? We were here and now, and that was fine. Charlie was a pain. I reached out for her again. She didn't stop me this time.

"I missed you," I said.

"We saw each other a couple of days ago."

"No, we didn't."

"Well, a few days ago."

"Six."

"Do you count? I hate it when you're like that."

I tossed her hair.

"Still missed you."

"Don't go all sludgy."

"I love you."

I kissed her.

"Love me?"

She smiled. It was a deliberate smile, part scorn, part affection, all beguiling. She didn't like to be forced. She had to control. When I forced, she fought.

"Want another coffee?"

"I said I love you."

"I heard."

"Well, do you love me?"

She sighed and raised her eyes to heaven.

"Yes—yes, I love you. Do I have to keep saying it? You know I love you. I sleep with you, don't I?"

"Is that a sign of love?"

"It is for me. I wanted to be alone this year. Why do you think I took this place? Look, Connolly, do you want coffee?"

"I want you to say you love me without me asking you."

"I can't now, you've asked me. Let's have a coffee."

"Why does it always have to be a game? You make fun of me, you know."

"I don't mean to."

"Don't you want to love me?"

"It's going to end, you know."

It was the first time she'd ever said anything like that. Direct. I hesitated before replying.

"Maybe."

"Yes."

"You telling me something? I love you."

She poured water in the pot and turned on the stove.

"You say it so easily."

"Does that lessen it?"

She shrugged.

"I love you."

"You keep saying that, like that's all that's needed. Say I love you and everything's fine. Say I love you and Chrissie will jump in the sack."

"I do. And it's not to get you into bed."

"Okay. I love you. I don't want to talk about it any more. Want to go to a film? We'll get a *Press* down at the Swan Centre. What's on in the Stella?"

I pulled her to the bed.

"Love you, Chrissie."

She closed her eyes and blew at me.

"Groan!"

"Don't mock."

"Don't be so sensitive. What would you do if I was pregnant?"

My mouth suddenly went dry.

"What?"

"See! No more love."

"Are you?"

"No."

"Why'd you say that?"

"To show you. So shut up."

"Bitch."

"Love."

I kissed her and she responded and we held it until the water began to spill over the edge of the pot.

"The water's boiled," she said.

Our lips were still touching.

"I'm boiling too," I said.

"Phallus."

She pushed me off and turned off the element.

"Sure you won't have another cup?"

"Chrissie!"

"Look at you. Tuck your shirt in. Work first, then down to Chrissie for sex. That's it, isn't it? I bet if you'd work you wanted to do, you wouldn't be here."

"That's not true. Why do you have to trivialise everything? You know it's not like that."

"Do I? All we ever seem to do is make love when you're here."

"Is that wrong?"

"Ask your mother."

"I'm asking you."

"No, I suppose it isn't. I'm sorry, I'm in a mood. Chrissie crisis. I should have a sign on the door. I'm scared—of you. I love you and I'm afraid of you.

Don't ask why. I want to see a film. I need my fix."

"Come here."

"Is this where we make love and everything's okay?"

"No. This is a hug. We haven't hugged properly yet."

"You're a shit, Connolly."

She made coffee for herself and took a drink. Then she put her cup down on a book at the corner of the table. A tear of coffee ran down the cup and stained the book cover. She sat down and tucked herself in close to me.

"Rub my neck," she said.

I massaged her neck with my thumbs.

"You smell nice."

"Perfume."

"It's nice. You're nice."

She turned around and kissed me.

"We could make love if you like."

"It's nice like this. Let's stay like this. If we make love then we make love."

"Okay. That's good. Right up under the skull. And do my head. Think we'll be doing this next year?"

I didn't want to answer. I didn't want to think about it.

"What do you think?"

"Feel like getting out of here. I can't stand this

place any more. Billy got beaten up."

"What?"

"He owes this guy a load of money. I think his nose is broken. I hate this place. Feel like getting out of here. I do."

"Where?"

"Wherever. It won't be the same, you know. Not like before."

My heart beat faster and my throat got drier.

"Yeah. That scare you?"

"Bit. You?"

I nodded.

"I want you to stay here."

"For what?"

"For me."

"Shut up, Liam."

We didn't speak again for ten minutes. We lay in each other's arms, face to face. I was fighting off a kind of selfish fear which was attacking me. It was a subdued fear, eased by distance, and I managed to conquer it and bottle it up. My selfishness became love and returned to selfishness several times, and when we made love it was because we both wanted it. The emotional pressure made it so that we could not do anything else. It was not skilled, and the physical pleasure was not as important as the being together, and we almost fought against the climax because the climax would mean it was over, and we could not be so close any more.

CHAPTER FOUR

We went to *Top Gun* in town and then bought kebabs and ate them in her bedsit. Chrissie was supposed to be a vegetarian, and when she was in the mood she made a big thing about eating meat and used to yell at me if I wanted to eat it; but if she wasn't too pushed she'd eat it so long as it wasn't dripping blood like a steak. Afterwards, we had a shower together and made love. Then she threw a sweater on and a pair of jeans and brushed her hair back and tossed it a bit and looked beautiful. She didn't need me to tell her she looked beautiful but I did anyway because I couldn't let it go without saying something, and anyway Chrissie would have said something if I hadn't. As it was, she told me it didn't mean anything, me telling her she looked beautiful, that it was all superficial, that it didn't last, that she didn't think she was good-looking at all, not as good-looking as Clare, that if all I was interested in was how good she was looking any particular time then my interest was shallow and she hated shallowness. It didn't take away from how good she looked.

I'd said I'd meet Tony in The Castle Inn in Rathfarnham village. So Chrissie and me got a 15A to Terenure, walked back to my house, got the car and went up to the pub. I don't know who the fuck told Charlie we were going there first. It was amazing how that bastard always managed to turn up when he wasn't wanted. Like a groin rash. He was sitting in the corner, to our right as we approached the bar, staring at a Guinness, and there was no way we could avoid him.

"Oh, God!" Chrissie whispered to me.

"You're late," Charlie said.

He smiled.

"You were supposed to be here at half eight. It's a quarter to nine."

He looked at his watch and laughed.

Fucking leech, I thought.

"Long time no see, Chrissie," he said.

"Hi, Charlie."

He took her hand and kissed it.

"Ravishing," he said.

"Shut up, Charlie," Chrissie said. "Don't be stupid."

"It's true. I only speak the truth. Amn't I right, Liam?"

I didn't answer.

"Ravishing," he repeated.

"Are you going to buy me a drink?" Chrissie asked

him.

"Sure. What? Liam?"

"Lager," I said.

"Tequila," Chrissie said.

"Tequila it is."

Charlie stood up.

"Don't go away," he said.

Maybe he thought we would. His breath belched beer.

"I didn't ask him," I said when he'd gone to the bar.

"Doesn't matter. Just ignore him. We'll go as soon as Tony gets here. He looks paler."

"Who?"

"Charlie."

"He's pissed."

"He can buy us a couple of drinks. He's rich enough."

He came back with our drinks, and salt and lemon for Chrissie and another Guinness for himself.

"Still here," he said. "You look great, Chrissie. Doesn't she, Liam? I can't get over it. It's been a while. I've been busy. Blackhall Place. Did Liam tell you I was thinking of dropping out? I'm getting sick of studying. Maybe go hitch-hiking. Around Europe or somewhere. Maybe Asia or Africa. Bit of danger."

He downed the rest of his first pint and then half

the other, and we let his words pass us by with the
time and watched for Tony.

"Like another?" he asked.

"We haven't touched these yet, Charlie," I said.

He looked at his watch.

"Only so much drinking time," he said. "Got to
get as much down as possible."

He'd taken my advice. I wondered what was going
on in his brain.

There was a silence.

Then he said it again.

"Jesus, I can't get over how good you look,
Chrissie."

He touched her leg, and she pulled away from
him.

"Would you get off, Charlie," she said.

"But it's true."

"We've heard it, Charlie," I said.

"Can't I compliment the best-looking girl around?"

He put his hand on hers.

She moved hers, rubbed some salt on it, licked it,
knocked back her tequila and then put the slice of
lemon to her lips.

"Great, Chrissie," Charlie said.

She raised her eyes to heaven.

I don't think he saw it.

"Listen, we must have dinner, Chrissie," he said.

"Maybe the three of us. That'd be nice. Have a chat. Haven't seen you for ages. We could go to—what was that place we went? Never mind."

He drank the rest of his pint.

"And Clare's off tomorrow. Another one bites the dust."

"You might get a dose of the shits if you go to Asia, Charlie," Chrissie said.

He laughed out loud and touched her leg again.

Chrissie's mouth tightened.

"I'm going to powder my nose," she said.

She didn't wait for him to comment.

I took a long drink to avoid having to speak.

"She's pretty catty," Charlie said.

"Don't have any more drink, Charlie."

"What are you, my nursemaid?"

He called over a waitress instead of going up to the bar himself and ordered three of the same. I said I didn't want another yet, but he ordered anyway.

Where the fuck was Tony?

Charlie'd downed another three pints of Guinness when Tony finally came. Chrissie and I had three full drinks before us on the table. Tony's hair was wet and he was carrying a blue sports bag. And whatever about us not wanting to meet Charlie, he definitely didn't. Even pissed. Charlie got nervous when Tony came. He nodded at Tony, and Tony nodded back and offered to buy a drink. We refused. Charlie accepted. Tony called the waitress.

"Sorry I'm late," he said to me. "They spiked my fucking feature. I did four days on that. Then they say they can't use it. Bastards."

"What was it on?" Charlie asked.

Tony didn't answer. The little waitress, whose cheeks were rosy, was back with a lager for him and a whiskey for Charlie. He paid her and took a big gulp of his drink.

"It was on car thieves," I said to Charlie. "He was interviewing car thieves. Joy-riders too."

"I got one guy who was eight. He was great. And they spiked it."

"If at first you don't succeed," Charlie said.

"What's that supposed to mean?"

"You know, try try again."

"When's the last time you had to fucking try?"

"I always do, Mr God Almighty Bruton."

"Money, Charlie," I said. "It all boils down to money. No print, no pay. I've done one story in the last month. Small bloody effort. We've got rent and phone and stuff."

"Well, there's always London. Plenty of company."

He burst out laughing and dribbled beer on the table.

"Better than here," Tony said.

He took a drink and slammed his glass down on the table.

"It's only one story," Charlie said.

"Drop it, Charlie," I said.

"Oh, I'm not allowed speak. Not allowed say how good Chrissie's looking and not allowed tell Mr God Almighty Woodward and Bernstein Bruton here he's making a mountain out of a molehill. You two think you're special. It's not fucking Watergate. Just some bloody joy-riders."

The truth in his words made both of us more angry. For a moment I thought Tony was going to ram his glass in Charlie's face.

Chrissie stepped in. I knew it was deliberate, and Charlie knew it was deliberate, but he couldn't say anything.

She tipped her drink all over his crotch. It got him right dead centre, and he jumped up and tipped what was left of his own pint all over himself too. Tony giggled, and Chrissie put on an apologetic voice and said how stupid she was, that the tequila must have affected her more than she thought. Charlie just cursed.

"There's a hand drier in the men's," I said. "Try and dry them under that."

"I'll have to take them off. I can't do that. I'll dry them in Clare's."

"Look at the stain, Charlie," Chrissie said.

His trousers were dark but the stain still showed.

"Looks like you've pissed yourself," Tony said.

"Fuck up, Tony," Charlie said.

"Dry them in the toilet, Charlie."

"You come with me. I'll take them off and go in the cubicle, and you dry them."

I looked at the other two. Tony winked at me.

"Okay."

We went in the men's, and Charlie fell over getting out of his trousers, and I had to help him up because he was legless. I put him sitting on the toilet and closed the cubicle door. Then I started drying his pants. He talked to me through the door.

"Chrissie's really looking lovely, Liam, isn't she?"

"Lay off, Charlie."

"Why?"

"Just lay off. I know what you're doing."

"Scared I'll get her back."

Two fellows came in to take a piss, so I couldn't reply. They smiled when they saw what I was doing.

"I'm making headway," I said when they'd gone.

"What?"

His voice was dulled.

"With your pants. Stain's reduced."

"Yeah."

"You okay?"

"Chrissie's lovely, isn't she? Shit, my head feels weak. I'm ratarsed. You told me to get ratarsed, so I did. You didn't go to work this afternoon. What was it like?"

"Ah, fuck off, Charlie."

"Fuck you. Fuck—"

I heard the sound of his head hitting against the wall of the cubicle. An old man came in, pissed, coughed a lot and combed his hair with a silver comb. Then a fellow who looked embarrassed. He tried to get in the cubicle. I told him there was someone inside. He left.

"Charlie, they're ready," I said when his trousers were as good as I could get them.

There was no answer. I knocked on the cubicle door. Still no answer. I threw the trousers over the door.

"Come on, Charlie, put them on."

I pulled myself up over the door. He was leaning against the wall, asleep, threatening to fall over. His pants were over his head. I jumped down. What the fuck? I thought.

"See you, Charlie," I said.

I went and got Tony and Chrissie, and we left.

CHAPTER FIVE

I figured Charlie would still be unconscious when they went to close the pub, that maybe no one would find him, that maybe he'd be there all night, only waking up when his head fell in the bog. We laughed about it while I drove up to Ballinteer. And I was happy we laughed about it because it meant we had a kind of unity, and that was what I wanted. At least Charlie had some use.

Clare was flying when we got there, on a false going away high, hiding an underlying depression. She had to be excited, I guess, there wasn't much else for her to do. Chrissie hit her with a dose of Meryl Streep, and she responded with an equally bad Scarlett O'Hara. They pissed about with each other and anyone else they could find to listen to them. Clare insisted I sit with her for a while, holding her hand, and Chrissie didn't seem to mind. I minded. I minded because Clare was looking gorgeous and I didn't want to want her or have Chrissie thinking I wanted her. It's awful when you're with someone you adore and someone you care a little less for but not so much that it makes a lot of difference when they're holding your hand and you're drinking. It made me want to take Chrissie and get out of that house, get away where there was nothing threatening us, where I could be sure. But that wasn't going to happen, so I had to smile and pretend I was enjoying myself when, in fact, I was about to explode.

Tony got on better than me. Probably only because he wasn't with anyone. It's great not being with anyone—no, it's not. But I wish it was. Anyway, he was pissed and pissed off and except for kissing Clare and giving her a big hug, he didn't speak to anyone much because he'd that story on car thieves he'd done a load of work on on his mind. He sat by the Heineken keg in the kitchen and drank and poured pints and messed with the cooler. At least he was having things turned down at the last moment. I don't suppose he saw it that way.

Don't ask me how Charlie got there. I couldn't believe it when I saw him. Like seeing gangrene reappear. He didn't come near any of us, and I figured he was sore about what had happened. I was going to go up to him but then I thought, fuck it, if he doesn't want to know me, then that's fine with me. That was what I wanted. His trousers had the faint outline of a stain. He went back into another room and I thought he'd done it to avoid us altogether and that he'd stay out of our hair all night. The place was black with people at that stage and it would have been easy to get lost. Get lost, Charlie.

It didn't work out that way. Clare disappeared to welcome some more people and Chrissie said she was going into the kitchen to dance on her own. I said I'd come with her, but she said she wanted to do it on her own. That pissed me off. That's when Charlie came up to me. It was brief.

"I suppose you thought you were being funny," he said.

"You were out of it. I called you."

"Like fuck."

"I did. Ask Chrissie."

"Piss off."

"Piss off yourself."

"You're a—"

"What?"

He turned and walked off.

I was left ready for something that hadn't happened.

Next time I saw him, about an hour later, he was lying on a couch in the sitting room with this girl who had straight jet black hair, straight like it had been separated strand by strand, black like beauty. She wasn't a pretty girl otherwise. Her face was too long. Gaunt too. And the lipstick wasn't right. She wore a short dress and you could see where she'd shaved near the ankles if you were inclined to look. I wondered if he was talking to her about Chrissie. Every so often he'd throw a glance at Chrissie, who was back from dancing and sitting with a new audience, and at me if I wasn't quick enough to avoid him.

Chrissie was trying on her Streep thing with everyone. I tried to get her to pack it in, but she said she was enjoying it and I shouldn't be such a stuffed shirt. Clare kept introducing her as a Pole. She was already drinking champagne and smoking dope, and Chrissie made it easier for her to let go. She loved Chrissie when Chrissie was acting. She once told me they used to stand in front of the mirror when they shared and put on faces for each other: pain, love, joy, sadness, all night sometimes. I wished I could have gotten into it. I just couldn't. Maybe Chrissie was right: I was too strait-laced. I didn't care much. She was going to go over to Charlie and his woman and do it on them but I stopped her. I don't know why.

Then Clare went upstairs with this fellow I didn't know. That happened out of nowhere and it shouldn't have hurt. But it did and I felt rotten. There were a couple of times I was going to leave but I couldn't. So I drank and watched Chrissie and wished she'd give up what she was doing and come and be with me.

Charlie and his bird went at each other on the couch, him with his hand up her skirt, her with hers down his trousers, basically pulling him off. I'm not a prude but they could have had the decency to go somewhere private. No one wanted to see them. She was making noises as low as she could, and he was taking these deep breaths, but we could all hear, even under the score of conversations. Eventually, it became part of the decor—Charlie and your woman humping each other in front of us—and it got ignored. Until the crowd started thinning out.

Tony started everything, even though he was too bottled to know what it was all about. And he probably didn't care. Anyway, it was about three, and there weren't many people left, and most of those that were were in the sitting room, on the floor, talking. Tony wandered in from the kitchen, maybe because there was no one much left in the kitchen or maybe because Wham were playing. It was a thing with Tony that he wouldn't stay in the same room where Wham were playing. He could have switched off the record and anyway you could still hear it in the sitting room. It was stupid but maybe Tony wanted to make something of it and be seen to be making something of it. Who knows what else was going on in his brain. I was talking to this fat cousin of Clare's over from

London. He was working in the City and was dying
to tell someone how well he was doing. His accent
was a bit affected for someone who'd only been over
there a few months but I gave him my ear anyway.
Tony sat by the brick fireplace, holding half a pint of
lager and opening his shirt. He made an attempt to
get into our conversation but gave up, probably
because he wasn't that interested. I lost sight of him
for a while. Next thing I knew he was trying to sit
down beside Charlie and Charlie's girl. They were
both lying immobile across the couch. Tony went to
move Charlie's girl's legs.

It happened quick the way these things do, so that
when they've happened you're not sure if they have
even though you know they have. Charlie lashed out
at Tony and caught him in the face with his boot.
Tony fell back against a bookcase behind him and
dropped his glass on the floor and pulled a few
encyclopaedias from the bookcase down on him.
There was silence. You could have heard a fly fart.
Tony was moving in a rubbery slow motion,
bewildered almost. His lip was bleeding and the blood
was running down to his shirt. He reached up and
put his fingers in the blood and looked at his fingers
as if to check he was right. Then his expression
changed. It became hard and angry like I'd never
seen it before. He picked up his glass and threw it at

Charlie, missing Charlie and smashing it against the wall behind him. Charlie's girl, whose name I never got, screamed a muted scream. Tony was already at Charlie's throat. They fell over clumsily on the floor, neither of them able to get a good dig in. The rest of us in the room were in a kind of suspended animation, as if watching something somewhere else. Chrissie must have moved sometime around then, because before I knew it she was pulling them off each other, roaring at them that they were ruining the party. I followed her and others followed me. I pulled Tony off Charlie just as Tony was about to give Charlie a knee in the balls. His knee caught me in the ribs instead and I groaned, more in shock than pain. The fat fellow I'd been talking to and a couple of others were helping Chrissie with Charlie at this stage.

"He's a fucking twat," Tony yelled.

I rammed him up against the bookcase and pinned him to it. The next five minutes were a slagging match. Three years into five minutes.

"Fucking pickled bollocks," Charlie said.

Ultravox were filtering through from the kitchen. "Vienna."

"Go in the kitchen, Charlie," I said.

"Why the fuck should I?"

"Because I'm telling you."

"Cunt!" Tony said.

"Shut it," I said. "Get in the kitchen, Charlie."

"Fuck off. Take his side. He started it. Why the fuck take his side? Fucking Bruton and Connolly. Close as two queers in a single bed."

"Get out, Charlie, or I'll belt you myself."

Chrissie slapped Charlie across the face.

"Shut the fuck up," she said. "Bastard!"

Tears were filling her eyes.

"Yeah, it's all my fucking fault. Fucking Bruton's out of his head. You're a bitch, Chrissie. Treat me like shit. Think everyone'll suck up to you. He threw a fucking glass at me. Fuck you, Chrissie."

She kicked him in the shin, and Charlie cried out and went down on one knee, gripping his shin with his hands.

"Fucking bitch!" he roared.

He grabbed her by her sweater and threw her across the room, ripping a piece from the sweater. She cracked her head against the wall, loud enough to hear. As soon as she'd hit the wall, his face changed from rage to fright. He was terrified.

I exploded. I have no explanation except that I wanted to hit Charlie and I didn't care who was watching. I booted him and caught him in the backside and sent him sprawling across the coffee table. An ashtray smashed under his weight when he fell on it. Then I was on top of him. It was as if every

frustration I had could be exorcised by beating the
fuck out of Charlie; like Charlie didn't really exist
except for me to beat the fuck out of him. So I hit
him in the face again and again, watching the blood
spurt from his nose and his face contort under my
blows and not feeling a thing or knowing that I'd
bruised my hands or strained my finger hitting him.
It was a few seconds though it felt like forever.

Then Charlie rooted me one between the legs and
I felt like I'd been stuck with a poker. I tumbled off
him in fierce agony, that shocking pain you get in
the abdomen when you've been kicked in the balls
taking my breath away. People were trying to get us
away from one another, but we were gone beyond
being controlled without hurting others. Tony came
behind Charlie when Charlie was trying to kick me
in the stomach. He threw himself on Charlie's back
and shoved Charlie into the door. As Charlie went
over, Tony punched him in the kidneys. Charlie
screamed in pain and buckled up beside the door.
Tony kicked him in the stomach and the balls, and
I lashed out at him with my fists, belting him across
the face and in the balls too. He screamed and curled
up. Tony was going to boot him again when three of
the spectators got hold of him and pulled him away,
cursing.

It ended not because they pulled him off but

because none of us had any energy to go on. Fighting takes a hell of a lot of energy. And the whole thing couldn't have lasted more than a couple of minutes start to finish. I was in fucking agony, and winded. We all backed off, and it was remarkable how we managed to disappear around the house, and the party just kept rolling along to its finish. I suppose that's humanity, or our brand of it anyway. Just goes to show you how much of an impact you really make on the world. Know when you're young and you think the whole world's watching your every move, only waiting for you to do something wrong? Well do something like have a fight at a party and see who really cares enough to notice five minutes later. As I said, it was a time of came and wents.

I got Chrissie up to the bathroom and took a look at her head. There was a bump but she wasn't feeling it too much. I'd got my breath back. My left index finger was hurting like hell. From when I'd hit Charlie. I couldn't move it. Chrissie ran downstairs and got some ice from the fridge, and we put the ice on the finger to stop it swelling too much. It didn't stop the swelling. Tony's lip was up like a balloon and there was blood all over his shirt and on my jumper. We didn't speak very much. There was some sense of shame for what had happened, and none of us wanted to say it. Clare came along kind of upset and kind of confused, and maybe a bit too drunk and high to make up her mind which, pinning up her hair, all apologetic for asking Charlie, saying what a dick he was and that she'd only asked him out of pity and that she'd gotten rid of him with her brother, and asking was Chrissie's head all right. Charlie seemed to be the fall guy for the whole incident, someone everyone disliked, and he'd hit Chrissie and hitting a girl was something you didn't do. Clare dabbed Chrissie's head with TCP.

The fellow Clare'd gone upstairs with came along and asked if everyone was okay, could he help? Clare dismissed him abruptly. He looked completely lost, and Clare made him feel like he should find a hole and jump in it. And you know what? I was glad she'd done it. I think we all were. He was an intruder.

And when he'd gone downstairs, Clare turned to me.

"Where'd he come from?" she asked.

I gave a shrug of ignorance.

She made a face.

When everyone else had gone, we sat in the kitchen and played old Seventies singles and drank hot chocolate and ate almond slices, an old ritual. Clare sat in the middle of the floor and flicked through a photograph album. Chrissie did a sketch of us in crayon and then made me dance with her when she knew I didn't want to dance with her. Tony just conked out in a chair with his hot chocolate still in his hand. He couldn't drink it with his fat lip.

Clare started crying at five.

"Eight hours left," she said.

She didn't get another word out. Chrissie was down beside her, massaging her shoulders, whispering in her ear.

"When shall we three meet again, in thunder, lightning, or in rain?" she said.

Clare looked up, smiling.

"When the hurlyburly's done, when the battle's lost and won."

Chrissie looked at me and gestured.

"Eh—something the set of sun."

"Come on, Liam, don't you remember it?"

"Not much."

"Fair is foul, and foul is fair: hover through the fog and filthy air."

"Shall I compare thee to a summer's day?"

I grabbed Chrissie and kissed her.

"Stop, Liam."

She shoved me off.

"Now is the winter of our discontent," Clare said.

"Made glorious summer by this sun of York."

"So you think you can tell, heaven from hell, blue skies from pain."

Chrissie knelt down and kissed Clare on the head.

"Can you tell a green field from a cold steel rail?"

"Will you keep in touch, Chrissie?"

"Yes."

"You won't. Change scenes. Put on another costume. I'll miss you. Both of you. Who was that guy I was with? If I get completely out of it, Chrissie, will you put me on the plane?"

"Sure. I'm leavin' on a jet plane, don't know when I'll be back again."

"Shut up, Chrissie."

"The play's the thing, Clare."

"Is that it with you?"

"What else is there?"

Chrissie laughed.

"In a billion years there won't be a trace that we ever existed. Nothing. And when the sun cools and the planets die, there won't even be a trace that anybody ever existed, that the earth ever did. No Plato, no Jesus, no Muhammad, no Elvis, no nothing."

She tapped the side of her head.

"Inside, Clare, that's where you really are. No shackles. The rest is costume."

Clare shook her head.

"Look," Chrissie said, "think of it like this: there's only the present really. Now. And the now when you go will be a now without me and Liam, and your man over there. But there'll be other nows and maybe we'll be in them. Just stick to the now you're in."

"All our nows," I said.

"In the end, we're all alone, Liam."

"Are we?"

"That's a pretty lonely notion."

"There's something radically Reaganite or Thatcherite about that. Individualism gone mad. What about the collective conscience? Collective humanity? Oneness? The great one? God, maybe?"

"Heavy!" Clare said to me, raising her cup. "I don't want to be one with Charlie fucking Shaw. What the hell did I ask that bastard for?"

"You are. We all are."

"Not me."

"You too, Chrissie."

"I'm unique."

"True. That's the beauty of it. Uniqueness within the greater whole."

"Bullshit. I want money," Clare said.

"And family and home and car and holidays in the sun," Chrissie said.

"Yes, Chrissie. Is that so bad? You make it sound bad. You're a condescending cow sometimes."

"Sorry."

Chrissie stayed with Clare, and I took Tony home with me. I'd rather have gone home with Chrissie but she wanted to stay with Clare. We left them sitting in bed together, both holding teddy bears. And on the way home in the car, with Tony snoring beside me, I kept thinking, why'd Tony have to start all that with Charlie? It all seemed unreal. Like it hadn't happened. Tony must have livened up in the damp autumnal air on the way home. He wouldn't go to bed without a coffee even though his lip was still swollen. Then he went on about what a fucking bollocks Charlie was, that Charlie was a twat, a whore's twat, poxed up. Fuck Charlie, I thought, fuck Tony for going for Charlie, and Charlie for being a prick. We had two lukewarm coffees and I stuck Tony in the spare room with a sleeping bag.

CHAPTER SIX

Tony and I woke up too late to go to the airport to see Clare off. We'd said we would, and when we'd said it we'd meant it, but when we woke up we weren't too pushed. By mutual consent, we didn't talk about Charlie, though Tony's lip was a constant reminder. We sat around the whole day, watching television and drinking coffee. And Tony read *The Phoenix* cover to cover. He stayed that night in our house, too. We drove into town together the next day. In the office, I made three or four disinterested phone calls to papers and magazines and got nothing for my trouble, and Tony drank coffee and looked through the stories pinned to the wall by whichever of the two girls had read through the morning papers and dug out anything we could use or follow up. The one who did the work got the pick of the bunch. The rest were torn out and pinned to the wall. They'd left phone numbers stuck to the phone. Cathy was wherever Cathy was, and I didn't much care. Anne was out with this anti-drugs fellow she knew. Kieran. The kind of five-needles-a-day zombie you wouldn't let your sister out with. Told us in all seriousness he'd worked as a rent boy to support his habit. Tony and I just cracked up. He couldn't understand it. Tall, thin, acned, wasted, he looked buggered out. A prick too far, Tony said. He was always calling in with press releases, as if we were going to get him the kind of coverage he wanted. He had a hankering to be a journalist but he couldn't string two words together properly, and we used to laugh at his press releases when he'd left. Tony kept pressing him to go public with his own story, saying that with a bit of work he could probably get it into the *Sunday World*. Kieran ended up in hospital with nearly every bone in his body broken with baseball bats. The Provos got hold of him by mistake after some residents of a block of inner-city flats complained about pushers. By the time the lads realised that they'd pulped the wrong fellow, it was too late. He still walks like he's held together with safety pins. The Provos apologised and sent him some fruit. They got the right fellow a couple of weeks later.

The weather cleared up during lunch and it turned into one of those October days that make you think you're in the middle of summer only you know summer's not like that in Dublin. Well, not much anyway. I wasn't even thinking of Chrissie, and maybe I should have been, but the way I was, work seemed more important then. Tony'd struck lucky and gone off on a story, and that made me feel bad. The envelope was sellotaped to the door, with my name on it. As soon as I pulled it off the door, I had a strange tightening inside me. Like I was getting ready to be hit. I sat down at one of our chipboard tables and carefully opened the envelope. Inside was a postcard with a picture of Meryl Streep on the front, and Chrissie's handwriting on the back.

"Mr Connolly,

Would you join me for an afternoon stroll on the pier in Dún Laoghaire? 2pm.

Please drain Dublin Bay as a sign if you can't make it.

Love,

Chrissie."

She was sitting on a bench on the pier, near the bandstand. Her hair hung loose around her shoulders, and the sun brought out the red in it. Her head was lowered. At the edge of the pier three kids were casting fishing lines into the harbour.

"Asleep?" I said.

She looked up and squinted.

"Dreaming."

I looked at the sky.

"It's nice."

"Yes."

She patted the bench, and I sat down beside her.

"Long time."

"Since?"

"We were here."

"Yeah."

"Let's go down to the water. I want to put my feet in."

We went down to the shore below the harbour wall. The water was dark blue, and the lazy autumn sunlight was dancing in little bursts on its surface. We sat down at the edge and Chrissie took off her desert boots and white socks and put her feet in the water.

"You didn't come to the airport?"

"No. We were out of it. Did she mind?"

"Yes."

"Damn."

"She said you're to collect her degree and send it on."

"You can do it."

"I won't be here, Liam. I'm going to go away soon— leave. I'm sick of things here. I'm going back to Dundalk for a while. This evening."

I got scared. Shit-scared. I think I'd known deep inside what she was going to say. I don't know how, I just did. And all I could think of was to try and talk her out of it. I came up with arguments to counter what she'd said. Loads of them. About love and loyalty

and need and all that. There was a part of me angry
with her too, for causing me a mess when I didn't
need it. She should have known that. That I didn't
need it. Fuck it, I loved her, and she knew that. I
didn't need this. And all the while I knew how
powerless I was.

"When did you decide this?"

"Last night."

"I don't want you to."

"I've gone over it: it's best we end it now."

"This is terrific. Don't you love me?"

"Liam!"

"Well?"

"I've made up my mind."

"And that's all that counts? You've made up your
mind."

Any logic I'd been planning vanished from me. A
terrible loneliness came over me.

"There's no point in going on, is there? I'm going.
It'll only be harder to do it further on."

"So when are you going away?"

"Maybe after Christmas. Maybe some time in
January."

"There's still time."

"Few extra fucks?"

"That hurt."

"Sorry."

I felt like the life in me was draining away with every word she spoke. Her voice had a clinical tone, as if she'd rehearsed it. And I wished she'd stop speaking because maybe if she stopped speaking what I was feeling would go away. And I wanted to love her; to impregnate her before it was too late; to leave her with something of me, something which would remind her I had once existed. A kind of oblivion faced me. Black and cold. And her voice was its instrument. The urge to take her was so strong in me, I had to fight to keep myself from doing it.

"Why can't you stay?"

"And do what?"

"What do you want to do?"

"Go."

"More than me?"

"I don't know. I must do. This isn't easy, you know. If we do this now, then it won't be so bad. What happens if we let it drift? I mightn't be able to let go, and that'll make it worse."

"Where are you going to go?"

"Everywhere. I want to get a bit more money together. That's why I'm going home. Cheaper to live. I'll get another waitressing job. Something like that. I'll need the money. You know what I'm like. Sure there isn't much here for languages anyway."

"Is that what's making you go?"

"You'd like to believe that."

"I don't want you to go."

"Please don't keep saying that. I need your support. At least give me that."

I put my hands on her shoulders and rubbed them, and then moved to her neck.

"That's good," she said.

"Who's going to give you these when I'm not around?"

"I'll find someone."

"Will you?"

"Mum's behind me."

"Do you need me then?"

"Nice to have your two favourite people behind you."

"You include me?"

"Piss off, Liam."

"Didn't know you cared."

"I said, piss off. You broke my hymen."

"Does that make me special?"

"Of course. Hymen-breaker."

"How do you know?"

"I know."

She pulled her feet from the water. They were pink. The water wasn't as warm as the day.

"We'll still be friends," she said.

"Don't be so fucking sarcastic."

"Sorry."

"Will you come to bed with me, one more time?"

What a fucking stupid question.

"No," she said.

"So what happens?"

"Nothing."

"I'll miss you."

Tears were beginning to fill my eyes, and I could not control them. Several ran down my face into her hair.

She sensed it.

"Don't do that. You'll have me going, and I don't want to."

"Do you have to want to? I'm not very good at this. I feel empty."

"And how do you think I feel?"

"So why the hell are you doing it?"

"I told you."

I wanted her to cry. Some desperate attempt to keep us together.

"Why aren't you crying?"

She turned and hit me on the face, and then she began to cry.

"There! Is that what you wanted?"

Heavy footsteps behind us made us look up. A sandy-haired man, with long sideburns and big ears, hands stuffed into a torn leather jacket, was using his heavy booted foot to guide his young son along the sloped walkway. The child was struggling to maintain his balance. The father whipped his eyes from us when we turned, but we caught the last of his uninvited gaze. He almost tripped over the child.

"Nosy bastard," I whispered to Chrissie.

"Did I hurt you?"

"What do you think?"

"Your cheek's glowing. You're a selfish shit, you know. If you want a wallflower, why don't you go after Clare?"

"That's a shit thing to say. She's not a wallflower. Anyway, I want you."

"How noble. That was a shit thing to say, you're right. I'll write to her. That's easy to say, isn't it?"

"Don't get off the point."

She touched my cheek.

"It's still warm. Sorry."

"I'll floor you next time. Can I buy you dinner?"

"Say that again."

"Can I buy you dinner?"

"No, I'm going to Dundalk. I told you. Are you in the car?"

"Yes."

"Give me a lift. To Busaras. And I've to pick up my stuff."

She was really going. I put my arms around her. I

wanted to be outside it. But I wasn't. Part of me was saying, do anything to stop her, Liam, beg her if you have to, don't let her go. The frantic part of me, below the surface, being held back by the colder, more detached, me, who refused to be hurt by her, who would let her go and never look back. And they wrestled inside me, turning my stomach around and squeezing tears from my eyes.

"You're the only one I get like this with," she said. "Know that? The only one. Anyway, you'll be digging up so much dirt on people you won't even know I'm gone."

"Won't I?"

"Give me your handkerchief. I want to wipe my face."

I dried my eyes and gave it to her.

She blew her nose in it.

"Love," she said.

We laughed a false laugh of relief.

She wiped her face but the area around her eyes was still inflamed. She thrust her feet back in the water and pulled out some seaweed and kicked it at me. It hit me in the face, and some of the salt got on my tongue and went down my throat. I spat until the taste was out of my mouth.

"That water's probably polluted," I said. "Look at the shit around those rocks."

Close in among the rocks there was a slimy coating on the water, and pieces of rubbish bobbed in the slime, moving back and forth a few feet with the lapping tide.

"Love," Chrissie said. "All for love."

"Don't make fun."

"Adesso, e all'ora della mia morte."

"What's that?"

"Italian."

"Yeah, but what?"

She put her hand to my lips.

"Now and at the hour of my death."

"What's that supposed to mean?"

"Love."

"And you're still going?"

"We're agreeing to part."

"Are we? Don't trivialise it."

"I have to."

"Is this what you did with Charlie?"

"Fuck off. Charlie was a good deed. He needed a girl on his arm and I needed someone to keep Lisa and Clare from plaguing me. Charlie served his purpose. Things were fine till you came along. Why'd you have to appear?"

"You didn't have to go with me."

"Didn't I? I didn't want to."

"Screw things up for you?"

"Yes. Charlie was easy. Out a couple of nights a week. Kisses when I needed them. Besides being a bastard, his breath always smells of cheese, know that? And he can't kiss to save himself. Then you come along and there's bed and all. I had to grow up with you. One minute I was a nice tight little convent girl, the next I was drunk on you. Strong stuff."

"So are you."

"You scare me."

"You?"

"You go deep, too deep. I'm not comfortable with it. With what happens. Losing control. Letting go. Depending. I don't want to depend. On anyone. It's okay at the time, but after, thinking, it's not so easy."

"I need you."

"I don't think so."

"I do."

"We'd better go. We're going to run out of light soon."

She picked up her shoes and socks.

"I'll put them on in the car. Will you buy me a bar of chocolate?"

"All right."

"You're very good to me."

She walked ahead of me. I watched her move in her tight black trousers. It was still the sexiest walk I'd ever seen. And she knew it. She turned after a few seconds and winked at me. I winked back.

"Billy still going out with your one from Finance?"

"Why?"

"Any dirt we could use?"

"I don't know if they're still going out. Anyway, Tony probably knows more than Meg."

"Tony's more your massage parlour type."

"Billy's enough problems."

"Yeah, I suppose so. Got to try and build contacts."

"Hack."

"It's a living."

"You look good today, you know."

"Fuck off."

"I mean it."

I said I'd wait in the car with her till her bus came but she jumped out before I'd a chance to argue. I thought she'd kiss me, and there'd be more tears, and maybe she'd reconsider, but she was gone before I could say anything, and I found myself cut off by the noise of the door slamming. She ran across the road, around two taxis pulling out, and went through a glass door to Busaras. I hung around to try and see her on the bus but it was dark and three or four buses took off together at the time hers was due to go and I didn't see her.

CHAPTER SEVEN

S he was gone.

I felt like a limb had been amputated. All the noises outside, and the people and the evening traffic, didn't exist. Only the slightest trace of her scent in the car with me. And that smell hung around in the car for days afterwards.

I drove to Burgh Quay and parked across the road from the *Irish Press*. I went around to the office to see if Tony was there. It was instinctive. I needed to be with someone and he was the best I could think of for the way I felt. I knew he'd go on about work and get caught up in whatever he was doing. That was what I needed. Tony mouthing on. I didn't give a shit what he talked about, so long as he kept talking.

He wasn't there. There was no reason he should have been but I cursed him anyway for not being there. I sat at one of the tables and took the phone in my hand. I held it for a few minutes, thinking. I couldn't figure out who I was going to ring. It was an automatic thing. Pick up the phone and ring when you get in. Hello, can I speak to so and so? And so

and so would either be out and never call back or full
of yeah, we were thinking of something like that,
listen, send us an outline and we'll see. We'll see. See
you.

When I got hold of myself I put the phone down
and shut the office and ran downstairs to the street.
I was trying to picture Chrissie like we'd just seen
each other for the last time and I had to preserve a
mental image of her. And I couldn't. I couldn't get
her face right. I must have looked foolish in the street,
in the rush-hour, trying desperately to fix a mental
picture of Chrissie in my mind. I could feel myself
fretting inside, like a little child who's lost and feels
he's going to be alone forever. And I was cold and
shivering even though it wasn't a cold evening.

I found Tony sitting at the bar in Mulligans, sipping
a glass of lager and reading the *Evening Press*. His
narrow shoulders made him look awkward on the
stool.

"How's the man?" he said.

"Okay—got something in that?"

"Some chance."

"Want to hit the town tonight?"

"Sure—what's up with you?"

Was it that obvious?

"Nothing."

"Okay. What'll you have?"

"Guinness. Pint."

"I might have something with the *Herald* tomorrow."

"Bully for you."

"Sorry."

He ordered my drink and another for himself.

"I've come up with a name. We can get a plaque done on the cheap. Anne knows this guy who'll do it."

"Shoot."

"Nuseek."

I didn't like it much but it wasn't politic to tell him. Maybe one of the girls would.

"Sounds like a pop group," I said.

"It's good. You come up with something."

"And we can get a plaque?"

"Sure—and cards too. How are you for cash?"

"Tight. Dad's given me a bit."

"Right."

"Don't want to take it."

"Come on, Liam, every bit counts."

"I know."

"It's only till we get going. Then we're off."

"Dad's not keen."

And they were squeezing him at work. Associate Director Sales stroke Promotions. What the fuck was that?

"Don't I know," Tony said.

"Yeah."

"Beggars and choosers—remember?"

"Right."

"How's Chrissie? She see Clare off?"

What the hell did he have to ask that for?

"Yeah. Fine."

Standard reply for shit.

"Right."

He drank some of his drink.

"Lisa's shacked up with a black guy. They're in a squat in Notting Hill. Colette says she met him her first day in London. Her mother'll go ape. She's such a stuck-up bitch. I'd give anything to see that old bat's face when she finds out. Cow."

Hearing about Lisa made me feel better, the way hearing about other people's antics always does. It didn't last long. I was too down to get that excited about who Lisa Bryant was shafting or not. Tony could be a real old woman with the gossip. Colette told everyone he couldn't get it up. I wondered if he knew that.

"Good for Lisa," I said.

"Should keep her happy."

"You still in touch with Colette?"

"She rings."

He had big eyes and a freckled face and for a

moment the eyes seemed to merge with the freckles.

As each hour went by, I thought of what Chrissie might be doing. I was talking to Tony and laughing as if I was totally engrossed in what he was saying, but I was with her, watching her move around her house, eat, sit down, watch television, listen to music. She would probably take a bath before bed. I'd taken them with her, and showers. She preferred baths. She'd have her hair tied up and maybe soap on her nose. And each drink I had accentuated my thoughts, so that by eleven I could almost feel her. I thought about ringing her, or jumping in the car and going after her. No, it was up to her. We got a taxi to Leeson Street. I was too jarred to drive.

I wanted to leave immediately we got inside Maxwell Plums. Tony made me stay.

"Give it a bit of time," he said. "It's the middle of the week. There won't be a big crowd."

I sat next to the DJ's hut, beside the small dance floor. Tony went around to the bar to get a bottle of wine, which was probably going to set us back as much as all the drinks in Mulligans put together. He liked coming to these places, to be seen and to pick up any gossip which might be floating around. And there were women. Jesus, he was a horny bastard. I could never stand Leeson Street or the people who hung around it. What did that make me?

I was sitting there alone, feeling out of it, when a pale man in a dress suit approached me and put out his hand.

"Haven't seen you here for a while," he said.

Declan. I didn't know his second name. He was one of the owners. I shook his hand. I'd been to school with his nephew and we'd come down a few times right after the Leaving to pretend we were grown up. He'd always been good to us, slipping us the odd bottle of wine free. We could never afford it.

"What are you doing with yourself?" he asked.

"Freelance journalist."

It sounded important, I thought.

"Good. You don't see Alan these days?"

"No. He's in Manchester."

"Yeah."

"He was home a while back. Didn't see him?"

"No."

"Quiet tonight."

He showed me his thumb and dropped it.

We stared at each other, trying to think of something to say. I didn't know him that well, and I was past the age where knowing a nightclub owner made any difference.

"Enjoy yourself," he said.

"Yeah, see you."

Tony came back with a bottle of white and two

glasses, and a huge smile.

"And you're talking about money," I said. "We'll be broke at this rate."

"There's two women over at the bar."

"Not interested."

"Come on, I need you. I'll bring them over, and you just talk to the other one."

"Fuck you."

"You don't have to do anything. You were the one who wanted to come out."

I gave in to his argument. He brought them around with two more glasses. His one was about thirty and mine was a few years older. It wasn't easy to tell in the strange light of the nightclub. My one had more make-up, so I figured she was older. Tony's had a pointed face and tiny nose. Neither of them was good-looking but Tony was too pissed to bother about that. My one had false eyelashes.

"I'm Linda," she said.

As if I could have given a fuck.

She put out her hand. Chubby fingers and long nails. There was a nicotine stain between two of her fingers. The hand was rough. Not like Chrissie's. Chrissie had good hands. They gave good back rubs. Linda sipped some of her wine and left lipstick on her glass. The lipstick was uneven on her lips. She smiled at me and I smiled back. Then we both stopped smiling and we looked at Tony and the other woman.

"I'm Tony, this is Liam," Tony said.

"Mary," the woman he had his arm around said.

I knew she'd be something like a Mary. Her hair was thinning and she was bulging from her blouse. Mary, Mary, quite contrary, the rhyme ran through my head. Tony's finger touched her breast. Linda looked back at me.

"So what do you do, Linda?" I asked her.

"Secretary."

"Right."

"Boring."

"Right."

There was a pause of maybe a minute.

"And what do you do?"

"Journalist."

"Which paper?"

"Freelance. We have a news agency."

"Sounds interesting."

The music volume increased and I had to lean over and make sure she'd said what I thought she'd said.

"What?"

"Sounds interesting."

She blushed.

"Yes."

She reached into her small white bag and pulled

out a packet of cigarettes. Silk Cut. She offered them around. We all refused. She took one out and put it in her mouth. She lit the cigarette with a gold lighter.

"I want to dance," Tony said.

He dragged Mary up and she made a pretence at refusal and then went with him. Linda sucked and blew hard on her cigarette. A group of five went past, and one of the girls walked like Chrissie. Not as sexy. Walk like a Chrissie. The Bangles ran around my head. My mind left the nightclub and went to Chrissie's bed. I could ring her. Fuck it, she could ring me. She'd left.

"Want to dance?" Linda asked.

"Sorry?"

"You're miles away."

"Yes."

"Want to go somewhere?"

"Where?"

"I've a flat."

"Big bed?"

"Yes."

"No."

She stubbed her cigarette into an ashtray and relaxed.

"Mind if I go back to the bar?"

"No."

Tony and Mary were lost in dance.

I took out a tenner and gave it to Linda.

"Will you give this to him?" I said.

"Sure."

"I'm going. Thanks for the chat. And give up smoking, it's bad for you."

"I know. Keeps me sane though. I—"

She stood up and went to shake but stopped herself.

I walked down towards the Green, past small knots of people going into nightclubs. I had to go down to the quays for the car. It was too long a walk, so I got a taxi. The driver had a copy of *The Sun* on his front seat. I took it up and looked through it.

"Busy tonight?" I asked him.

"Nah! Few wagons out on the make."

CHAPTER EIGHT

I got a chest infection before Christmas and was laid up for nearly six weeks. It was a real bitch spew up green phlegm kind of dose and it took my mind off Chrissie and killed off the pain of her leaving, because I'm pretty self-indulgent when I'm ill. Up to that I'd been living right on the edge of ringing or writing or just going after her. Except that something was holding me back. Maybe that pride. She'd told me to get lost. I wasn't going chasing her if I could help it. It was up to her. And if she didn't want to do anything about it, then—well, I didn't think that far ahead. I might have given in to my need for her if I hadn't been sick but once I was, she sort of slipped into the background, and before I could make up my mind what to do about her once I was well again, things changed.

FitzGerald's coalition fell apart over food subsidies. His Labour partners felt their virtue was being compromised. It was a boom time for us in the office. Things had been lousy up to Christmas, and Tony'd been talking about going to London before I got sick.

The election put us back in business. Suddenly everyone wanted hacks. We even got work from the BBC, arranging interviews and stuff. It was crazy. Sometimes we slept in sleeping bags in the office. Mostly we didn't eat much. During that time it was easy to forget Chrissie.

Then, as quickly as it came, the election was over, Haughey was back in power, the inmates had handed over control of the asylum to the outpatients, and we were pretty much redundant.

Two nights after my twenty-second birthday, I was lying on my bed in the dark, listening to my Walkman, feeling sorry for myself and thinking fractured disjointed thoughts about Chrissie and work, and just wondering. I might have been sleeping a bit, too. It was a cold night on our cold quiet semi-detached road. Even numbers on our side, even numbers and copper beech; odd numbers across the road, odd numbers and cherry blossom. And for twenty-five years, the same families in the same houses, save the occasional extension, for ten houses up from us on either side. We were the last house on our side.

A stone hit my window. And I immediately thought of Dad. I'd often had him outside in the small hours of the morning, throwing stones at my window when he'd forgotten his keys or was too drunk to fit the key in the hall door, but he usually threw a few stones together, and harder, the way drunk people throw things when they can't judge force or distance. This was a single stone and just right. Hard enough to make the required sound, gentle enough not to damage the window. And it made me jump up.

In that moment it was as if someone just slammed the whole part of me I had left in neutral back into gear. I stood there too gobstruck to shout or even say anything, waiting for it to sink in or go away.

Chrissie was sitting on the grass, her legs in a lotus position. The grass was sodden from all the rain that had fallen during the day, but she just sat there, smiling and waving at me. I watched her for a few seconds to make sure she was real. I knew she was but I had to check. The pause before the leap. And I looked around at the road to see if anyone else was watching. Any signs of gaps in the curtains. Neighbourhood Watch. Our sticker was hanging loose on our lounge window. Dad and my brother, Cormac, were in there, shouting at a soccer game, and the noise of them and the television drowned my coming down the stairs—our stairs creaked and groaned at every conceivable point. I eased the front door open and fought hard to be calm.

"Hello, darling," she said. "Happy birthday."

"Get off the grass. You'll catch your death."

"Pleased to see me?"

I didn't know how to answer that.

"You're supposed to be gone somewhere."

She plucked a blade of grass and chewed it.

"I'm here. I'll go if you like."

"No."

"I have a present."

"What?"

"You'll see."

"Okay."

"You could have phoned."

"Could I?"

I wanted to be cold with her.

"You left, not me."

"Yeah, but I thought you'd phone. I missed you. Miss me?"

I said nothing.

She tossed her hair back and smiled.

"Think I look like Meryl Streep?"

I went over to the grass and stretched out my arms and pulled her up. She made no effort to help me. I had to pull hard to get her standing. I looked at her backside.

"It's soaked," I said. "Come inside."

"I love you when you're masterful."

"Fuck off."

She put her arms around me and we kissed, not long because I was too aware that people might be watching.

"Get inside."

I got her a pair of jeans from my wardrobe and took off her trousers, a pair of old combats, and put them in the hot press, on the immersion.

She sat cross-legged without putting the jeans on.

"Your mother will think we've been up to something if she sees me like this," she said.

I was turning on the electric fire.

"She's very understanding. Anyway, I'd rather risk it than have you die of pneumonia. Put the jeans on."

"You're very good to me."

"Fuck off, Chrissie."

"Don't be so rude. I'm worshipping you."

"Don't."

"My knickers are wet too."

"Take them off."

"I don't know. What would Mummy say?"

"Take them off."

"Who can resist a command like that. Wow!"

"If you don't shut up, I'll lay you here and now."

"Is that a promise?"

She lay down on the rug beside the electric fire and spread her legs.

"Chrissie, for God's sake."

"Chicken. If you loved me you wouldn't care."

"Behave yourself. Anyway, you broke it off."

"No, I didn't. We agreed. Why didn't you ring? You look lovely."

"You been drinking?"

"No, of course not. Where's the Connolly clan?"

"Dad and Cormac are inside watching television. Mum's upstairs, reading."

"What were you doing?"

"Listening to my Walkman."

"I didn't think you were in."

"I didn't expect to see you."

"I haven't gone yet."

"So I see."

"Do you hate me? I'll go."

"I said, no."

"I'm waitressing here again. I didn't do anything at home. Just hung around. Dutiful daughter bit. There's a lovely old man who I serve every day. We talk a lot."

I was losing the fight. Her magic was casting its spell on me again, no matter how much I tried to be matter-of-fact.

"How's work? I saw a couple of articles by you."

"Brilliant during the election. Now—well, now's not so good."

"Giving up?"

"Maybe. Who knows."

"What else have you been doing? Tell me, please."

"Got sick. You?"

"Nothing. Was it bad?"

"Not now."

"Give me a hug. Small one if you're not keen. For me."

"I don't know what to think, Chrissie."

"Don't. Hug me."

Some fish must bite willingly, knowing what is concealed in the bait. They must bite because the bait is infinitely more desirable than the hook is frightening. And maybe the hook won't catch them.

"Can you get the car?"

"Yes. Why?"

"I want to take you camping. My present. I have my tent. It's at the wall. There's this little place in the woods, past Enniskerry. Will you come?"

"It's eleven."

"Quarter past."

She grinned.

"I don't believe this. Are you serious?"

"Yes. Is this really you?"

She took my stained communion photograph from the mantelpiece.

"Yes. My head's too big."

"Still is. But I forgive you. Want to dance?"

She crawled over to the stereo, beside the sideboard, and sifted through the albums.

"Simon and Garfunkel?"

"If you like. If we're going camping we'd better move. You're beautiful."

"Shut up. One dance. Pull the curtains and turn off the lights. I want to be alone with you."

I pulled the curtains and turned off the lights and we slow danced to "Scarborough Fair."

It was wild, her turning up like that, just picking me up like nothing had happened and heading off into the mountains, and that was what made Chrissie what she was and why it was so hard to say no to her. She sat behind me, rubbing my neck and licking my earlobe on the drive to Enniskerry. I had to tell her to stop licking my earlobe, it was distracting me. I had the lights on full in the darkness of the country roads and our world was the furthest extent of the lights. We drove through Enniskerry and along the road towards Knockree, stopping in a small lay-by. I nearly missed it, and Chrissie screamed at me that I was passing it when we reached it. It was a fairly clear night except for some clouds over the mountains. Long thin clouds. The wood was across the road, over a wall. We pitched the tent between the trees. Shadows moved with the trees in the wind, and the sound of the wind in the trees was a gentle whisper in the night.

Chrissie wanted it to be good, and it was because I wanted it to be good too. She had a sleeping bag to keep us warm, and after, I lay on top of her, stroking her face and combing her hair with my fingers. We didn't speak for a long time. I didn't want to speak and I didn't want to hear what she had to say. All I wanted was for us to stay there, lying naked together, breath on breath, holding and held.

She broke the silence.

"What are you thinking?"

"Why?"

"Why what?"

"All this."

"Present."

"That it?"

"I thought you'd ring."

"You were supposed to be going."

"I thought you'd ring."

"Why?"

"Do you want to make me squirm? You can be a bastard, Liam."

"I don't mean to be."

"I missed you. I missed this. You don't know how much."

"You think I didn't?"

"I was outside your office yesterday."

"Doing what?"

"Watching. You could have rung."

"But you left. Do you know how I felt?"

"Sorry. I felt the same."

"You're not going away, then?"

"Not yet."

"What's that supposed to mean?"

"What it does."

"Why the hell'd you do this, then? Why didn't you just stay away? Why don't you just leave me now, then?"

"That what you want?"

"No. You know it isn't."

"It's always up to me, isn't it? If you care so much, just let me be. Just accept things for now."

"That's easy for you to say."

"I shouldn't have come."

"You did."

"And you want me to pay?"

"No. I want you to stay. That's all I've wanted."

"And if I did?"

"I don't know."

"See, you want me for a wallflower."

I rolled off her, holding her hand.

"Marry me."

It just came out. I didn't plan it. I'd thought of it

before, sure, but I didn't think I'd say it. Chrissie buried her head in the groundsheet. I couldn't say anything after that until she spoke. And I didn't even know whether I'd meant it. I suppose I did, in the charged state I was in, in that tent, lying beside her, sure, I meant it. Maybe not immediately. But I'd had plans inside me somewhere for us.

"What sort of a fuckwit thing was that to say?" she said. "Did you say it to make me feel bad?"

"I don't know why I said it."

"Fucker."

"I'm sorry."

"And don't say that. It cheapens it all. Why'd you have to come along now? It'd be funny being married to you. Getting up every morning with you, eating with you. And we'd sit down every night and talk about work—probably your work—and make love every night—well, not every night but most nights. What am I going on about? I'm too young for this. Look at the way you have me thinking, Liam. You're a manipulative bastard. Why couldn't you come along later? And we'd meet in some park or café somewhere and start talking. Why'd you have to happen now? I don't want you now. We could have met later. It'd have been splendid."

"And it hasn't been?"

"It has, damn you."

I lay my head on her breast, wondering if she really would go, telling myself it didn't matter to me if she did or not, knowing it did, that she had me again, hoping she wouldn't go. In the half sleep which follows loving, I didn't care. There was only the warmth and total intoxication of her.

When it was still dark, we crept out over the wall with the tent, shivering. We jumped up and down on the road beside the car to get warm, and I put the heater on full all the way down to Dublin. She had a new bedsit in a terraced house near Portobello Bridge, and we went to bed and then sat up, wrapped only in a duvet, dunking almond slices in hot chocolate. And when I had to go, she sat on the doorstep and waved and blew kisses, and I almost turned around and went back. As I approached our house, I turned the car engine off and dimmed the lights and freewheeled into the driveway. The paper was in the door. I slipped the key in the door with the same care a lover slips himself into his love. Turn the lock. Open. A click and a few seconds to see if anyone was disturbed. No interruption in the snoring. Upstairs and close my door behind me. Everything over the back of the chair.

CHAPTER NINE

S o it was back fine between us again, just like that, like it had never not been fine, and that was good and I didn't question it because I was getting no work again and I really needed it to be fine. Tony got some work, not much, but not much was more than the rest of us, and I guess I was angry at that, even if I didn't say it. Chrissie helped keep it down below the surface. She got back into part-time acting, still with those friends from Dramsoc who weren't my friends, only there were fewer of them now, and she was all into workshops and stuff in her spare time. I was able to fit myself into her schedule because I hadn't much else to do and often I'd wait all afternoon or half a night for her because it was easier than hanging around at home. I was still going into the office and contributing to the bills with what I'd earned before and some help from Dad. Thing was, Dad's help came with why don't you give up this messing and get a career I didn't put you through college for this strings. It was never said direct, and maybe that was worse because if I kept my head down like I was I could avoid it coming to a head. I'd have moved out of home only I couldn't afford to keep myself, and Chrissie said she didn't want me moving in with her, that it would ruin things. Her new place could have done for both of us. It had a fridge and its own shower. But I didn't press it. Maybe I was scared of what would happen. I didn't want to antagonise her. I needed her there, the comfort of knowing she was around, that I could go to her when I wanted. And I think she was glad to have me there. She said it and all but I'd learned you could never take Chrissie at her word. Not that that stopped me believing everything she told me. When you love someone you so desperately want to believe in them, like it's believing in yourself. Problem is, you can deceive yourself. It was a happy limbo for us, neither of us pressing the other too much, both of us taking what we needed, what was freely available.

The day I got the feature on funerals, Chrissie'd already gone down the country with her drama people to this theatre festival. I think it was Cork. She was pretty high about the whole thing because they'd been working on this play for ages and were pretty sure they'd win a prize or something. Jesus, I'd to sit through about fifty rehearsals of it. It was American and not well-known, and I didn't think much of it, but Chrissie was in it, so I didn't say. Anyway, she was really happy going down, all theatrical, full of kisses, deep heavy kisses, and smiling like only Chrissie could smile, a smile which made you lose a breath and want to follow her anywhere. Jesus, she was lovely when she smiled and her eyes filled everything, and you drowned in them or wanted to drown in them. She was still real into Meryl Streep, though more subtly now. She'd talk about her films and maybe criticise her so I'd respond, but I knew what she was at.

I was in the office with Cathy and Anne, trying to do this feature I'd got, finding it hard to get anything down on paper. That's the way it always is. Someone turns your idea down and you've got the whole thing already written in your head and it doubles the disappointment. As soon as you get the okay you can't get a word down on paper. And this was a commission, filling for someone who was sick and couldn't do it. I was going to get paid. I'd made a couple of phone calls to undertakers and stone masons, got a load of information and couldn't string two words together. Tony might have been able to help only he was off researching a piece on the army for *Magill*. Cathy was reading *Image* and sulking the way she did when the rest of us got work and she didn't. We all sulked when the others got work and we didn't, but she always did her sulking in front of you, making you feel lousy for getting work. Anne was finishing off going through the papers, sticking a few stories on the wall.

"Well, there's fuck all here," she said.

"I'm blank," I said.

I threw a pencil at the wall.

"Fancy a bit of unemotional sex, Liam?"

"Where?"

"The floor."

"It's a bit hard. My knees aren't up to it. Anyway, sex without love is a shallow experience."

"But as shallow experiences go, it's one of the better ones."

"Indeed."

"Would we enjoy it?"

"I don't know."

"We'd have to enjoy it. There's nothing worse than not enjoying it."

"The floor's definitely a problem then."

"Listen, you'll love this: I was banging this guy the other night and I'm telling you, I haven't had a fuck like it for ages. He must have had a foot of dick. I'm banged out. I was coming like a hyena and I tore his sheets. With my nails. And his pillow. Know when you're wild and the two of you are panting and sweating, and you know you're sinning and you're enjoying sinning and sweating, and it's like you're going to burst, and you're just fucking for fucking's sake and—Jesus, I'm getting excited just thinking about it. God, I love it."

"Don't be disgusting," Cathy said.

"Who's disgusting? I'm only voicing what everyone thinks deep down. Right, Liam?"

"Right."

"See."

Cathy sighed and went back to *Image*.

Anne giggled.

I stuck a sheet of paper in my typewriter.

I wrote something sublime about epitaphs and thought of Jim Sloane in Mount Jerome. A loving son: James Arthur Sloane, died June 12, 1984. Not much of an epitaph for Jim. Sloaner the loaner. They had to cut him out of the car. He used to try and run me over with his bicycle on the way to school. I had my first fight with him. Everyone called him a mad bastard. It was true. Him and Ryan wanking in the toilets when they hadn't got anything to wank with. All of us outside breaking ourselves laughing, and the two of them racing away. Then Brennan found them. Jim won by default. Ryan pulled his foreskin back too far. Maybe that should have been put on his stone: Champion Wanker, 1977. I'd wanted to tear the lid off his coffin, to make sure it was him. They might have got it wrong. He might still be living in some mountain cave in Tibet. That would be Sloane all over. Old Sloaners never die, they just fade away.

The knock on the door brought me out of my daydream. None of us got up to open the door. There was another knock, less forceful. The door opened slowly. I knew who it was before the head was fully in.

Clare.

Her hair was cut shorter and tied at the back with a ribbon.

"Hi!" was all I could say.

I was genuinely surprised.

"Liam!"

"Come on in. How goes it?"

"Fine. I didn't know if I had the right place."

"Excuse the decor."

I stood up for her.

We embraced and I kissed her kind of on the cheek but near the lips.

"The exile returns. When'd you get in?"

"I'm only home for a few days. Dad's not well. His heart. He's had a by-pass. They're down in Galway. I'm on my way down."

"God, I'm sorry. I didn't know."

"Neither did I till a couple of days ago. Still wearing that old jacket? Are you ever going to get a change of clothes?"

"It's part of the image. This is Anne by the way—and that's Cathy."

Clare nodded to both of them. Cathy nodded back. Anne shook her hand. Clare turned back to me.

"Tony not around?"

"No, he's out chasing soldiers around ditches. Kind of thing he likes."

"Are you free?"

"Yeah—why not? You buying?"

"Of course."

She smiled at Anne, and Anne smiled back and gave me the kind of look I didn't want or need. Cathy was still buried in *Image*.

We ran between the cars to get across D'Olier Street, then down Fleet Street and between the cars again across Westmoreland Street. Sitting in Bewleys, we sat looking at each other for a minute or so, stirring our coffees to disguise what we were really doing. I was damn glad to see her. Out of the blue like that. The kind of morale-boost you always want when you can't get anything on paper. It was like she'd never been away. Like it was the next day after we'd last met. Except for her hair being a little shorter.

"Well?" I said.

"Well what?"

"What's happening?"

"You got my letters. And I got your letter."

"Sorry. It's just—"

"No need. It's lovely being back. I'm doing a night course in accountancy. Imagine! Me doing accountancy. The firm's paying."

"The world and his mother's over there now."

"Nothing here, is there?"

"Too right."

"Work shit?"

"Pretty. That's why I made that crack about paying. We were fine during the election. It's been awful since then. The worst thing is getting paid."

"Heard from Chrissie?"

"She's here—well, she's down the country at an arts thing, but she's back in Rathmines, and doing some waitressing."

"I thought you said she was gone. She hasn't written to me."

"C'est Chrissie."

My eyes caressed the curves of Clare's figure. I broke my rule and began comparing Chrissie and Clare. Chrissie still had it by a pair of eyes. Clare's odds had dropped though. My heart raced. The first time my heart had been sent racing by Clare had been in first year, our first tutorial, when McCarthy made us tell about ourselves. Her skirt rode up to her thighs, and she saw me looking and tried to pull it down and talk about herself at the same time. A whole tutorial talking about ourselves and wondering what lay under that skirt. And after, all that nervous chat and manoeuvring, the looks, the slight touches and brushes, the waiting, the hinting and expectation, and nothing.

People were coming through the restaurant, wet, with steam rising from their coats. Two men shoved themselves into the seats beside us and made us aware of ourselves. I was looking at Clare for any signs she might be giving me, unconsciously at first, but when the two men sat beside us, I became aware of what I was doing the way we had both become aware we were talking about things which only concerned us. Clare nodded at me twice before I took the hint.

We headed down Fleet Street to the Auld Dubliner under the cover of various shop fronts.

At first, we didn't talk much more over the beers than we had over the coffees. We had reached the line between gossip and small talk, and more intimate exchanges, in Bewleys. There were pauses now, in studied deliberate sentences. More jokes too. Jokes are a good way of hiding what you don't want known. But the screen was coming down, slowly, with each drink. The pub filled up over lunch, but we didn't notice and we didn't eat, and after lunch it emptied again. And by the time we were thrown out for the holy hour, we were both pretty gone. And I could smell her perfume like it was the only smell there, rich and intoxicating so that I had an erection. And we stirred our drinks with our fingers and licked our fingers and laughed because we were both drunk in the afternoon and it felt good being drunk in the afternoon.

"I'm supposed to catch a train," Clare said.

"When?"

"Ages ago."

"Oh!"

"I'm blitzed. I'll get one tomorrow. I can fly down maybe. My head's dreamy. I haven't been like this since—since I left. Do you remember that?"

"Who doesn't."

"We'll have to eat. Want to eat? Am I holding you from work?"

"I don't think I'd be able to now."

"Good. And I want to buy you a birthday present. I never got you one. I've been wanting to."

"You needn't."

"I want to."

She put her hand on my leg and held it there, close to my erection, and I thought I might erupt. And the liberating feeling of the alcohol sent my eyes wandering around her legs, and the rest of her, and I thought about being in bed with her, touching her skin and it was hard to stop.

We walked up to Grafton Street, and the weather got dirty again at College Green, heavy showers gusting with the wind. Everyone hurried. We ran to Brown Thomas, and Clare rushed through the shop, giggling, nearly falling over a couple of stands, till she got to the man's section. She pulled two ties off a rack and held them up.

"What do you think?"

"Fine."

"What do you mean, fine?"

"They're lovely."

"Which one's best?"

"That one. It's less aggressive."

"I like that. You absolutely sure?"

"Yes."

She took the tie to the counter and paid for it. I amused myself with some trousers.

"Happy birthday," she said.

She gave me the tie in a bag.

"Birthday present. Sorry it's late."

She kissed me.

"I didn't want you to."

"I did. Now, do you have a pen? A good one?"

"Clare!"

"You need a good one. A Cross."

"Please, there's no need."

"I want to. I do. Let's go across the road."

She wanted to go to Weirs but I persuaded her to go to Byrnes on South Anne Street because I knew one of the staff and I knew he'd give us something off. It was about the only contribution I could make but it made me feel better.

She gave me a bigger kiss with the pen.

"You shouldn't have," I said.

"Why not? They're paying me loads. Shut up. Where do you want to eat? It's fabulous being home, know that? Even the rain. London's such a piss pot. I wish I'd more time. We're going to go mad tonight. You'll stay out, won't you? Chaperon me?"

"Sure."

"Terrific."

I should have had more wine when we ate. We ordered three bottles but Clare drank most of it, and I had a huge pizza which helped me sober up too. And sobering up made me feel guilty, a latent feeling it didn't take much to bring to the surface. I'd done nothing to feel guilty about but still I felt guilty, for enjoying being with Clare and for allowing my mind to fantasise about her. Like I'd never done that before. Most of first year at college had been taken up with wild dreams about Clare. Incredibly erotic. Maybe if she'd known about them, she'd have run a mile. Or maybe I'm a product of my upbringing: nice girls don't. If she was anything like me, she was thinking what I was thinking. There'd never been any problem like that with Chrissie. You know the way people are when they want each other and there's nothing holding them back? There was something holding me back from Clare, and even being tipsy on wine couldn't force me over the edge. Maybe if I'd been blasted, so blasted that I had no control, maybe then I would have gone as far as it was going to go. Without thinking. But that wouldn't have been me, at least, not all of me. And that would have made it bad. Wine's okay when you're going to bed, just enough to highlight the senses, to prolong it, to make you feel warm like there's a fire in you, but not so much that you're out of it, because then it doesn't mean anything and not meaning anything when you care is pretty rotten.

"It gets fairly lonely over there, Liam," Clare said when we were having coffee. "Like, they pay me well and I've got a good flat, and Fiona—she's my flatmate—she's lovely, but I'm prone to the Sally O'Brien syndrome."

"Only for a while."

We both knew that was a platitude.

"With Dad the way he is, I hate being away. You feel shit, like you're running out on them. I'm glad he's down in Galway. It's easier than here for him. He's going to retire early. The bank's become a sweat

shop for him. He wanted to be a singer, you know.
He's a real good singer. He's a tenor. Sang on radio
when he was younger. That's what he wanted to be.
But then he married Mum and that was that. Safe,
secure and a by-pass at fifty-four. You should hear
him sing. Shit, if anything happens to him. Well, if
anything does—I'm boring you, amn't I?"

"No."

"I am. I can see it in your eyes. Do you wish Chrissie
was here? I'd like to see her. I've got a feeling I'll
never see her again. Yeuch, I'm so morose. Let's go
dancing. Would you mind? I want to and I'm the
guest, so let's go dancing. I'll show you how to let
loose."

"You on the make?"

"Yeah."

"Dublin watch out."

"I want pleasure. I've had six months of solid graft
for her majesty, Maggie. Maggie's glory girls, that's
what we call ourselves. Work all day, watch videos at
night, maybe get a drink at the weekend if we can
summon up the energy to go down the pub."

"At least you're being paid."

"Poor Liam. Listen, you can always join the rest of
us over there."

"I might have to."

"No, do, I mean it. Come over, stay with us. Work

hard, watch videos."

"We'll see."

"Sorry."

"Nothing to be sorry about."

"Yes, there is."

"No."

We didn't go dancing. Clare went off the idea the minute we hit the street. Said she wanted to go home to Howth. I said we should go dancing so she could sober up—I was pretty sober by then—but she got angry and said she wanted to go home and me to take her home. She started hailing taxis, pulling me by the hand around Stephen's Green.

"Come on, Liam. Viens!"

She looked at me.

"I want you to come—with me."

In the taxi, on the way to Howth, she leaned her head on my shoulder and ran her hand through my hair. I opened the window to let in some air. The sea air filled our lungs, and Clare took deep breaths of it because I made her.

"You're lovely, Liam," she said.

"So are you."

She held my hand and stroked my fingers, and I was so erect I thought my pants would rip off if she touched me any more. Her warmth and her smell and the curves of her body against her clothes were mixing with the drink still left in me, and it was so alluring I could almost taste it. Just there, put my hand so gently between her legs and that would have been that. But I couldn't. I couldn't do that. Christ, why the fuck was I so bloody boy scout moral? So shagging decent gentleman don't let Chrissie down? Clare was opening the front door of her house. I could go in with her, forget the world, just do it, so that I wouldn't regret anything—it's shit to regret things—just follow her. Sure she was the one who wanted it. I'd be doing it for her.

She turned and took me by the hands again.

"I won't come in with you, Clare," I said.

I felt such a chicken.

"I kind of figured."

"I—"

"Don't say anything."

"No."

"See you. I will see you."

"Yeah."

"I mean it."

"Me too."

I kissed her on the cheek.

"Say hello to your folks."

"Yes."

"Bye."

"Bye."

I got the DART back into town, and this old fellow puked up in my carriage. I was fifteen minutes waiting for a 16A. The queue filed on. Me, two lovers and a sad woman. The sad woman sat across from me, staring out the window, upstairs. Maybe stood up, I thought. Lousy to be stood up. Chrissie'd stood me up a couple of times. I was in the third seat behind the stairwell. Aine loved Tommy. It said that in red marker. That and Tiocfaidh Ár Lá; and fanny's tit. There was more, but the writer needed lessons. I leaned my head against the window and thought. Two girls ahead of me looked around and turned back quickly. Ugly. Back of the vehicle we were in. How much is that doggie in the window? I was still dreaming. Of Chrissie. Waiting tables, black skirt, white blouse. I would take them off. I would take them off and move my lips over her body, and she would—

And Chrissie became Clare for a second and then Chrissie again.

Siegfried Sassoon ran through my head.

And hope, with furtive eyes and grappling fists, founders in mud. O Jesus, make it stop!

CHAPTER TEN

I'm a liar. To myself. To others. My lie at this time was that I had refused Clare out of some noble sense of fidelity. That I could have gone through that door, had her, walked away and thought nothing of it, if I'd wanted. Only I was an honourable man. So are we all, all honourable men. And honourable men don't do that. They don't betray. How could I betray Chrissie when I was in love with her? An honourable man would never do that.

I had betrayed Chrissie in my mind a thousand times. And the only reason I hadn't gone on with it, through that door with Clare, was that I couldn't have coped with it. It was for me I held back, I know that now, for no one else. For me. The thought of playing some double game with the two of them, the emotional commitment required, scared the hell out of me, scared me so much I wasn't even able to conquer it with the thought of having Clare for a night. There was nothing grander as motivation than my comfort. And my comfort was with Chrissie. Chrissie who'd come back to me, whom I did love, who was my safety. Clare was too much for me. I would have to work to love her. And it might never happen. I wasn't brave enough to risk that. Hadn't the bottle. Of such things are ordinary mortals made.

They were bad days for being brave. There was a constant drip of people leaving after the first early dash. It became almost routine, even boring, to go to going-away sessions. You couldn't think about it or let it get to you. So you laughed and made jokes about what they'd do over there, wherever over there happened to be, and you left the sadness behind. They were only an aeroplane ride away. Only a plane ride. A world measured out in 747s and 737s. These weren't big people, they were ordinary innocuous people, some not even very close friends. Bit players, walk-on parts, the odd co-star. But the stage was emptier with them gone.

I didn't sleep well for three days after Clare left. Wondering what might have been. In the end, when I'd worked it all out in my head, I felt pretty good about myself. I didn't love her, so I was right to have done what I did. I was right. What a bloody good feeling it is to be right. And when Chrissie rang, and before she spoke and I only knew it was her because it was from a phone box and there was a pause before she got through, I was on a high.

"Liam!"

"Hi, how's it going down there?"

"Shit. I'm back."

"You sound rotten."

"Liam!"

"What, Chrissie?"

"Liam!"

"Come on, Chrissie."

"Darling."

"Chrissie!"

"I'm pregnant."

"What?"

"Pregnant. Up the pole. In the club. What the hell else do I have to say, Liam?"

My legs nearly went from under me.

"Are you sure?"

"Course I'm sure. I wouldn't be telling you if I wasn't. And don't go asking me some stupid question like, how? I don't know why men always ask that. Like they haven't a clue what's going on. I was late and I puked a few times. So I had a check."

"Shit."

"Thanks."

"I didn't mean it like that."

"Yes, you did. Don't pretend. You don't have to pretend."

"Chrissie, I'm not pretending. It's just—"

"A real belter."

"You could be wrong."

"No. Come down. I need you here."

I finished my breakfast, knocking over the tail end of my orange juice and staining the table-cloth and my finished manuscript on funerals. Oh, fuck, I can do without this, I thought. I was going to take a look at myself in the mirror, but I knew what I'd see and I didn't want to see it. I was shaking and I must have been pale, and I just wanted to run, as far away as I could, just run. I had to sit down for a while. My breathing was fast. Any illusions of being pretty much able to stand up to whatever was thrown at me, of being so capable, were crumbling. Jesus, I can't describe how small I felt, how completely useless and impotent, how I wanted to cry. Like it wasn't my fault, like I was the victim of a crime, of someone else's action, a conspiracy; and I felt angry because I needed to feel angry or feel something, but even the anger was draining from me like the rest of my feelings. Oh, fuck. Shit. Crying fuck. My mind began to calculate. Months, how many months?

She was lying face down on her bed when I got to her bedsit. The bed. I just stood there, over her. She might be wrong. She might be wrong. And I wanted her to say it was all right, that it wasn't my fault, that I could go, that she'd take care of it. That she'd take care of it. Take care of it. It was easy. Take care of it.

Quick and easy. Before it got a chance—to what? To grow. Was this some sort of cancer? Yeah. A cancer, attacking our lives, that was what it was. Just a little boil. I'd seen pictures. You couldn't tell what it was if you weren't told. A boil. And you lanced boils. Sure, it had—

What?

Nobody'd know. If she took care of it now. How many times had I argued with people about the sanctity of life, about all that what would you be if your mother had thought that about you. But this wasn't like that. Wasn't a nice neat little moral speech over coffee. This was so real I could feel it. This was growing up, families, changing nappies, midnight feeds, crying, wind, clothes, school, all that. Jesus Christ, whatever it was, it had to go. And now, while only we knew about it. She hadn't told anyone else? No, not Chrissie. Oh, Chrissie, what the fuck's happened to us?

"How are you?" I asked.

"Okay. It's natural. Most natural thing in the world, Liam. You look like you're dying. Do you hate me?"

"No, course not."

I caressed her face. She was crying.

"Hold me, Liam," she said.

I put my arms around her and tucked in close to her.

"What—"

I stopped. I was going to ask her what she was going to do.

"What what?"

"Nothing."

"What am I going to do?"

"No."

"It's—he—she—been growing inside me for weeks. I got a book to see what it looks like now. It's still tiny."

She touched her little finger.

"I thought—"

"What? You thought what?"

There was anger in her voice.

"Come on, what did you think?"

"Nothing."

"Fuck you, Liam. You thought I was on something. Leave it to Chrissie. Too sordid for our Liam."

She reached over for her bag beside the bed.

"See this? It's my diaphragm. Ridiculous-looking thing. And these are my pills. You've never once asked me if I used anything. Do you know that? Never once. You were quite prepared to bed me without ever bothering to see if I was protected. Let alone ask if we should use a condom. Not that I wanted to use one of them. But it would have showed you cared enough. Too much for romantic Liam. Well, it's all very well being romantic but this is the bottom line. See! A big hunk of rubber for stuffing up myself. And these damn things may or may not do me damage. Well, I forgot, Liam, or something like that. I suppose I didn't think I'd be—what's the point explaining? This is your birthday present, love, my little surprise for you, and I hope to Christ you remember it because I'd hate to think we got all this without some enjoyment."

"I'm sorry."

"For what?"

"Everything. Being so powerless."

"I knew I shouldn't have come back to you. I should have gone when I said I was going. Damn you, Liam, why do I have to love you? Jesus, I was so romantic, so full of—"

"I love you."

"Brilliant!"

"Sorry. I do."

"I ached without you. Do you know that? Do you know how many letters I wrote to you, how many drawings I did of you. God, I ached for you. And you didn't phone. Maybe if you'd phoned—"

"Sorry."

"Don't keep saying you're sorry."

"I wish—"

"So do I, Liam. You know what I really wish? I

wish I'd never clapped eyes on you. And I don't like it. And I wish I could pull it out of me, just reach in and pull it out of me."

"Don't say that."

She got up from the bed and went over to a washbasin in the corner and filled it a little with cold water and rubbed the cold water on her face. When she had finished she took a small hand towel and dried her face and tried to smile.

"I tried, Liam."

"What?"

"Stupid little bitch that I am, I tried this."

She reached into the wastepaper bin and took away a sheet of paper. Underneath was a whole pile of tissues and cotton wool, stained with blood.

"Jesus, Chrissie," I said.

"I tried to scrape myself. Old wives' stuff. Christ, Liam, I was in the shits. Last night. I used a fucking coat hanger. I couldn't get it up myself. I was virgin tight. So I drank gin—I'd heard that helps, too, I don't know where, maybe in a film, but I was in such a state that it didn't matter. Anyway, I couldn't get the damn thing up myself. Tight fucking virgin, that's me, Liam. Going to scrape away at myself like I'm going to scratch a spot. And I cut myself. I was scared to shit. I soaked all this tissue and cotton wool in gin and stuffed it up me. It stung like hell. I had to use the mirror to see where it was. It wasn't far up. Just a cut. Then the gin made me puke. You know me and drink. I can't drink. Oh, Liam, I just sat there and puked on the floor and stuffed tissues up me. I thought I'd die. That they'd find me in a pool of blood and puke with a damn coat hanger beside me. It was kind of tragic, don't you think so? I was going to write you a letter in my own blood. Never say die sort of stuff. Don't worry, it was only a small cut, I didn't get up very far. I can't remember when I last had a tetanus though. Do you think I should get one? Do you think I might get infected? It was a tiny cut but I thought for a while I'd done it. I shouldn't have drunk anything. I didn't know what I was doing really. And when I thought I'd done it, I was sad."

"Chrissie, for God's sake."

"You're not going to get all moral with me, Liam? Because if you are, I couldn't stand it. I used to think what it would be like to be pregnant. I can't believe it. Was I like that? I can't have it, Liam. I couldn't stand having it. I'd be useless. It'd be all so awful. What the fuck am I going to do? It's not your fault. Don't feel it's your fault. It's my fault. If I hadn't come down. If I'd gone away like I said. And the play went well. I had to cry off. Said I was really sick. They got someone else. That was a good play. Don't feel it's your fault, Liam. I'll sort it out. Just don't be all moral with me. You're not, are you? Remember we used to joke about having kids? Well, it isn't a joke, Liam. It's hard to believe it's happening. In there. Maybe I should see a doctor."

"Yeah."

"No, this is my problem. Hear that? My problem. Sounds like a maths question. Is it a baby, Liam? What do you think? A baby? Like the little ones you see around? It's too small. It couldn't be. It's not really alive. Only a foetus."

"I don't know, Chrissie."

"That's you all over, Liam. I need you. I need your support."

"Do you want me to say it's okay? Then it's okay. Do what you have to."

"Washing your hands, Connolly?"

"No."

"You are."

I didn't reply. She was probably right. I needed time to think.

"I remember the moment of conception. Do you? Do you remember the exact moment? Right at the moment? You said you loved me. Remember? I love you, Chrissie. I remember. God, I felt so close to you, Liam. So close. Like I was part of you. Do you remember? You do, don't you?"

"You can't know which time, Chrissie."

"I can. I do. It was the first. It's always the first. I could feel it. I knew then I'd get pregnant and I didn't mind. I knew it. Jesus, Liam, I knew it, didn't I? Why did I do that? How did I know? You think there's something special here? Maybe I should have it."

"Maybe. Is it what you want?"

"What do you want?"

"What you want."

"Bollocks."

"Look, I'm sorry, Chrissie, I don't know what you want. I can't force my views on you."

"That's real easy."

"No. I remember I said I loved you. I remember that."

I didn't.

"Did I say I loved you? Can you remember that? I don't. I would have though. We were making love. I would have said it. You don't make love and not say it, and that's the time you say it, isn't it? I love you, Liam!"

"Yeah, you did."

She reached out and took my hand.

"Hold me."

I held her.

"How'd you vote?" she asked.

"When?"

"The referendum."

"I was away."

"I was too. Yeah. Good. That's good."

"Yeah."

I kissed her and ran my hands up and down her body.

"I love you, you know?"

"You don't have to say that. Like—"

"I do. It's true."

"I just want to go, Liam. Go. Like I said."

"I know."

"The play was crappy. We had a whole pile of rows. I wanted to get away anyway. I hate the stage. It's all so stupid. It's better having the whole world to play to, on your own. That crowd are useless. You were right."

"Not all of them."

"No, they all are. It was stupid. All of them talking as if they're stars. Jesus, stiff as boards. About as much chance of getting a card as a corpse. I'm better off away from them. It was a crap play. You knew it was a crap play. I could tell from your face. Did you miss me when I was away? I wanted to see you again. I came up for that, too. To see you. I love you, you know. I'm sure I said it when—"

"You did. Look, I think you should see a doctor if you cut yourself. Just to be sure."

"It's over. It's only a small cut. We'll see. I feel a

bit better. I'm worn out, you know. You can only worry so much. I'm worried as much as I can be. Will you stay tonight?"

"Sure."

"Celibate?"

"Yeah."

"Though I want you. Do you think that's mad? I want you. With all this, I want you. Maybe there's something the matter with me. But the want is there. I can't say it isn't. I want to be close to you like the moment it was conceived. That close. Do you remember?"

"It's okay. I'm here."

"Are you?"

"Yes."

"Was I good?"

"What do you mean?"

"That night in the tent?"

"Chrissie!"

"Was I?"

"Yes, of course."

"Good. I couldn't bear not being good. It had to be the best. It was the best, wasn't it?"

"Don't, please."

"I know it was."

"It was."

We sat a while together, singing songs from

musicals, mixing up the lyrics, making up our own. Chrissie sang "All I Want Is A Room Somewhere" and burst out crying, and I sang "Don't Cry For Me Argentina." Then she broke into "Consider Yourself," and I joined her. We finished off with "The Bare Necessities," her scratching her back against the wardrobe door, me bashing out a rhythm on a pillow. It was easy to love her then, to feel we were both together against some terrible unseen enemy. The whole world against us. I firmly believe that's how we viewed it, and I felt good being behind Chrissie, somehow honourable again, knowing that in the end the decision didn't lie with me, that even if I'd wanted it, it was not in my power to do anything, enjoying the freedom of adopting whichever morality I chose without ever having to take responsibility for it. In such causes do the small assume epic proportions.

In bed later, we talked about other things.

"Clare was over. You missed her."

"When?"

"Earlier this week. She's gone to Galway to see her dad. He's had a by-pass."

"Shit, I didn't know. I haven't written to her. I said I would. How is she?"

"Great. We—she—got plastered."

"She's always getting plastered."

"Only here. I'd say she'd like to be home. With

her dad and all."

"Yeah."

"She was sorry she missed you. She might be back on the way over to London. If she doesn't fly direct. Can you fly direct?"

"Think so. She's so—so directed. Don't you think?"

"Maybe. I don't know."

"She loves you."

"Don't be silly."

"I know she does. She was always talking about you in second year. Always."

"Get off."

"I'm serious. We thought you were a thing."

"Would that have mattered?"

"No."

"She's very fond of you. You should—"

"I know. It's just, well, you know. Will you run your hands around me? I want to feel you touch me."

"If you do."

"Okay. Even here?"

"Yes."

"I'm very tired, Liam."

"Me too."

I felt so good about Clare. About not—

"Love you," Chrissie said.

"Love you too."

"What's the furthest place away from here in the world?"

"Where you can live?"

"Yeah."

"New Zealand or somewhere like that, I suppose."

"Well that's where I want to go. Somewhere near there. An island in the south Pacific. Preferably where no one else lives. Would you come?"

"Sure."

"No, I mean it."

"Do you?"

"Yes."

"Okay, Chrissie. We'll go in a giant snail like Doctor Doolittle."

"Or a giant turtle shell."

"Or one of them."

I woke before Chrissie. She shifted closer to me and muttered something in her sleep. I got out of bed and went to the window. I pulled the coarse curtain back. It was raining. I could only see the rain on the window and close to the street lights, and there were puddles on the street. The bedsit was warm. I sat, looking at the street, staring at the car across the road. I'd have to go soon, to have it back. There is a moment of transition, when night is receding and morning is breaking, and the world passes through a timeless umbra. This was that time. It was easy to feel safe at this time, cocooned, entombed, as if in the womb again. Chrissie stretched out and except for one of the sheets covering her around the hips, she was naked. Her body seemed to melt in the soft light. And my mind drifted and wondered what was happening there, in her body, and it all seemed so distant.

CHAPTER ELEVEN

C hrissie went to talk to someone in town about everything, and what they talked about was against the law. And when Chrissie went to these meetings, she was alone, and I didn't argue with her to allow me to come because I didn't really want to be there. Maybe if Chrissie had done it right away, it would have been easier. Maybe. Maybe I'm only saying that. I got a couple of features after my funeral thing appeared, and that made what was happening with Chrissie more difficult for me, even though I didn't want it to be difficult and I thought I'd be able to act pretty okay, and that she'd appreciate what I was doing, especially since I was getting more work and had to fit it in around the work. We saw a lot of each other then, and she was always on the phone to home or the office. I cared. I don't want anyone to think I didn't care, but when she'd ask me if I thought she was doing the right thing, I never came right out and said what I thought. Not straight, the way she wanted. I didn't go against her either but she was looking for my total support, and I did everything

but give it to her. I just couldn't. I hadn't the nerve.
To be involved. To say, okay. Even though that's the
way I felt. I guess I felt so shit about it, I wanted to
avoid it, leave it to her, because deep down I thought
it was wrong and even if it wasn't wrong, I was wrong
for wanting it. For wanting the easy way out. The
convenient solution. The final solution. So long as
no one knew about it, then it was okay. Thou shalt
not get caught.

We stopped making love. It was a mutual thing,
and neither of us questioned it. I still slept with her,
but we only ever lay together. And she started really
hating Dublin again. You know, finding fault in
everything, saying there was much better in other
countries, that she was going to go somewhere, she
didn't know where, but somewhere, get out of Dublin,
that it wasn't her town, that she always felt an outsider
in it, that she might as well be in another country. I
didn't take that too seriously. I should have but I was
more concerned with other things and, anyway, she'd
said it all before and gone and come back. She must
have felt so alone, more alone than I could ever
imagine, even lying with me; and knowing I couldn't
feel what she was feeling maybe it's understandable
she was intent on doing what she did. That didn't
make it any easier.

It was a very hot still day early in the summer,

uncomfortable and thick with fumes the way Dublin is when it's very hot and still: thick so you can taste it, hot like you're standing too close to it, still like nothing wants to happen in it. Days when people don't want to do anything, when they hate having to work or anything like that because they know there mightn't be another one like it all summer and they're going to miss it.

Chrissie was sitting on the wooden floor outside our office when I came up the stairs. She was wearing shorts and a green singlet. And her hair was clipped up. She had dimples in her cheeks, and her eyes were far away. They were still lovely but they were far away. I was sorting through the mail.

"Good morning," she said.

"Hi. How're you feeling?"

"Okay. Little sick this morning."

"Sorry I couldn't come last night. Deadline. I had to get it in. I was here late. I was going to call in but it was too late and—"

"It's okay."

I crouched down and kissed her. Then I got up and opened the door of our office.

"I'm going tomorrow," she said.

"What?"

I didn't have to say that. I'd heard her.

"To have it done."

"What?"

"You heard me."

"But—"

"But what? I don't want to hang on, Liam."

"Where?"

"London."

I was opening a letter and I tore it.

"Oh!"

"That all you can say?"

"Jesus!"

"Not much better."

"I suppose—up to now, I didn't—well, you know. You really are?"

"I thought you were for it. Christ, Liam. We've done nothing but talk about this. I need you, Liam."

"Yeah. Give me a chance to think."

"What's to think about? If I think now I won't do it."

I sat down.

There it was, spread out before me. And it looked dirty, so dirty. Up to then it had been academic, all talk. Oh, Christ, I thought, did it have to be like this?

"You want me to come with you? I'll come with you."

It was a gesture. No more.

"No."

"I would."

"I'm not coming back this time, Liam."

I threw the letter down on a table.

"What?"

"You heard!"

"I thought—"

"You thought what?"

"Where are you going?"

"Anywhere!"

There was such a sound of release from her in that word when she said it. Anywhere. She was serious. Dead firm serious. Christ! I had never seen Chrissie so serious. I reacted from instinct. Old instincts. I had to say something. Get her to reconsider. Give me time to work on her. I didn't care about anything but keeping her with me.

"Couldn't you think a bit more? Maybe you're rushing. You have time."

"No! Don't be stupid. I don't want that. Stop it now. Before it becomes real."

"Yeah. But—"

"But what? It's my decision, Liam. I want your support. Do I have it?"

"I feel lousy."

"You feel lousy! Poor fucking Liam. I'm so sorry for you. Offend your sensibilities, do I? Damn you, you fucking fairy. Mummy's little Liam. Grow up, you bastard. I'm the one that's doing it, Liam. It's me

they're going to poke at. Jesus, Liam, I don't know
what to make of you. I have to do it. For you too."

"Do you?"

"I don't believe this."

"It's all so quick."

"You don't believe that. At least, I hope you don't.
Do you think I haven't thought about it. It feels like
a million years to me."

She was right. I didn't believe it. I wanted to,
though. If it could keep her there.

She gave me a look of scornful affection which
always left me confused. Where love was hatred for
loving and being loved.

"All planned?" I said.

"I've been planning a lot."

"Yes. And I don't fit in?"

"Don't be like that. You know what I'm doing. I
have to get out of here and I don't want to come
back. I can't, Liam."

"I could come."

"Sure! Thing is, I don't want you to. I don't."

"Chrissie!"

"Don't act the prick, Liam. You can't do this with
me. And you don't want to. I want to get away from
you, Liam, for I don't know how long. Longer perhaps.
I'm in too deep. I told you before: I don't like what's
happening. And all this. Jesus, Liam, just be nice to

me today. I feel like I'm falling apart. I'm about this much away from going crazy. I got really sick this morning. I'm afraid, Liam."

I put my arms around her and held her close to me. Inside, there was another me, totally calculated. How long would it take to forget her? Who would replace her? What would I do instead of calling down to her? If work really picked up I'd have no problem. My calculations were struggling in hurt but I wasn't going to break. She wasn't going to break me. And after six months, a year maybe, if I could stick it, she'd be out of my head. Cold turkey. Chrissie cold turkey. There'd be pain, sure, but no more than I'd had before. I'd get over it.

"You'll need me after," I said. "You'll need someone. You will."

"No."

"So sure?"

She sat on the table.

"Do you hate me?"

"No. Does it matter?"

"Of course it matters. I'm a bitch, amn't I? I know I'm a shit. This is hurting me too."

"You seem to like that."

I wasn't thinking straight. I couldn't.

"I'd like you to see it from my point. Can't you try?" she said.

"I don't understand. I really don't. I thought we were in this together. You say you love me and you still do this."

"Are we? I'll still love you."

"Okay, go."

"I want to spend today with you. Are you free?"

"Why don't you just go?"

She got off the table and went to the door.

"You don't mean that."

"Don't I?"

"Sure?"

"Yeah. Go. I'm sick of this."

"Okay. Bye."

"Yeah."

The door shut, and I heard her footsteps pick up pace in the corridor. I cursed myself and tried to stop myself going after her. It didn't work. I ran after her, skipping stairs and nearly falling over. I caught her at the foot of the stairs. She shook me off.

"Fuck off, Connolly. Just fuck off."

Someone in one of the ground floor offices dropped a pencil. I saw it roll across the floor through a half-open door. I held Chrissie against the wall.

"I'm sorry," I said. "I'm angry."

"Let me go."

"Let's go somewhere. I'm sorry. I love you."

"If you say that again, I'll fucking belt you. So

help me, Liam, I'll stick a knife in you. If you love me, why don't you let it be?"

"Don't start that again."

"You did."

"I just thought we'd stay together."

"And that's it?"

"I'll miss you."

"There you go again. Nice trite phrases. You'll miss me like you'd miss a favourite coat, or a hat."

"That's not true."

"Isn't it? I'm sorry. I'm upset. Another Chrissie crisis. Big fucking Chrissie crisis. I shouldn't have told you. I should have just gone. Sent a letter. Maybe I should have just done it a long time ago."

I considered her there in the hallway. In its shade, she wasn't so attractive, against the wall, strained. Was she?

She wanted to go to MacDonald's for a chocolate milkshake, but we turned left at Bachelor's Walk and wandered back over the Halfpenny Bridge without noticing what we were doing. We went into a small coffee shop in Temple Bar. Neither of us touched our coffees. We just sat facing each other, staring, and tearing up serviettes. I was trying to think of all the bad times we'd had, not really caring about what she was going through, only what I was feeling, but all I could remember were the good times and I was filling up on the good times. She reached over and stroked my hand but I couldn't feel her touch. I was gone. I faked a couple of smiles.

A withered man sat at the table next to us, with a coffee and a hunk of cheesecake. He opened his newspaper, and I saw a ten-centimetre story of mine, on deserted wives, on page three. No byline. Hacked back from nearly thirty. The subs. Wreckers. Send in a good piece and they'd change it out of all recognition. Tell you you got something wrong. Always bloody questioning and changing. Are you sure this is right, Liam? Doesn't sound right. And the pedantry. Sound interested, Tony said. Make them think they're helping you. Keep on the right side of the subs. What do they do but fuck around with our copy. And the bloody headlines they come up with. Those who can, do; those who can't, sub. Not real journalists.

The man reading the paper, whose face was long and angular and ashen, saw me looking.

"Shag all in it," he said.

"Yeah, not worth it."

"Do you want to have a gawk?"

"It's just that piece on page three. In the corner. It's mine."

He went to page three.

"This one?"

"Yeah."

He read it up close, his eyes moving rapidly across the text.

"Shag all in that," he said.

"Yeah—it's a living."

"Much screw for that?"

"Not much."

"Good working there?"

"I'm freelance."

"What's that?"

"I do things for different papers."

"Freelance?"

"Yeah."

He kept his eyes on me for a few moments and smiled at Chrissie, who was stirring her coffee with her finger. Then he opened the sports pages.

We sat on the steps of the Central Bank for an hour, watching what went on around us. Chrissie sat one step below me, wiring a piece of costume jewellery she'd bought from a hawker on Grafton Street. I didn't like it much. The pieces were too big. And it ruined her neck. She always insisted she hated her neck. I wasn't inclined to believe her because she was continually buying things to wear around it. She'd had a small string of imitation pearls, and I'd liked them, but they fell off one afternoon in the Phoenix Park when we were trying to set up a photograph of her and a deer. She tripped and fell in a ditch, and the pearls were lost. I got one shot of her with the stag. It wasn't a bad picture.

"Are you going to talk to me, Liam?" she asked.

"What's there to say?"

"You could ask me if I'm happy."

"Are you?"

"What do you think?"

"No point in asking."

"That's it?"

"What else should I say?"

"Are you happy?"

"Don't be stupid."

"Do you want to be?"

"What sort of a question is that?"

"A normal one. You're not normal. Do you think we'll see each other again? It could be a while. Imagine if we passed each other in the street and didn't know each other."

"I'd know you."

"You mightn't. You might be married."

"I asked you to marry me. I don't want anyone else."

"You will. You'd have died if I'd said yes."

"So sure?"

"No. I'm not sure of anything. I'm not sure I'm doing the right thing. I need your support, Liam."

"You're kidding?"

"Sulk. Think of me as being posted away."

"I don't want to think of you at all."

"That's hurtful. Do you want to hurt me?"

The sun went in and came out and went in again in a matter of seconds. And the colours, and the mood of the street and the buildings and the traffic and the people, changed. And when the sun returned, they were not the same as when it had been out before.

"So you're going tomorrow?"

"Yeah, tomorrow."

"Tomorrow."

"I've moved out of my place."

"Where are you going to stay tonight?"

"A hostel."

"You could stay with us."

"And have your mother pawing all over me. No thanks."

"She needn't know."

"We'll see."

She finished with the jewellery and put it around her neck.

"What do you think?"

"Sucks."

"Sourpuss."

"That's me."

"I don't think I can love a sourpuss. So it's better

I go now."

"Yeah."

"Are you sulking? It'll cramp my hitching style if I keep having to worry whether you're sulking or not, Liam."

"It's dangerous for you to be hitching."

"Crap. I clocked you a couple of times."

She made a fist.

"I'm well able to take care of myself."

"I suppose you are. That's one of the things I adore about you."

"I'll be thinking of you."

"You won't. I know that. You'll be with someone else by the end of the year. And that will be that."

"Do you believe that?"

"Do you not believe it?"

"Que será."

"I don't want to let go."

"You have to."

"No."

"You're a pig-headed bastard, Liam. If I didn't go, you'd probably dump me in a few months."

"No. I love you. I feel like someone's scraping my heart with a needle. Stay."

"Bastard."

My instinct and my calculations were allying.

"I'm not sure about this, Chrissie."

"What?"

"I'm not sure."

"About what?"

"Having it done. The abortion. Whether it's right. I don't feel good."

Neither of us had used that word before. We'd been avoiding it. It made me shudder.

"Oh, great!"

"Don't be like that."

"You said you were with me all along. Now you choose to say all this. Why the hell say it now? Jesus, Liam. Go to fuck. I've been working myself up to this. Do you have any idea how I've been working myself up to this? No, you don't. Because you can't feel what I feel. You can't know what I know. Fuck you."

Tears were streaming down her cheeks but it wasn't grief. They were tears of anger.

"They're going to cut my fucking insides up and scrape out whatever's up there, growing in me. They're going to dump it all in a bin or something like that, and then I'm going to walk out and pretend there was nothing there in the first place. That's what's going to happen, and I've been going over and over it for weeks now, preparing myself to do that, because the alternative—well, the alternative is impossible. I couldn't cope, Liam. And neither could you, and you know that. And if you say anything more like what you've just said, I'll never speak to you again."

"You're not going to anyway."

"Piss off."

"But what do you think it is?"

"What?"

"Inside."

She wrestled inside.

"I don't. Look it's my body. God, that's what they all say. Cliché."

She touched me.

"You were with me, Liam. I thought you were with me. We agreed. We both agreed it's for the best. What the hell would we do with a kid? We can barely look after ourselves. Do you believe in reincarnation? Look, if there's reincarnation and it's real, then it'll get another chance. You know. And there'll be no chance for it to do wrong, so it'll get a better deal. Shit, I sound like a right bitch. Please don't go getting emotional, Liam."

"I don't know. I feel like I'm a criminal."

"For what? You're doing nothing. Anyway, I'm going. It's my life, Liam. This is what I was getting at about you. Too close. I have to check everything with you. It's like I don't have any control over me any more. Too deep. Too damn deep. I'm sorry, love."

"Are you?"

"You're trying to hurt me. You're feeling sorry for yourself and you're trying to hurt me. Why didn't you say all this before?"

"I was going to."

"Rubbish."

"I was, Chrissie. I feel. Half of it's part of me."

"Half of what?"

"The baby."

"So it's a baby now. Sometimes I hate you."

"I'm just saying what I feel."

"Shit."

"I feel left out. Powerless."

"Oh, yeah, you were screaming at me to have it when I told you. If you'd had a knife you'd have cut the fucking thing out yourself."

"Don't talk like that. Please."

"I'm upset, Liam. How do you expect me to talk?"

"Is that what they do—cut?"

"Or suction. Or drugs. Miscarriage things. I can't remember. I'd prefer drugs if it didn't make me sick. I don't want to talk about it—Liam, I need you."

"No, you don't."

"Who are you to say?"

"Yeah."

"For God's sake don't sulk."

"I'm not."

"What would you do if I had it?"

"Adoption."

"Great."

"Well, we could have it."

"You're kidding."

"Maybe in a few months—"

"Maybe what?"

"If you'd hang on for a few months."

"This won't hold. They have limits."

"Then why can't you come back after? You'll need me. Need someone."

"After? After, I'll want to be as far away from here as possible. I hope on another planet. Here's useless."

She threw her arms up dramatically and put on an accent. "It's cramping my style."

"What accent was that?"

"Katharine Hepburn. Don't you watch films?"

"Who am I going to watch them with when you're gone?"

"We haven't watched one for ages together. Remember Derek's video? He's in the States now, illegally. He's going to try for a green card."

"He was a faggot."

"So what?"

"Nothing."

"Jealous?"

"Of what?"

"Exactly."

We had lunch in Marks Bros, soup and sandwiches upstairs. Chrissie had a bottle of mineral water with hers and I had a coffee, black with one sugar.

There was an element of absurdity about it all, like most serious things in life. You don't want to admit that when you're being serious but it's there and you know it's there, laughing at you, telling you you're not so important.

"I want to give you something," Chrissie said.

"What?"

"Poetry. A book."

She reached into her bag.

It was a small pocket book.

"I got it on the quays," she said.

There was a bookmarker in it. I was supposed to open it at that page. So I did.

It was Shakespeare.

Let me not to the marriage of true minds admit impediments.

My name was written in pencil before the first line. I read it right through, and then again. It should have done something for me. Any other time it would have done something for me but I wasn't into it doing something for me. I was switching allegiances. I looked at her belly. It was no good to me any more. It was the cause of all the mess. Get rid of it now and it's gone. An idea was fighting its way through me.

Something Chrissie'd said. I had a knife at my fingers. Cut it out. It would be no more than they'd do.

Love is not love which alters when it alteration finds,

Take the knife and cut into her belly and rip it all out. And that would be that, an end to it. Only taking back what I had given.

Or bends with the remover to remove.

I was chewing on my sandwich and thinking of this. Strange the sort of dreams you have about people you love. Makes you think about love and altruism. Is there really such a thing? Or is every act selfish?

O, no, it is an ever-fixed mark that looks on tempests and is never shaken;

If I couldn't have her no one could. The kind of melodrama claptrap Channel 4 shows on Friday afternoons in winter; the kind of bread and butter low-grade soap thrives on. Maybe that's why we denigrate soap: too close to the bone, and not the serious bone, the foolish bone, chewed on once too often, showing us how stupid we really are.

It is the star to every wandering bark, whose worth's unknown, although his height be taken.

Liam giveth and Liam taketh away. I could see she wanted me to be impressed. With her love. The fact that she'd given me this book. And Shakespeare dedicated to me. And I would be impressed. But not then. Then I was hurt and lonely, reading an obituary.

Love's not Time's fool, though rosy lips and cheeks within his bending sickle's compass come;

Absence makes the heart grow fonder. Wrong. Absence makes you forget. Love is immediate. There, in the breath, in the touch; love needs a love to be loved. Otherwise it is a dream. My thoughts of cutting into her flesh were making me feel bad, so I struck the idea out.

Love alters not with his brief hours and weeks, but bears it out even to the edge of doom.

Damn it for fucking us up. Damn it. If she hadn't gotten pregnant, we'd be okay, and she wouldn't be going. No, Liam. She was always going. Chrissie was nothing more than a breeze that cools you on a summer's day. And maybe I'd write better when she was gone, do better work, get more work. The uncertainty. I couldn't stand it.

"What do you think?" she asked.

If this be error, and upon me proved, I never writ, nor no man ever loved.

"I think we did it for the Leaving."

"That's not what I meant."

"What do you want me to say?"

"What you feel about it."

"Not much."

"Can't we love each other still? Even if we're not

together. Even if we never see each other again?"

"Is that what's going to happen?"

"I don't know."

"Thanks."

"Do you hold it against me?"

"What?"

"This."

She touched her stomach.

"I don't think I count."

"You don't want to."

"You've made all the decisions."

"I've had to."

"I love you."

"There you go again."

"What?"

"With all that."

"I can't say anything with you."

"Not true. I used to be a bit scared of you."

"What!"

"I guess I still am. Not much."

"That's rubbish. I've never touched you."

"Not that way. There's other scareds. I told you."

"What?"

"Don't force it."

"I'm not."

"You see?"

"No."

"Then drop it."

"You brought it up."

"I know. And I want to drop it."

"Fine. Have it your way."

"There you go, Liam."

"What?"

"Screw you."

"Screw you too."

We were going to shout. And neither of us wanted to shout. Not there. Not in that place.

"How are you going?" I asked.

"Plane."

"When's your flight tomorrow?"

"Ten."

"Where you going after?"

"Doesn't matter."

"You won't tell me where you're going?"

"No. It's better. I'll write from—from wherever I get to. I'll write. I promise. It's all for the best, Liam. You can see that, can't you? Like, I wouldn't be doing it if it wasn't. If I hadn't worked it out. If I hadn't thought about everything. It'll be quick. And I won't feel so bad. And I'll be able—to—to—you know—have kids, like. It won't damage me."

"Yeah."

"You?"

"I won't come to the airport."

"No."

"I'll miss you."

"Don't."

I was going to say something more, about our baby and stuff like that, but I couldn't do that, not to either of us, me maybe more than her. She said she'd buy me dinner, and I agreed, except that I wanted to pay my way. Chrissie said that was fine. I didn't want her to.

CHAPTER TWELVE

Thoughts of dinner vanished in the frustration of an afternoon of avoiding issues. If she had forgotten, I wasn't going to remind her. There was no more to be said, really. I was growing more and more angry with her. For destroying my dream. Betraying my trust and destroying my dream. We can forgive almost anything else but the destruction of dreams. Dreams are hopes, and without hopes there is nothing. That nothing was rushing at me fast, a frightening emptiness. I kept trying to think of all the other things that meant anything to me in life, all the things I'd had before Chrissie and during Chrissie, and would have after Chrissie. But somehow they paled into nothingness. As I watched her go towards O'Connell Street in the last light of day, I wished to Christ she would turn and come back and say it was all a joke, that I was an idiot to fall for it, that she would never leave, how could I ever think she would leave? And we'd hold each other in the street, not caring who was around us, and I would feel her close to me and feel I was whole again. I watched her go, waiting vainly, until I lost her in the fading light and the evening crowds. I waited for a while after I'd lost her, in case she did decide to change her mind, so she'd be able to find me, and there were times when I saw people in the crowd I thought were Chrissie and my heart would pump for a moment until I knew it wasn't her. And you know what hurt most? Knowing I'd backed off, let her slip away, through my own weakness. Knowing that. Being ashamed of that.

I found myself standing in the street, staring into space. I literally found myself there. And for a moment I didn't know myself. For a moment.

I thought about going into the office and doing some work—I'd a film review to do. I wasn't in much of a humour for doing a review, and the film would probably suffer unjustly for my mood. Work could wait till morning. I was hurt and angry—and kind of relieved. I can't say which was the strongest feeling, they came in different orders and combinations.

I took my jacket off and rolled up my sleeves. Around Trinity, up Nassau Street, I stopped across the road from Lincolns Inn and thought about going in for a few minutes. A tinker woman sat on the footpath near me with a cardboard Mars box beside her and a child in her arms. She was swarthy and furrowed. I dropped ten pence into her box, to add to the fifteen pence already there. It was too late for her to be there. She should give up and go home, I thought, if she had one. Up Merrion Street, past the back gates of the Dáil, across the road and around the corner to Doheny and Nesbitts.

There were some press people in Doheny and Nesbitts, and maybe that's why I went in there. I pushed myself from the door to the bar. Ray Meehan was there, talking with Terry Lamb, who was editor of *Magill* then. Meehan had been a year ahead of me at college and the editor of a magazine I'd been involved with in second year before Tony and I started ours. He was on a six-month contract for the *Sunday Tribune*, and Tony and I envied him for it. It wasn't his fault but we had to have someone to envy and bad-mouth, and he was the best candidate. He wasn't a bad fellow. I always got on with him. He was pissed and slapping Lamb on the shoulder and laughing too loud, when I managed to get to the bar. Lamb was nodding politely but looking like he'd rather be somewhere else. I knew Lamb vaguely. I'd rung him a couple of times, trying to get work, but he was never interested. I didn't mind that. I'd cursed him every time but I didn't mind. Tony had done a few pieces for him and knew him better than I did.

"Liam, you cunt," Ray yelled at me.

I nodded to Lamb and offered to buy a drink. The way Ray was, I knew he'd buy. He was good that way.

"I haven't seen this cunt in years, Terry," Ray said. "Do you two know each other?"

"We've talked on the phone mostly," I said.

Lamb smiled his spare smile.

"I've got to go, Ray," he said. "I'll see you, Liam. Ring again if you get a good idea. Something good though."

"Sure."

As soon as Lamb had gone, and Ray and I were drinking, I knew I shouldn't have come in. Lamb had done the wise thing. Ray wasn't fun when he was drunk. He went on about stories he was working on, and I made a mental note of some of them, in case they might be useful to me, but really I wasn't interested. I just watched his big mouth move and his rough hands slap the counter of the bar every time he made a point. I stayed long enough to drink five of his drinks and hear six of his stories. None of them was anything I could follow up. I was going to buy him a drink but I thought, fuck it, I'd stayed listening to him boring my balls to sterility, why the hell should I buy him a drink? He should buy me some more.

I looked at my watch several times.

"I've got to get going, Ray, I'll see you."

I gave him a shove to show him I meant it. He spilt some of his pint on the counter and some more on another fellow's shoulder. The other fellow didn't notice. He was too much into this peroxide blonde sitting beside him. Ray said he was going to Belfast at the weekend. I slapped him on the arm and wished him good luck.

"I have to go now," I said.

"Okay," he said, reluctantly. "We'll have another sometime. Maybe I can get you some work. Tell Bruton he's a slimeball."

"You tell him. He loves compliments."

Two car lights blinded me on the street. I nearly stepped off the kerb. Chrissie was on my mind in glorious alcoholic technicolour. I leaned back against the front of Doheny and Nesbitts. My eyes were stinging from the smoke in the pub and the car lights. Two girls with slit skirts walked by and I followed them with my sore eyes. I wanted to have sex. Not love or love-making, sex. I was going to do it, even though I was scared of it all, I was going to do it. Yeah. I could go around to Fitzwilliam Square and see if there was anything to pick up. I wasn't drunk enough. I needed more drink, much more drink.

Larry Murphys wasn't as packed as Doheny and Nesbitts. I had Irish to make me drunk quickly. There was a girl in the corner at the door, and I tried to eye her up but she wasn't interested. I had wind too, from the stouts, and I was trying hard to fart in silence.

I had four whiskeys and I belched hard before I left. I don't think anyone heard my belch. My head was lifting off and I was numb. My face was probably red, the way it always goes when I've had too much to drink.

I thought about going down to Leeson Street. No. It had to be certain. I could walk down that way and see if there was anything on Fitzwilliam Square. I didn't know if there'd be anything around. Would I be able? I'd be letting Chrissie down. That was a laugh. No, I wouldn't. There'd be no feeling. Nothing. Purging, or something complicated like that. Pick up something and screw it. Cold screwing. Chrissie was wherever she was, doing what she wanted to do, not caring a shit for me or what I felt, and I was where I was, doing what I liked.

She was standing against the railings, under a shelter of a tree from the square, almost invisible. I passed her three times before I went up to her. She had a country accent. I didn't look at her too much, and she did all the talking. She had a good walk but her skirt was too short and her legs weren't good at the thighs. Her hair was tied tight in a bun at the back of her head, and her chest was flat.

Her chest preyed on me all the way to the house off Pembroke Road. I like good chests on girls and I wanted her to have a good chest. I hadn't noticed it at all before we'd started walking. Then it was on my mind, the same way Chrissie was on my mind, telling me I shouldn't be doing what I was doing. I tried to get her out of my mind, saying I was doing it mechanically and it didn't mean anything. It didn't mean anything. It was just what I wanted to do that night. I couldn't give a crap about this girl, who she was, what made her do this, if she loved anyone. It was the way to do it. It didn't get Chrissie out of my mind.

The basement flat was functional and my country girl, who didn't smile when she undressed and showed me her flat chest, took my money first and turned off the lights and lay down on a bed with no sheets. The walk had made me think more than I wanted. I wanted to piss too. I was scared I'd piss inside her.

"No money back guarantees here," she said. "Do or don't, but no cash back."

"That's okay. I don't want it back. It's only money."

"You going to stand there? There's other punters. Time's a living."

"How much do I have?"

"One go."

"How long's that?"

"As it takes. And here, wear this."

She threw me a durex.

I undressed and placed my clothes on a chair across

the room. I lay on top of her and tried to think of something else other than what we were doing, and not to piss inside her. She had bad breath, not very bad breath, and the hair under her arms wasn't shaved. It was sweaty and the odour made me swallow.

It didn't last more than a couple of minutes.

PART II

THE MAGI

CHAPTER THIRTEEN

Thirtyanythingish and English, tall and taut and very thin with butter-blond hair combed from the centre in waves, sallowish face stretched over sharp prominent bones, excited ice-blue eyes, reluctant sardonic mouth, smooth elegant hands, gentle with a strong handshake, and a purplish scar near his right temple.

I met Ian Lester at seven thirty on an August evening at a péage about twelve kilometres south of Avignon when the sun was low, balanced on the tops of the trees, and I was starving. He appeared from a field at the side of the road, eating an apple, like a mysterious stranger in some arty continental film no one ever watches, strolling over to me as if in slow motion, as if he were being drawn.

He gave me half his apple, and we shared a lift to Paris with a couple who were going to divorce when they got there. They were sorry people and they didn't talk more than ten words all the way. Not that they had to. They'd given us a lift. But you expect talk when you're hitching. You gear yourself up for it. So

Ian and I talked. And he had two more apples we shared. And when we were worn out talking we went to sleep on each other's shoulders as if we'd known each other forever.

I had spent the summer wandering. Wherever I felt like when I woke up. And each place I came to I was a different person. It was easy to fool people on a foolish continent in a foolish world. That was how I saw it. Them and me. And except as an audience, I wanted no contact with them. Just to be alone, detached. I went to Paris and then down to Nice, where an old man who must have been eighty bought me my only decent meal in three days because he believed I would give him a blow job and feared he would die without ever having had one. When I asked him why he didn't just get a whore, he said he'd never paid for it in his life and never would. I found it hard to believe him, and when I had eaten more than I needed, and packed some more away in a supermarket bag, I told him I had to go to the ladies' room. He had blotched leathery skin and sunken pools for eyes, and crooked teeth. I hated the crooked teeth the most. I didn't go back to the table. There were others, like Albert, who found me in the rain beside a petrol station near Mons, headed back to Paris again. He bought me two meals and gave me two hundred francs and told me I shouldn't be hitching alone, it was dangerous. I told Albert my real name, and about myself, some of it, because he was special. He was so quiet and distinguished, and I dreamed of him being forty years younger. Paris, Nice, Rome, Naples, Venice, Belgrade, Split, Budapest, Vienna—Vienna, *The Third Man*, Harry Lime, dark wet streets, Carol Reed, haunting music, the Borgias, the Renaissance, the Swiss, the cuckoo clock and a midnight waltz with Daniel after *The African Queen* and the rest of his bread and cheese: Daniel who was so afraid of being Jewish in Europe, unable to enjoy himself for fear of being what he was. And he looked so Jewish, so bloody Jewish, that he couldn't have hidden it in a million years. People don't like us, he'd say. They don't like us here. He'd been to Dachau, for fifteen minutes. He couldn't take it for any longer. Not because it was so horrible. Because it was clean, too clean. I didn't know enough about Israel for him. The waltz was wonderful.

I was supposed to be going to India, to find myself or something like that, because India's a place you go to find yourself when things get on top of you and grind you down. I wanted to make up for things, all sorts of things I felt were wrong. It was there in my mind somewhere that I should do something to make up. And India was a good place to go to make up. I had schoolgirl visions of being needed and helping out. Making amends. The poor or something. Mother

Teresa stuff, a self-imposed sentence, an open prison. It was as if I was trying to exorcise whole chunks of myself and prove something. And there was Liam. Even an abortion couldn't get rid of him. It might even have made his hold on me stronger. He was at the back of my mind all that summer. I didn't want him there but he was there the way he'd been there before. It could have been the reason I went for Ian. One of them, anyway. Who knows. That and the kind of redemption I was playing with. Resurrection of Chrissie Halloran. All a bit Tolstoyan. You laugh at it until you're in it. We all have such a dreadful need to feel good with ourselves. I don't know. Ian needed me. Like no one else—definitely not Liam.

Ian had a room near Austerlitz, and he offered it to me to share for as long as I liked, as long as I didn't mind classical music and Moroccan dope—tumble weed, he called it—and too many books. He'd been teaching English in Spain for two years and was in Paris for a break. He had a house in Andalucía too, a small farm with a hundred vines in a tiny village near Ronda. And a flat in London. He was divorced from a girl who'd been to school with Fergie. They'd been married for three years but he didn't go into it very much. His family was rich but he didn't have much to do with them.

I expected Ian to make a pass at me when I took

him up on his offer. Like all the others. I wouldn't have held it against him if he had, I'd just have left and thanked him for his hospitality. But he didn't. And he was so gentle and courteous and uninquisitive. That was lovely in a world that isn't happy till it's sucked you to the marrow. I could have given him any one of my personae, and he'd have accepted it. So I told him the truth too. The economy version. He said it was good to have company, he needed company, and Paris wasn't a good place to be without company. And I fell for him even though I wasn't sure what exactly made me do it. He needed me to fall for him. I know that. And I know I was glad he needed me to fall for him. It wasn't the love of want, like with Liam, where the want was so strong it was unbreakable except at a great distance, and there's no explaining the want except that life is unliveable without it. That frightening love I fought so hard to break and even there in Paris with this guy who needed me, I knew I had not broken it. But Liam was far away and there was all that had happened between us, all that I felt bad about and couldn't change, for which I wanted so much to make up.

I said I'd stay a week and I stayed a month, and in that month we busked at the Pompidou, mimed in the Luxembourg Gardens, drank wine into the early hours in a Vietnamese café near the Opéra and walked

the streets together and talked of life and death and
the things that should be talked about in Paris. Often
we didn't sleep until we were too exhausted to stand.
Ian had the money and he shared it freely with me,
who had none, so that I never had to ask him for it.
It was there for me to take. I cannot express how
good that felt, that someone trusted me so much,
and I was so careful spending, watching every centime.

"Money's to be spent," he'd say when I'd been
skimping. "Just get rid of it, Chrissie. There's more
where that came from. I told you, I'm rich. And I
don't want to be rich. Not that rich anyway. You
know what my father says when we meet? He says,
'Buster'—that's what he calls me—'Buster, mate, you
don't stay with money unless you keep it.' Tight
bugger. Well, I want to get rid of it. Have nothing."

I felt such a duty towards him it scared me. Like
he was a replacement for something I had lost. I
knew what it was but I didn't dwell on it. It would
have been morbid to dwell on it. Better to get on
with things and possibilities. But there was a loss.
Definite yet indefinable. And the gap needed to be
filled. So I filled it with Ian. In a way, it had to be
him. Almost written. A stranger in a strange land
who knew nothing about me except what I told him
and was willing to accept me for what I wanted to be.
Whoever I wanted to be. I felt free. And Ian didn't

mind what I called myself, or who I played, so long as I told him so he'd be able to play along. And sometimes he thought up a different character for himself. I thought of Liam less with Ian. I was caught up in something he wasn't part of, far away, and it was like thinking about a dead person. The feelings were always fond feelings, like those about a dead person, but they were faraway feelings.

Ian's room near Austerlitz had no beds, just his mattress up one end and mine down the other end. I did some sketches of it and of Ian, and I still have them. When we were going to sleep, whether it was night or day—we didn't care about time—we used to chant Hindu mantras. A lot of the time Ian wouldn't go to sleep even then. Instead, he'd sit up reading—things like Kierkegaard—smoking dope and humming Peter Paul and Mary songs. I don't know for how long he'd do that but he didn't like sleeping, that was obvious. Several times, I sat and read and smoked with him for as long as I could. And we'd hold hands and hum together. And that was fine. When he was drunk we couldn't do that because he wouldn't allow me. He'd drink and drink until he couldn't hold any more and then he'd throw up in the toilet. I'd hear him but there was nothing I could do about it.

I saw him have the nightmare the night he offered me the job teaching English. The offer wasn't altogether out of the blue. He'd been skirting the whole subject for a while, touching on it now and then without ever coming out with it straight, telling me stories about Béjar, the town he worked in, saying that even though it wasn't a pretty town, the countryside around it was beautiful. So he was probably planning it. I'd actually been thinking about heading off, but I was finding it harder to make the effort, putting it off. So I must have wanted him to ask me. Anyway, I listened to his pitch.

It was a small town, about two hundred kilometres west of Madrid and seventy-odd south of Salamanca, in the lap of the Sierra de Béjar, at the edge of the Gredos.

He spread a map on the floor.

"The countryside is fabulous, Chrissie. Honestly. And there's a medieval wall girding the old end of town and some nice old buildings around the Plaza Mayor," he said.

I felt he was somehow apologising for imperfection.

"It used to be a big textile producer but the textile barons got fat and lazy and let themselves be overtaken by places like Barcelona."

He drew a sketch on the map.

"It's elongated, split in two by a river, the Cuerpo de Hombre, see? It runs down from the sierra and then wraps itself around one side of the town in a small gorge. It's all decaying whitewashed houses at the old end, above the river, capped with reddish-brown terracotta tiles. They make it look like a rotten tooth in a bad gum. Don't worry, it's not as decayed as it looks on that side. At the other end there's solid tower blocks of pisos—flats. The old end of town does look like it's hanging on at the edge of the gorge, though, going to fall into the river."

He looked at me with the eagerness of a small boy.

"It's beautiful countryside. I swear. You'd love it. The sierra dominates the town and the whole surrounding area. Up to eight thousand feet. Like a wall. It's all lush and green on the lower slopes, chestnutty. Higher up it's scorched and windswept. There's year-round snow over the ridges at the top, in a gorge, under a cliff overhang. And then down from that there's the lagunas. The Lagunas del Trampal. They get their water from the melting snow. The biggest, the Laguna Grande, is the best for swimming. You have to swim in it, Chrissie."

He got up from the floor and went over to one of his bags. He dug around in it and pulled out a postcard which he threw down on the map as if to prove what he was saying.

"The far side of the river, as it wraps itself around the side of the town, is all rocky brown heights. They're not as nice as the sierra—I think—and not as high, but they're a good contrast."

He rang a woman called Paoli, as soon as I'd said yes. He said she was his boss. They spoke French and Spanish and German. I didn't understand the German. He was supposed to have gone to England to recruit so he made up a story about me for Paoli.

I didn't sleep that night myself, thinking about it. I'd had too much to eat and drink too, and I wasn't feeling so well. At first, I thought he was talking to me. And I kept saying, what? Then he began to raise his voice. I propped myself up on my elbow and watched him. He was moving, jerking, twisting his head so far that I thought his neck would snap. I got up and went over to him.

"Ian!"

He didn't waken. Instead he became more furious. And when I studied what he was saying, it was Spanish, cursing. There was sweat all over him. It was a warm night but not so warm that you would sweat that much. And when I touched him his body was tense like it was being pulled apart. I shoved him and shook him and tapped his face. Suddenly his arm came out from under the covers and swiped at me. I ducked, and it missed me by a fraction of a centimetre.

"Jesus, Ian!"

I thought he was awake now. But he wasn't.

No matter what I did I couldn't wake him. I sat

beside him and watched while whatever it was went on inside his brain. His anger and fear were apparent on his face, combining in terror, rigid terror, and I thought he might suddenly rip apart. But he didn't. And after a while he began to relax, very slowly, breathing heavily, and when I put my head on his chest and listened to his heart, it was beating madly. I left my head on his chest and listened to his heartbeat recede and felt his body relax. I didn't get in beside him. I just lay there, my head on his chest, until he was back relaxed and sleeping normally. When daylight came, I got a damp cloth from the bathroom and wiped him on the forehead and face and chest, very gently. And then I tapped his cheek with my finger till he woke.

"Hi."

"Chrissie?"

"You were having a bad night."

He looked around. Like he was checking.

"Yes. I do sometimes."

"You've had them before?"

"Yes. This was a big one."

"That why you don't like sleeping?"

"Yeah. Sometimes."

"You okay?"

"Fine. It's not as bad as it looks. The real thing was worse."

"It scared me."

"Sorry."

"What is it?"

"It's okay now."

"Come on, Ian."

He looked around again.

"I was in the war."

"War?"

"Falklands. Malvinas. Whichever you like. Thatcher's great crusade. I used to be in the army. I was in Belfast too. I didn't tell you in case—in case you held it against me. I'm not in it any more. Unfit for duty."

"What happened?"

"I killed someone."

"Oh!"

There was a strange bonding in those words. Like he'd said them for both of us.

"I was at school," I said. "I saw it on telly."

"I was suffering from the trots. I got a chill the day after we landed. We were advancing. It was raining and getting dark. They were dug in, the Argies— Argentinians. They hit us with mortars. Two of my lads were blown to bits. I could see one chap's leg near me. The other one was screaming this terrible lonely scream. I can still hear it. All that firing and noise and smoke and smell, and I can still hear the scream. I kept going. Had to. They were well dug in, so we had to scramble from cover to cover and ferret them out hole by hole. But we were never sure we'd got them all. I had this sneaking feeling there'd be one behind me. I kept looking behind me, so much so that I didn't see this bloke right in front of me. He was standing up, dark and dirty, aiming his rifle at me when I turned. About five feet away. Someone yelled a warning—I think it was my sergeant—but he'd fired at me by the time I'd heard it all. The bullet creased me. I felt this crack at the side of my skull, like it had been cleaved open. I was lunging at him with my bayonet. Right into him. I heard it, I think, and a sickly wheeze. His eyes screwed up and blood came out of his mouth, and I twisted it into him. He fell back and I fell on to him in the mud, and he cursed me. He was so bloody young. Should have been at school with you. I can't remember much after that. I passed out. That's the dream."

"Oh, shit."

"They gave me a medal and shipped me home, and then I attacked someone one night and they gave me six months suspended and a score of visits to a shrink. And I know what you're thinking—you're thinking, who did he attack and will he attack me? I'll save you the trouble. I attacked my wife. My lovely Kate. Kiss Me Kate. I hit her with a bottle and split her head open one night after I'd bum-fucked her. She hated to be bum-fucked—"

"Don't, Ian—"

"Don't? I want to. She hated being bum-fucked; more your missionary was Kiss Me Kate. She was kissing everyone, you see. We had an open marriage when I came back. I couldn't do it—get it up, get it in—not the proper way. That sounds ridiculous: the proper way. So Kiss Me Kate fucked everything in trousers. The shrink told me it was all to do with what happened—over there, eight thousand miles from home. The most barren lump of waste I've ever seen. Where was I?"

"Please don't."

"I'm sorry. I haven't told anyone this for a long time. I wasn't going to ask you to stay because I was afraid, of myself, of this. You see, I enjoy the dream now."

He lifted off the covers. There was semen all over his penis and on his legs and his stomach. He scraped it off and held it up for me.

"Wanker."

He laughed.

"Ian."

"Not my fault, the doctor says. Just happens. Something funny inside me. Don't worry, I don't feel very good about it when I wake up. Like now. I don't

use bottles any more. Not on other people. Kiss Me
Kate was the last. I feel rotten about that. It didn't
damage her though. Her looks. I did myself with the
next bottle. Didn't work though. I'm still here. Will
you grab my balls and squeeze them till they hurt—
and belt me?"

"No."

"Good. I thought I'd ask. I need it. I can't love.
Like—I hate that word—like normal. There was this
bloke, Alex, for about a month. Nothing happened.
That's when I started bum-fucking Kiss Me Kate. I
hated her for that. For doing it. Why'd she do it?—
you can go if you like. I'd understand. I'd go if I were
you."

"Oh, lord, Ian!"

"No pity. Please. I love you. Know that? You make
me feel good, Chrissie."

I kissed him. He didn't respond, but then I didn't
need him to respond.

"I'll wipe you," I said.

I got some paper from the bathroom and cleaned
him off. He lay still while I cleaned him, and when
I had finished wiping him with the paper, I rubbed
him with the wet cloth and ran a towel over him.

Later, I left him sleeping and went walking and
went through my options. As if I had any. I thought
about Liam, what he might be doing, allowing fond

faraway feelings to massage me. And I thought of Ian, sleeping peacefully now. I'd done that for him. I made him feel good. I did. Those were his words. There was a swelling feeling in my chest that I hadn't felt for so long I couldn't remember the last time, and walking through the streets of the Fifth and Sixth, I felt good about what I'd been able to do, about what I might do. He needed me. I was strong beside him and that felt good too. It was all very little-girlish, wondering if I could help him more. Be a sort of saint. I used to look at the saints and think it would be fantastic to be one of them. I think girls go for saints the way boys go for soldiers. With the same naïveté. It was a *Magnificent Obsession* sort of thing. Only I didn't have the problem of having caused it. I had others. Mine.

I imagined a kind of comic strip idyllic setting, where I could be a hero. I'd always wanted to be a hero, riding through people's lives, making things better for them. When I was a kid I loved Robin Hood and Daniel Boone, and when we played them I always wanted to be Richard Greene or—what was his name?—Fess Parker. But Billy never let me. You're a girl, he'd say. Girls can't be heroes. I hadn't seen Billy for nearly a year. The favourite. He got everything he wanted. And the shit that went with it when things fell apart. Perhaps that's the price of getting everything you want. I drank coffee and read a paper and bought some chips and sat in a corner of Shakespeare and Co on Rue de la Bucherie for the afternoon and read a book and thought about my options.

CHAPTER FOURTEEN

We lived in a top-floor piso on the Plaza Mayor in Béjar. A plaza mayor made redundant by the fact that it was too far up the old end of town to be used by people from the new end of town. There were a few bars around it, an old fortress used as a school, and a brown stone church with storks nesting in its tower, but only the children going to school gave it any life. There was a tiny park between the church and the old fortress but it was too small for anything to happen there.

The piso was small and low-ceilinged, the floors tiled and the walls stonewashed. The roof leaked in several places, mainly in the hall area and the bathroom. If it rained heavily, we got flooded. There were cracks and big black damp stains on the ceiling above the hallway. I thought the ceiling might collapse once when the rain was really heavy. The living-room ceiling had no leaks but it slanted down sharply on one side and it was easy to knock your head on it. There was a round table in the centre of the room, with a quilted rug draped over it and a small electric brasero fitted into the base of the table to keep your feet warm. The piso looked out over the reddish-brown roofs of the old town, and they were shadowy outlines through the window at night.

Our landlady, Concha, a short middle-aged woman with broad shoulders, lived in the piso immediately below us and always had her door open, whether as a sign of friendship or to keep an eye on our comings and goings, I don't know. I don't think she approved of unmarrieds sharing—even platonically. But then we existed in our own world with our own laws. Extranjeros. Part of the town but not part of it. Concha took our money anyway and sold us bottled gas for our cooker and wood for our fire when we needed them. We showed her the damp stains, and she put her hand to her mouth, muttered something and called her husband, Manuel, who did little odd jobs in a room beside their piso. They studied the damp and told us they'd have to do something about it, but they never did in the time I was there. It was only a problem if it rained heavily, otherwise we could live with it. There was always a smell of cooking from Concha's place.

Paoli was more fragile than I'd expected. That was Ian trying to build her up as a boss figure when she wasn't. They were partners. Ian's money and her effort. He left most of the decisions to her. She'd

been born in Germany and had an Italian mother
somewhere but she hadn't been out of Spain since
coming back as a child. Perhaps that was why she'd
married an American. Her hair was jet-black and short
and straight, and her eyes were bright white around
the pupils, which, with her hair, gave her a sort of
shocked expression. And she was too pale for someone
living in the sunshine. Ian said she didn't like going
out in the sun. She was attractive but too frail. On my
first night in Béjar, she and her husband, Tom, who
had an Eastern European surname that was unpro-
nounceable, gave a dinner for me. He was a painter
with an accent somewhere between Salamanca and
Brooklyn, a neat moustache, a pedantic attention to
detail in the things he was interested in and a
contempt for the things he wasn't. He wasn't much
interested in anything outside painting—except
perhaps language. He was a good painter and he
offered to give me lessons if I wanted, but he was
unhappy. Mostly at being in a small town like Béjar
when he felt he should have been somewhere else
like back in New York. He'd come to Salamanca to
study, met Paoli there and married her. They had no
children—he'd had a job done— and they hadn't
slept together in eighteen months. Ian told me all
this. Paoli was glad I'd come and she played big sister
to me, showing me what was what, and I played

along because there was nothing else I could do and I rather liked it anyway.

The school was a nondescript grey building, with paint peeling on the front walls, squashed into a side-street off Calle Mayor, the main shopping street. Calle Mayor was actually three streets, Mayor de Pardiñas, Sanchez Ocaña and Mayor de Reinosa, but we called it all Mayor. It was dark and narrow, and one-way for cars when they were allowed up it, even though there was barely enough room for one car. When you were walking along it with the traffic, you had to keep your wits about you and watch your back, in case a car caught you unawares. In the evening time, when the heat was heavy in summer, there was a strong smell of coffee from the side-streets and pig meat from the butcher shops, and frying and boiling from the houses and pisos. The old women and the children sat in their doorways down these little streets off Calle Mayor watching whoever chanced down their capillary in the soft evening light.

There was a small metal plaque on the door of the school, with its name in black lettering. The door was wooden and split on one side. Inside there were three classes off a central reception area. The floors were wooden and untreated, and the wood was decaying and splintering. The walls were painted light blue and the paint was uneven up higher. Each of the classes had a magic marker board and a table with a plain veneer chipboard top. The rooms had only one heater each, attached to the wall, and in winter we froze. In summer, it was pleasant because the sun never shone directly into the classes and the blue walls kept them cool. There were French windows leading from two of the classes and the reception area to a balcony which looked over a garden one level below it. The garden was overgrown and it had roses along one wall and nettles along another. There was a sunken pond in the middle of the garden. But it had no water. The third classroom had no windows and the light had to be on all the time. It was the coldest room in the building.

Paoli had her desk in the reception area, and a typewriter and a black phone. She had shelves behind her, next to the French window, with books for teaching English and German, and novels and cassette tapes. We had three tape recorders for the tapes. Paoli's heater was on wheels behind her. The wheels meant she could move it closer to her if she liked. There were some spare chairs lying around the reception area and some posters of Spain on the walls. And Paoli had a radio.

There was only one toilet and the bowl was unstable to sit on. The door wouldn't shut properly either and you could see in if you were nearby at a certain angle. The younger boys used to follow the girls down to it and try and look in if they could. We got a few complaints from mothers over that. When I first had to go, I tried to keep the door closed using my belt. I failed and held myself for a bar, later.

Under Paoli's desk we kept a kettle we'd rigged to fit a two-pronged socket. Paoli considered us Philistines for making coffee with just water. We didn't care. We kept sugar and a tin of powdered milk in one of her drawers. We had coffee in the school when it was too inconvenient to go to a bar, or when we were too cold to go out without a drink inside us. Paoli would sit with us but she never took our coffee.

Everything was lovely with Ian for a while. And for a while I was glad I'd agreed to come. I settled into my classes easily. He was right about it being another stage. And a different audience every hour. A different Chrissie for a different audience and never the same performance any two days. The minute I was in class I was in my own world, in complete control, and I loved it. I used to feel wiped out at the end of a day, the way I'd felt wiped out after a play, but completely exhilarated, totally fulfilled. And I had a new friend in Paoli, who needed a friend because her best friend, her husband, did not want to be her friend any more. I felt good about Paoli. And good about Ian so long as he appreciated me. So long as he appreciated me,

I felt I was doing him good. And I was. He was more stable and he even slept well and didn't have any more nightmares like Paris. There was a certain peace about him.

The change began when I started going to painting lessons with Tom. Part of it was that Ian hated Tom and he felt I was somehow letting him down by taking lessons. He'd sulk and get kind of manic whenever I said I was going. I found I could control it most of the time by threatening to walk out, and it generally worked except when he'd tear his watch off and show me the scar on his wrist. Then the nightmares returned, but I was working now and tired and sleeping in another room, so I left him with them. And when he'd ask me if he'd been having one, knowing full well he had, I'd say I'd been asleep and hadn't heard anything. It was wearing me down and the spontaneity and mystery of Paris was gone. I was finding out more about him too. That his family were Industrial Revolution money from the Home Counties, he'd been to eight schools, loved music and hated games, had been to Cambridge, joined the army because he'd nothing else to do, hated the army, had married his wife, Kate, because it had been expected, had some shares in a merchant bank his family had an interest in and had a brother who'd been killed in an air crash.

There were other things: I found out from Paoli after she'd broken down in front of me that he'd been screwing her most of the previous year. And others too. Students. Some under-age. She thought I was one of his flings. I felt a certain superiority telling her I was not. The mystery was replaced by a frightening ordinariness. Best to get out before you reach that.

Bang went my good intentions. I started having this vision of myself having to look after Ian forever, as a kind of eternal penance. And that began to haunt me the way it hadn't—or I hadn't let it—before. Like one of those terrible punishments in the ancient underworld. I'd wanted to believe I could do something to help him. But I was slowly realising that Ian was going down, and there was a rollercoaster determinism about it all and if I couldn't do something I'd go down with him.

He definitely started to look on me as his due. Like he'd done me all the favours. And that annoyed me. I started avoiding going home to him. And to avoid having to go home, to avoid being with him in the piso at night, I'd end up going home with Paoli, to her empty piso, and watching television with her until Tom came in or I grew too tired to stay awake. It was one of those evenings she told me about Ian and her. After three bottles of wine. I wasn't surprised.

She tried to tell me more about it. What he'd made her do. There were marks on her hips, big marks, and on her legs, where he'd hurt her, made her cry.

She pointed to her bottom and made a sign of sex with her fingers.

"Here. I don't like that. I feel—"

She shivered and sank back into her chair.

"Why?" I asked.

She shrugged.

"I need—you know. I am lonely."

"Yes, I know."

"You?"

"No."

"I thought—"

"No."

"I am glad. He is nice. You won't say."

"No."

She pointed to her head.

"He is—"

"I know."

"Please, you won't—"

"No, of course not."

I held her and comforted her.

The wine made me angry and want to confront Ian, to take him on. Not for me, at least I don't think so, but for her. She still wanted him. And when he asked again, she would do it. I'd asked whether Tom knew. She'd just laughed. So I wanted to clock Ian. Tell him what a bastard he was to her.

At home, I knocked on his door. There was no answer. I knocked again and didn't wait for an answer. I shoved it open. He was sitting on the floor, naked, against the wall, legs crossed, covered in semen. There was a glass of water beside him and his fist was clenched, like he was holding something, tight.

"Hello, love," he said.

I didn't reply.

"I've been dreaming. Buster's been dreaming. Can't you tell? Dream dream dream. All I have to do is dream. Where were you? Where were you when I wanted you? When I needed you? Avoiding me? Avoiding old Ian? Not quite right up top, old Ian. You and her been saying that? She been talking about me? She's a funny woman. Can't get enough, you know. Mad for it."

"Shut up."

"Sorry. You two been talking? I figure you have. It's written all over you. I've been drinking. Have you? Twenty beers. I can hold my beers. I can. That's pretty Irish. Drinking. Impressed?"

"No. Ian—"

"It was bad tonight. I came three times."

His head sank.

"I didn't want to wake up. I didn't. Look, I'm

covered in it. Fuck, Chrissie, is this ever going to stop? Touch me."

"No."

"No. You're right. I know you try. Thanks. Well, no need any longer."

He opened his hand. There were a load of pills in his palm. I looked around for a bottle.

"Enough to do an elephant in."

"Ian!"

"I'm not an elephant."

"Give me them."

He shoved them in his mouth. A couple hit the edges and fell to the floor. I moved towards him.

"Ian!"

He lifted the glass to his lips and smiled.

"Bastard!"

I threw myself at him and knocked the glass from his hand. The water spilled all over him and mixed in with the semen. I shoved my hand in his mouth and tried to force it open. He was still smiling. I tore at his mouth, yelling his name, splitting his lower lip with my nails.

"Ian, for fuck sake!"

He opened his mouth and showed me the crushed pills. He had them wedged in a mush between his lip and his gum. There was blood all over his mouth from where I'd cut him. He slammed his mouth shut again.

"What the fuck is this? Ian? What?"

"Love me," he said.

"What?"

"Love me."

"I—"

"I love you. You know that. I thought—can't you love me?"

"I do care."

"Then love me."

"Not like that. I won't. We agreed."

"I need you."

"I can't put up with this. You hear? I can't. Why the fuck do you do this? Like this? You—"

His mouth stayed open. I reached out and touched the crushed mess of pills and blood. He didn't close it. There was gathering moisture in his eyes. I scraped the pills out with my finger. On the floor. The tiled floor. He spat out the rest. I stroked him and then got him into the bathroom and washed his mouth out.

I put him to bed and went and had another drink to calm me down. I wasn't going to sleep. I drank a bottle of wine from the fridge and smoked some of Ian's Moroccan weed. He kept it in the tea caddy, at the bottom. My mind was racing, really weird, and I wanted to be emotional but I couldn't. Anger and care had fought themselves to a standstill. Care winning on points because I still wanted to believe I could help. And he was so vulnerable. He did need me. You don't know how attractive that was to me. To think I could make such a difference. That was what I was thinking—that if I—well—if I could do it for him, make proper love to him perhaps he'd— well, it was all like that.

I finished the wine and got some more dope and my head was swinging from the ceiling. I could do it. I could make him better. I was sure I could. It only needed me to help him.

I made love to him because it had become a challenge, a challenge I couldn't resist, to rescue him from wherever he was caught. It was my choice and it was more difficult than I'd imagined, so difficult that even with the wine and the dope, I couldn't loosen up. And there was Liam, back there in the distance, fading, and it was hard to let go of him, so hard that I don't think I did. And Ian, naked, limp, and my mouth on him, trying so hard, and nothing but the heat in me rising until—no, that's not what I want, Ian, I want to make love, proper love, tender love, not this, please don't make me do this, okay just a bit, there, harder, Christ, harder—until I obeyed him and squeezed him so tight he screamed and his prick came up and something deep within me broke free and I rushed to sit on him and get him inside me, pushing him even though it hurt me; and then he was in and I was moving, slow first, still squeezing his swollen balls, squeezing them and him in agony and crying, and it was warm, flooding warm and I was swelling, and he asked me to hit him, asked me louder, begged me, and, oh Jesus, I was coming faster than I'd thought I would and I hit him, around the face, soft then hard, then harder, and he raised hands and took my hair and pulled me to him and pushed up at me, and I raised myself so he could push up more, and we were doing it together: I was coming, Jesus, I was coming, and so was he, I could feel him throbbing, so I squeezed harder and belted him all over, and he smiled ecstatically and thrust up hard into me, moaning, and I moaned with him, oh God, I moaned and I came high on a wave, so high I thought I'd fall off, high, holding him, feeling him come, hearing him cry and call my name, and, oh Jesus, I love you, Chrissie, I love you, Ian, I love you, I love you.

I stayed the night in his bed, holding him. I didn't sleep. Ian did, and no nightmares. He looked so peaceful there, sleeping, like the weight of the world had been taken off him. And I was disgusted. With myself. With what we had done. With knowing I'd failed. I thought of times with Liam and wished to God he was with me. I never knew I could feel so lost, so out of it, miss anyone that much. I had never missed anyone before him and I thought time would take care of Liam, time and distance, but wherever I'd gone he'd always been there right behind me, right there.

I drew sketches of him in a notebook when I went for walks alone in the woods of the lower slopes of the sierra. I remembered the first time I'd tried to leave him. The pain of knowing he was so near, telling myself I had to break that pain, get free of it, then snapping. If he hated me, he had reason. His face when I'd left. God, they were all so possessive. Always wanting you to be there. To commit. It was claustrophobic. Like you were going to smother. And dependent. And I don't like dependence. It's false, and when it breaks down you fall apart.

And now Ian was pulling me in. Did it always have to be like this? I felt trapped there, with him, trapped as if in prison. I hadn't intended this. A few weeks, some fun, not this. There was a need to get away, and the knowledge that I couldn't, that if I got away, well, Ian would—I didn't want to think about that either. I had to get away though, from this, not to be sucked down. I knew what he'd do. And he'd mean it. That's the worst, knowing they mean it.

Liam wasn't in when I phoned. I was out walking by the river, sketching the textile factories, redundant and working, which lined its banks. The empty factories looked like discarded insect skins and the river sometimes changed colour below the working factories if one of them discharged chemicals into the water. It was a dirty river below them but clean further up on the sierra. I suddenly had this terrible urge to ring him. Bad feelings, perhaps. No more than that. And I missed him. Having him there. I wanted to hug him. I left a glib message with his mother and told myself it was ridiculous ringing Liam because he was gone and that was that. I still missed him. Ian was sitting by the window when I got back, throwing stale bread at some birds.

At that moment I despised him for what he was doing to me, for what he would do to me. I hugged him and ran my fingers through his butter-blond hair and thought about how I might get away from him.

"I want to leave, Ian."

"No."

"Last night—"

"It was wonderful, Chrissie."

"No, it wasn't. I was pissed and doped. I feel disgusting, Ian. I want to leave."

"Please."

"I can't take this."

"I'm sorry, Chrissie. I didn't—I thought you—"

"Enjoyed it?"

"Yes."

"No. It was for you."

"I couldn't bear it if you went. I promise I won't do anything like this again. I promise. Stay. You like it here."

"I know. I love this place. But not here. Not with you."

"Please don't."

"I want out, Ian. I thought I could help."

"You do, love. You do."

I had to use Liam. To really hit him.

"There's someone at home, too. Someone I haven't ever let go of."

He tossed what bread he had left out the window and took in five or six deep breaths.

"Do you love him?"

"Yes."

"I see."

"Do you?"

There was silence between us. Ian got up and went into the kitchen. I heard him open the fridge. If he expected me to follow him, he was wrong. I stayed put until he came back. Drinking a glass of milk.

"I'll move out, Chrissie. I'll get another place. Okay? Another piso. I'll leave you here and still pay my half. How about that? Then it'll be okay. And anything you like, I'll accept, I promise."

We talked about Liam for an hour, and I found myself holding Connolly up as some kind of superman for Ian. Shit, the things I do. I know what I was planning, I knew it then but I didn't say.

I only called Liam again to hear his voice, find out how he was. That's all. At least that's what I told myself. He was depressed the way he got when life wasn't working out the way he absolutely wanted it. He cared a lot about home. About what was happening. Tabloid philosopher. Though he would never accept that. I couldn't really get worked up over it all. People left me and I left them, that was that. My problem. But Liam felt all the mess at home personally, and that made him depressed. And he'd counted on me, and I'd let him down. But I picked up the phone anyway, after a session with Paoli. Along with what I was planning, I had this want. For Liam to fill. To be treated tenderly. Loved tenderly. To cleanse myself of Ian—his ways made me feel unclean just thinking about them. And I'd been part of them. Just that once. But to be loved properly. To enjoy every touch. I'd tried with Ian. I had tried, and there'd been a little, hadn't there. But—

"Hello, darling!"

"Chrissie!"

"Hello."

"Where the hell are you?"

"Typical. Couldn't you ask me how I am?"

"How are you? Now where are you? I thought—"

"Miss me?"

"Of course."

"Good. I miss you."

"What? The line's bad."

I raised my voice.

"I said, good. How's work?"

"Shit. We had a strike. That was shit. It's over now. The girls have gone. Anne's gone to Sydney and Cathy's gone to the States. We're on our own. Tony's getting stuff from the Indo. I'm getting nothing. Look, where the fuck are you? It's been months."

"Spain. I've a job teaching English."

"What? Speak louder."

I yelled.

"Spain! Teaching English!"

"Right. God, it's good to hear you. How are you? I mean—"

"I'm fine. Everything's fine. Listen, it's beautiful out here. You should see it."

"Where's here?"

"Near Salamanca. Do you know Salamanca?"

"I've heard of it. I'd have to look at a map."

"How's home?"

"Same old two and four. Tony's got legal action

against him. Wasn't his fault."

"That's typical."

"Chrissie—"

"What?"

"Nothing."

"Go on."

"Did—"

"Yes. It was quick. Hate me?"

"No. You're okay? You never said."

"Fine. Don't talk about that. Past. Leave the past to the past. You should see it here. I wish you could."

"Me too."

"Why—"

"What?"

"Why don't you come?"

It was what I wanted. Just then. The way I was feeling.

"Right now I'd love to. It's rotten over here. The only time I ever go out is to see someone off. If I go to another going away, I'll scream."

"Poor darling. Mum and Dad okay?"

"Yeah. Carry on regardless. That's their way."

"Cormac?"

"He's going to go to London. Most of his friends are gone. He could stay fiddling about but what would be the point?"

"I miss you. It's been yonks. I've been everywhere.

I hitched everywhere. All over the place. God, I've so much to talk to you about. Talk, will you. I need to hear your voice. Just talk."

"About what?"

"Anything. Just talk."

"You plastered?"

"Why?"

"You sound it. Anyway, this is pretty sudden."

"A little bit. We've been on the piss. You screwing anyone?"

"Chrissie! What sort of question's that?"

"Sorry. I miss you."

"Yeah. Me too."

"Love you."

CHAPTER FIFTEEN

It was wrong and I knew it was wrong but I kept ringing Liam. And I knew what I was doing to him, I could tell by the sound of his voice. I knew what I wanted even though I wouldn't admit it. I'd ring and be terribly happy even if I was feeling shit, and I knew he'd be sitting in that office, looking out at the rain when I was talking about sunshine in late November. I knew I had him, that I could do what I wanted with him. I knew I was bleeding him. I knew he was weakening. I knew what would happen. I told myself he had a choice. He needn't come if he didn't want to. And if things had been better, he might not have. But I knew he would.

He arrived the same day as the snow. The snow beat him by a few hours. Ian and I had been in Salamanca for the weekend. It had been good and we'd even kissed a few times, and he'd enjoyed it. Small affectionate pecks. Friend pecks. Salamanca is a jewel and has one of the best—if not the best— plaza mayors in Spain, and because it's a university town it's always buzzing, which suited Ian. We toured the bars at night and drank coffee in the Plaza Mayor all day. And Ian pigged out in Burger King, which was probably the real reason he wanted to go to Salamanca. For his fix. He got another fix too, in a bar near the Plaza Mayor.

I nearly dropped when I saw Liam. I'd planned it, wanted it, but it still caught me off guard just seeing him there. In front of me. I'd been briefing Ian about him for a couple of weeks, telling him how he should act if Liam came. I wanted to be in control. Ian was being perfect. That was the only reason I agreed to go to Salamanca with him. He'd moved into a small piso near the school and it was easier to deal with him there. Concha raised an eyebrow when she found out, then smiled and said nothing. I did my best to avoid her after that. I didn't know how I was going to explain Liam. And then he was there. Right in front of me.

I'd been out running like I always did when I could. Body beautiful. And there he was, sitting on his rucksack beside the door to our building, covered in snowflakes. I dropped the barra I had in my hand, in the snow. I bought a fresh barra every day in the same bread shop, from a fat woman who never looked you straight in the eyes when she was talking to you. Wide-eyed, she was always rubbing flour from her thick hands on the plain wooden counter which was the only indication that the single room with bare stone walls and stone floor was indeed a shop. She had the barras in milk crates behind the counter and she calculated bills on odd pieces of paper with a biro. I liked to get down early or late because if I went down in between then I'd get caught in the queue and I would be stuck behind a group of women who had come as much for a chat as for bread. Shopping in Béjar was a social event. Ask for something, have a chat, ask for something else, have another chat, and so on. It was fine if you'd the time.

Liam got up and picked up my barra from the snow and dusted the snow off it. We still hadn't spoken. I'm sure my mouth was wide open.

"Hello, you," I said.

I always said that if I wasn't ready for him. It was ridiculous and I wished I could come up with something better, but it always came out, as if I was a little girl. My legs were jellying fast. He handed me my bread. At least a quarter of my response was an act.

"Hi."

I fumbled with the barra and nearly dropped it again.

"Where—"

"Surprised?"

"Yes—no. I don't know. I didn't expect you today.

Why didn't you say? I didn't think—"

"I wanted to surprise you. I brought the weather. You said I should come out. I said I was coming."

"Yeah, but—"

"But what?"

I emptied my lungs. He was heavier, I thought. But that could have been all the clothes he had on. His hair was long, well, longer, and he was a bit red but that could have been the weather. He still had that same pained smile.

"Don't I get a kiss?"

I kissed him quickly.

He grabbed me by the shoulders and kissed me longer. Warm in the cold. It tasted of chocolate. I told him.

"Breakfast," he said.

"I'm going to have mine now."

I was dead excited. And trying hard not to show it. I must have shown it. Sure I couldn't get the door open for ages.

Liam stood watching, smiling, not helping. Expecting something.

"So, are you going to stay there? Or are you coming up?"

"Chrissie!"

"What?"

"Chrissie!"

"What's all this, 'Chrissie!'?"

"You're—"

"What?"

"Not much warmer than the snow."

"Oh! I'm sorry. It's just—well, you're here. Right there. Bang. Wallop. Die!"

I threw my arms around him and gave him a quick hug.

"I'm glad to see you, I am. It's just here. Come on up. I am glad to see you."

I scraped my shoes at the door and climbed the stairs in twos, trying to imagine what would happen upstairs. God, Concha. I had to get him by Concha. Liam struggled up with his rucksack. Manuel was working in his small room, bent over, his beret blocking any view of his face, a stringy column of smoke rising from under his beret. He was planing wood and his little terrier was playing in the shavings. The dog barked when I went by. I think Concha had it trained. Her piso gave off a smell of olive oil and garlic and fish. I thought she might run out when the dog barked. She often did. So I moved faster and hoped Liam would move faster. I could do without Concha talking to Liam. Manuel didn't even bother looking up. Why the hell did he have to arrive now? I kept thinking. Why not at night? Shit. And I'd classes at one and two.

When we'd been sharing, Ian and I used to watch *Dynasty* at midday if we didn't have any early classes. For a laugh. And then dress up and play the characters. Simple dialogue, childish plots and plenty of overacting. Who could resist? We'd flop back on the couch, sipping coffee and nibbling bread. I was really into it. I'd have loved a part in it. Anyway, automatically I turned on *Dynasty*.

"Shit," Liam said. "I come all the way here for that."

"Ignore that," I said. "Well, what do you think?"

He looked around.

"Nice. Very nice."

"I always watch this with breakfast."

I put on an Alexis Carrington mouth.

"Do you know what I'd love?" I said. "Almond slices and hot chocolate. We—I—have some. Want some? With breakfast?"

"Terrific!"

I put his rucksack in my room, why, I don't know, just mechanical, turned on the brasero, put on the percolator for coffee and the milk for hot chocolate, put out the bread, the butter, the apricot jam I always had, and, of course, the almond slices. All for breakfast. Liam followed me around like a shadow, not saying anything, and I couldn't think of anything to say to him. How long are you here for? No. Stupid. You can stay as—could he? He could. I watched him out of the corner of my eye. There was something bizarre and amusing about it. If Ian called over. He'd the eleven o'clock. Finished now. If he called over. A kind of mischief flowed through me. Ian and Liam. Cruel, I know, but I'm like that.

The percolator belched that it was ready and when I came into the kitchen again, the milk was bubbling tiny bubbles around the edge of the pot and coffee was running down the side of the grey metal percolator and spitting and bubbling like molten tar. I turned off both gas jets and used paper towels to lift the pot and the percolator. They had a habit of heating at the handles, and if you lifted either too quickly you got burned.

The snow was falling in heavy lumps outside, gathering on the window ledge, and condensation was forming at the corners of the window. On the red roofs the snow was settling in furrows, giving them a striped look. Further out, towards the sierra, the weather had closed in, so you couldn't see much except falling snow.

"Hungry?" I said to Liam.

"Not much."

"I am. Sit down."

We sat down, and I cut bread and buttered it. I put jam on it. He poured the milk for hot chocolate.

"Leave that. Dunk," he said.

He gave me an almond slice.

I squeezed the piece of bread in my hand, and the apricot jam spilled on to my hand and slid down to my sleeve. I swore and got up from my comfort at the table, and went into the kitchen for some more paper towel. When I came back I joined him, dunking almond slices.

It was like waiting for a time bomb to go off. Strapped to it. I could almost hear it ticking in my head. There was something of the French farce about it all, and I smiled to myself when Liam's attention was on the telly. The whole situation was crazy. What the hell was he doing here? I tried to be serious, see the seriousness of it, but I think I was too happy he was there, regardless of what would happen, and that meant I couldn't be so serious.

"I can't believe you're here," I said.

"Well, I am. I thought you were going to faint."

"I was. Why didn't you say?"

"Spur of the moment. I just went out and bought a ticket. Just like that. I didn't tell anyone till I was going."

"I thought you might come next year. No one?"

"No one. There was a fierce row at home. Shit, you wouldn't believe it. You'd swear I was some kind of kid. Then Tony blew up at me. He'd no right to say—

Jesus, it was shit. But fuck them. I'm here now and I don't care. I don't."

"Yeah? You big sludge. Just like that? I didn't think you had it in you. I'm impressed."

"It was getting impossible. Tony's going to London anyway. He's got a couple of interviews. And home was shit. I missed you."

"Yes."

"I said I missed you. Am I going to have to scrape a reply from you?"

"No. But—I bet they hate me at home."

"No."

"It's cold, isn't it? You cold? I'll put on a fire. It's just the fire's awful."

"It's okay, this is fine. Just fine."

What was the last thing I wanted? The thing I'd have sold myself to the Devil to prevent right then? Ian. That's what. Ian turning up the way he liked to turn up after an eleven o'clock and drink coffee and chew bread and watch *Dynasty*. Every footstep, every voice had me on the edge of my seat. What for? They were going to have to meet. Not even I could stop that. And Ian knew what to do. I'd told him about Liam and he'd gone along with all my conditions. All my conditions. They were my conditions for staying, for being around him.

As it turned out, I was engrossed in *Dynasty* when

he did come. I didn't even hear the first bell ring. Liam had to tell me.

I swore under my breath. Perhaps it was Concha. With some firewood to sell. Would I tell her? Why'd people have to know about me? Why should I tell her?

"Morning," Ian said.

He had his hands behind his back and a big grin on his face.

"Hello," I said.

He pulled his hands out from behind his back. He had snowballs in each of them. Before I could protest, he fired both at me, point blank in the face. I backed off towards the living room, trying to clear the snow from my eyes, and Ian came after me and caught me at the door of the living room and lifted me and spun me into the room. When he saw Liam, he stopped dead and let me drop on the floor. Crack. Right on the tiles. I think I bruised myself. I picked myself up and spat snow from my mouth.

"This is Liam, Ian, Liam Connolly, a friend of mine from home. Liam, this is Ian, another teacher. He's English."

Ian threw his hand at Liam.

"How do you do? Just get here? She didn't tell me. I'm sorry, I'd have been up sooner."

"It's okay, she didn't know. I kind of came

unannounced."

"Okay, yeah. Any coffee? My head's singing. Bad weed, you know. Tumble weed. Bad weed, man. You got class now, Chrissie?"

"Yeah."

I poured him coffee. Then I poured some for Liam and me. And I cut some bread and put butter and apricot jam on it.

"Liam. What's that?"

"William."

"Bill."

"Yeah."

"And you're over from Dublin. It's snowing. Outside. You know that, don't you? This place is great in the snow. So how long you over for, Liam?"

Liam made a facial gesture.

"For a while," I said.

"Jesus, this coffee's strong, Chrissie. She makes tar, don't you think?"

"It's okay."

"Bit cold in here. Wait till you have a shower, Liam. Just wait. Freeze the balls—oops, sorry—freeze you solid. Not worth it. Better stink."

I scowled at him but it made no difference.

"Hell, I don't want to teach any more today," he said. "I don't want to teach. You a teacher, Liam?"

"No, journ—"

Liam looked at me.

"I was a journalist."

"Were you, by God? Sleaze merchant. Vicars and nighties."

"Nothing like that."

"No, not in Dublin. Not in Catholic Ireland."

"I told you it wasn't like that," I said. "You've been there, you know what it's like."

"Surely, to be sure, mam."

He looked at Liam and smiled. Liam didn't smile back.

"No offence, mate. Kidding."

"It's okay."

"I see she's got you watching Joan."

He nodded at the television.

"Yeah. It's gas."

"You got anything at one, Ian?" I asked him.

"No, love."

Jesus, why'd he say that?

"Would you do me a favour and take mine?"

He looked at Liam again. There was tension in every muscle in his face. I wished the ground would swallow him up, right there. Why hadn't Liam told me he was coming today? I could have had everything arranged. Why couldn't he have told me?

"Could you take my classes, Ian? Liam's just arrived. It's only Yolanda and her lot, and a particular with Pilar. They're all nice."

"Nubile."

He laughed at Liam.

"Don't be like that," I said. "They're too young for you."

"Ripe."

"Don't be disgusting."

He laughed again and shoved his hand into Liam's. Then he put on a John Wayne accent.

"Sure, I'll take your classes. Welcome, pilgrim, to our town. It may not be much, but we call it home."

"It's fine," Liam said.

"Fine, to be sure."

"Shut up, Ian."

"Yes, mam."

He saluted.

I wanted to chuck a cup of coffee at him. Right in his stupid face.

"Welcome, friend," he said to Liam.

Liam laughed and saluted.

"Thank you very much, most civil of you."

The bomb hadn't gone off. When Ian had gone, I made more coffee and Liam and I sat under the rug at the brasero and talked like we were the only two people left in the world. And all the time, I was wondering what he was thinking, and knowing it.

"D'you've any plans?" I asked him.

"No. I'm only waking up to the fact that I'm here. I'm thinking about home. And Tony. I don't feel so good about it."

"Welcome. It's marvellous to see you. You look good."

I kissed him.

"You too. He's fairly intense."

"Ian?"

"Yeah."

"He has problems."

I put my finger to my head and had the sense I was betraying both of them.

"He was in the Falklands."

"Was he?"

"Don't mind him too much. Sorry it's so cold. You brought winter with you. It was fine up to last week. Cold at night and a bit chilly during the day, but fine. What do you think? Does it live up to expectations?"

"Yeah. I thought I might write a book."

"Really? What?"

"You know, a book."

"There's a typewriter at the school. You could use that."

"I haven't—"

"What?"

"I don't know. I feel a bit of an intruder."

"You're not. Still hate me?"

"I've never hated you. What makes you say that?"

"You know."

"I told you, don't talk about that. It was for the best. I don't want you getting worked up about it. I know it was hard for you. But it was for the best. I wasn't much help, was I?"

"Not much, but then how could I expect you to be? We shouldn't have expectations. Okay?"

"That a warning?"

"No. A fact. Don't you think so?"

"I guess so. Can we go to bed?"

I was completely thrown by that. Straight out with it.

"Liam!"

"Do I offend you?"

"No, it's just—"

"You'll have to some time."

"Do I? I want to give it up. I don't like it. I don't think I could. Not after—"

I did want to bed him.

"I shouldn't have asked like that. It just came out. I'm sorry. Where'll I sleep?"

"We'll see."

"What?"

"You angry?"

"Should I be?"

"We could lie down. In my room. If you like. For a while. I'd like to hold you. It's just—"

"Have I interrupted something?"

"What?"

"Nothing."

Why the hell did he ask that? I kept saying that inside. Why the hell? This was what I got from Liam. Like I had to answer to him for everything. I got really angry with him, inside, really annoyed with him, and I didn't want to lie with him any more, even though I knew I would sometime if he stayed long. I knew I'd want to lie with him and make love to him the way I hadn't been able to with Ian. Perhaps Liam was the only person in the world I could make love with. Imagine that, I thought. And him going through all his bad feelings about leaving home. I could do without all that love of motherland tomorrow belongs to me rubbish. I did want to be loved by him, though. You know: tender touch in out in out low moan pant sweat tongues hard thrust heavy wet come.

Paoli took to Liam the minute she saw him. I could tell. It was exactly like with me. Her eyes got even whiter. We were at the counter in Bar Sol, one of the best bars in town. It was right at the heart of things, on the Plaza de España, between Calle Mayor and the municipal park. The park wasn't very big but it was shaded in maple and chestnut and a good place to meet people. Whole families walked around together on Sundays and summer evenings. In winter, when the wind was sharp like a razor, the old men walked up and down the centre of the park in a line, dressed in heavy coats and berets, and carrying canes. Sometimes they linked arms to keep out the cold. The old were small and round, and many had bow legs. Their skin was leathery, and when the wind got at it, it broke and the veins showed. Their eyes were deep and sodden and a bit sad.

Pablo, one of the two brothers who owned Bar Sol, and Pepe, a tall barman with a large nose and an acid tongue, were asking Liam about himself. Pepe was making jokes. I was translating and Ian was interrupting my translation, saying my Spanish was shit even though it was better than his. Paoli bought Liam a load of beers and kept laughing at everything he said no matter whether it was funny or not. She'd been on the wine since lunchtime, hadn't gone home because Tom was off giving classes uptown and it was too cold to be home alone, she said. Qué frio, she kept saying, faking shivering. Liam insisted it wasn't so cold. I was past hot and cold. I was drinking hot port and thinking about being in bed with Liam on clean sheets because hot port always made me think like that and hot port in the snow doubled the fantasy.

When Tom came along, he was drunk. He bought all of us a drink and grilled Liam for about fifteen minutes. Ian butted in and got into an argument with Tom. This allowed Liam to escape. But Paoli got him again. She'd scored a kind of victory.

I rescued Liam from Paoli when her mind drifted across the bar after a little baby who could barely walk. She went vacant for a bit. Empty. I wanted to go over to her and help her, but it would have meant exposing me. I wasn't going to do that. Liam was the easier option.

"Happy?" I asked him.

"You always ask me that."

"Are you?"

"Are you happy, Ian?" Liam said to him.

"What?"

"Chrissie asked me if I was happy. I'm asking you."

"Overjoyed, old man. Overjoyed. Your nubiles have filled out since we began, Chrissie. Nice women."

"Rubbish. Shut up, Ian."

"Hard woman you have there, Liam."

"Sometimes."

"Shut up, both of you."

"Yes, mam," they both said.

Liam winked at me. I could remember that happening before, years ago, somewhere, but I couldn't place it. I winked back and we settled the

sleeping arrangements against the door of my piso
with the lights still on in Concha's place below us.

CHAPTER SIXTEEN

T he snow got heavier. Mountain winter heavy.
And every time he could, Ian pulled me aside.
"I'm doing okay, aren't I?" he'd say.

That was it.

Liam took the typewriter from the school, wrote a page, tore it up, wrote another and sat looking out our living-room window for two hours. I was with him, reading *As I Walked Out One Midsummer Morning*. Ian had given it to me, saying it was the best book ever written on Spain by a foreigner. He said things like that. He wanted us to retrace Laurie Lee's footsteps. I was half in favour of it. Though going with Ian put me off. But he was so enthusiastic about it, frenzied almost. And Liam had to go and encourage him by agreeing it was a great idea. Poor Liam. Spain didn't turn out like he wanted, I think. Not the great romantic adventure. My fault? Or he simply wasn't up to it. Wanted too much from himself. Far too much. He wanted to write about home and how he felt about everyone leaving, or having to leave, and how none of us ever expected this to happen to us, all that sort of bleeding heart faith of our fathers muck. I told him no one would be interested. No one cared. I suppose I made him self-conscious about it all. And he was probably right. It was a sad thing if you thought about it. I just didn't think about it. What you don't think about isn't there, right?

He tried writing again but he hit a wall after ten pages and no matter what he did he couldn't breach it.

When he found he couldn't write, he started coming down to the school with me, hanging around, sitting in on my classes. It was okay. I'd have thought it would have been shit, but it wasn't, and it was nice to see him there after class, waiting for me; and we'd go for drinks or coffee together, or with some of my students, or Ian and Paoli. It was very uncomplicated. Very clean. And I liked living with him then. More than I ever thought I would. For those moments. I might even say we were happy. But it was a fragile happiness, just waiting to be smashed.

We made it into the new year. Till the second week. We'd had a good Christmas. Everyone giving dinners for everyone else. Sometimes Tom and Ian would get too heated, but we always found a way to cool them down. And Tom knew more about Ian than Ian realised. He knew what Ian was about.

It was thick with snow outside. And I wasn't keen

on going to school. Not at all keen. Liam and I were sitting at the brasero, wondering who should take the shower first.

Because we were on the top floor, the shower was crap, and in winter it was worse. It trickled out of the nozzle, warmed by the gas heater in the kitchen, which made more noise than it generated heat. You had to keep moving around under the nozzle to make sure you got wet. And while one bit of you was being wet by warm water, the rest of you tensed up and froze. There was the bath if you were prepared to boil water in the kitchen and fill the bath with pots. There was never enough hot water straight from the taps. Liam took baths with boiled water but it took so long to boil each pot that the water boiled earlier had cooled considerably by the time a new pot was ready. He never seemed to mind. I just rushed in when I'd enough courage and threw myself under the shower.

The bathroom was freezing and the floor was always wet because of the leak in the roof there and a fault with the washing machine. I lifted my arms and sniffed under them. Not very ladylike but a good way of knowing if I needed a shower. There was an odour. And Ian was in my head, and the scar at his wrist. I wondered what the smell had been like for him. It was a foolish thought but the shower brought it to my mind. I was delaying. I looked over at Liam.

Let him go first. Then I could have a look at him. I wanted to have a look. To see him.

"You go first," I said.

"Okay. How long have I got?"

"Ten minutes."

"Want to join me?"

"Too cold. I'll go after you."

I had to see him. To study him. I'd really only seen him in the dark, at times when I wasn't particular. When he'd finished and was wrapped in his big yellow towel, I watched him through the crack at the door hinges. He didn't see me. He was shivering.

"It's bloody freezing," he said to himself. "Jesus!"

The mirror over the washbasin was fogged up and clearing slowly. Beads of condensation ran down the glass, revealing more of him to me: hungry eyes and a gentle offended mouth. There were changes too. His jowls were weightier, and as he moved the towel around his body, I could see I was right: he was heavier. It was gathering at his flanks, in layers only distinguishable if he made a move. If he stood tall and held himself in, you could not see them. His belly was a bit weaker, and swollen, but that could be disguised too. He had not reached the point where it could not be corrected. His arse was too big, too, and it had stretch marks. They were pinky purple, like scars, and when he tensed his buttocks, they cratered the white skin. And he was hardening. I watched it rise and felt something inside me build. Then he stopped rubbing himself and wrapped the big towel around himself again. Everything in the bathroom was wet. The walls were running with condensation and there was a hazy cloud sitting above Liam across the ceiling. He needed a haircut. His hair was falling badly, becoming unmanageable. My turn now.

On the way up Calle Mayor, snowflakes settling in our wet hair, we found the snow untouched except for two small birds poking their beaks through it at a shop door. The shop was stocked with coats and scarves. It had Rebajas posters on its windows, hanging loose. Across the street, next to a deli, a lingerie shop displayed the kind of women's underwear Ian called passion-killers. The size of tents, the colour of battle camouflage. A car came down the street with no regard for the conditions or us, or the beauty of the virgin snow, ploughing two deep furrows in it and spraying the white blanket with black sludge. I stepped to one side. Liam got splashed with slush and swore. The two birds took to the sky and hovered before returning to their foraging. I looked behind me, at our footprints, and saw that we too were culprits. I kicked some snow and walked on.

The clouds clung like stale breath to the side of the sierra. And still the snow came down, relentlessly.

"Chrissie," Liam said.

"What?"

"Do you mind me here?"

"No. Why do you say that?"

"I feel a bit like a—like I don't belong."

"Going to leave?"

"Want me to?"

"You must do what you want."

"And what do you want? We—"

"I want you. Right now, here. I want you. Enough?"

"It'll have to be."

We turned off for the school above the civil war monument and the bare maple trees beside it, covered in snow. The graffiti on the monument was obscured by snow. Outside the school, people were throwing snowballs at each other, faces disappearing behind exploding balls of snow. My ears were raw and I placed my hands over them and felt the cold transfer from my ears to my hands. I saw Ian chasing after a girl in a thick blue coat and throwing a snowball at her. The snowball missed and the girl in the thick blue coat quickly scraped a ball together, and Ian ran right into it. He sat down in the snow.

"What happened to class?" I asked.

"Good day to you both. We've decided to extend the curriculum."

A snowball hit me on the back of the neck and the

snow ran down my neck and into my clothes, to the small of my back. I swung around to see who'd done it. Another snowball hit me on the side of the face. Two girls were calling my name and yelling in Spanish. I wasn't going to retaliate but I couldn't resist. I scooped up two snowballs and went at them, roaring. They ran in different directions, and I followed the smallest and hit her twice on the head with the snowballs before knocking her to the ground and heaping snow on to her face. She laughed the whole way through her ordeal. The second girl came up behind me when I'd finished, and hit me again. I fell back in the snow.

"She's cancelled classes," Ian said, "we can go tobogganing. I'll drive us up. What do you think?"

"Brilliant!" I said.

"What are we going to use?" Liam asked.

"Wait till you see, mate."

"Do you have a toboggan?"

"No. Big metal tray thing. Only thing is, getting the car up. Paoli's inside. She's not well. I said she should go home. She's puked twice. She says it might be something she ate."

And when Liam had turned his back to throw a snowball at a girl who'd hit him twice, Ian whispered in my ear.

"You look lovely in the snow, darling. I'm going

to steal a kiss."

"No, you're not!"

"Just one."

"No."

"You'd fucking kiss him. Wouldn't you? Ian's got to get it somewhere else. Somewhere else. Anywhere. Get it."

"Ian!"

He'd been crying. There were marks around his eyes. I pulled away from him and went towards the school door.

"We've been at it over an hour," he yelled. "I tried sliding on it. It's not hard enough yet. Paoli's hyper. All full of advice. You'd swear the world was about to end. I'm high. Don't say anything. High as the proverbial kite."

Liam hit me from the side with a snowball and then launched himself at me in a dive tackle, knocking me over.

"Hi," he said, stuffing snow down my mouth.

I fought to shove him off.

"You're beaten," he said.

"Get off."

"No. You're beaten."

"Ian's been crying. Go mess with him. Talk to him, Liam. He wants to be friends."

"We are."

"Yes. He's dying to go tobogganing. I hope the Deux Cheveaux will do the trick. It's not the best at gripping. You look wonderful. Handsome."

"Shut up. What would you do if I took you here and screwed you in the snow? Would you mind?"

"You might have a problem. Things contract in cold weather. It could be nice though. I'd want something to lie on."

I threw snow in his face.

"Glad you're here?"

"Yes."

"Ian says he knows a good place up past Candelario where we can toboggan."

"Fine."

Candelario was four kilometres from Béjar, higher up on the sierra, surrounded by small farms and woods. A jumble of clinging whitewash and terracotta, scratched with narrow streets, some of them stepped, most of them cobbled. Getting a car around Candelario was a real achievement. Most of the postcards from the Béjar area pictured Candelario because it was that kind of village and the people in it, who were very old and very young, were village people. The gutters on the main streets were deep and flowed with water from the sierra for most of the year, and if you were driving, you had to avoid putting your wheels into one of these gutters. The water, like all that from the sierra, was clear, fresh and freezing, and if you had to put your hand in it at any time when it was flowing, your hand would flush red and probably purple and you'd have to blow on it for a few minutes to get it warm again. The houses in Candelario dated back two or three hundred years to when the village got rich on chorizo, a hard oily salami.

The school floor was covered in melting snow. Paoli sat behind her desk, wearing a heavy coat and a coloured scarf. Ian leaned on the desk, smoking. He stared past Paoli, at a poster of Andalucía.

"I think it's better to have no more classes today," Paoli said when we came in.

I shook myself like a dog and the snow on me fell to the floor.

"Come on out," I said. "It's terrific."

"It's too cold."

She hunched up.

"We've been falling all over the place," Liam said.

"Me voy a casa."

"Por qué?"

"Porque it's freezing. I hate it. I hate it."

"The Deux Cheveaux able to make it, Ian?" Liam asked.

"Yeah, mate."

"Let's go get coffee first," I said.

"The kettle."

"No, we need a bar, where it's warm; this place is like a fridge. Have you got the heat on?"

"She's right up against it. I keep telling her she'll get chilblains. Few more days of this'd do me fine. Did you ever have days off school in winter because the pipes were burst? We had this ancient Georgian building. The pipes even burst in May. They were always going. Then we'd go mad."

"Let's go get coffee first," I said.

"You feel better, Paoli?"

She shook her head.

"Little bit. It's not good."

"You should eat more," I said. "You don't eat enough. In winter, you should have two hot meals a day. At least. No salads. Eat more, Paoli. We'll cook you something fattening tonight. How about that? You and Tom come round. Ian too. All around to our place for a fattening meal. Fondue. How about fondue? We'll buy a big hunk of cheese and loads of wine. It'll be terrific. How much bread do we have?"

"One and a half."

"We'll get some more. Would you eat fondue? Would Tom come? Ian, the bread shops are closed now, aren't they? Do you've any decent bread? I can't stand the other stuff. I'll ask Tom if he'll come."

"A lo mejor. If my stomach is right. Tom may

want to paint," Paoli said.

"Screw painting. This is time for fondue."

"I'm with you, Chrissie," Ian said. "We can mull wine on the fire too, if we can get the bloody thing going. Plenty of grog. Get pissed and stuff ourselves with fondue."

"Come home for coffee with me," Paoli said.

"We're going up to toboggan—on Ian's tray."

"You are children."

She looked at Ian, hoping for support.

"It'll be magic," he said. "You could come and watch."

"Oh, no. You'll all come home for coffee."

I sat on the desk and put my hands on Paoli.

"You come with us."

"I'm going home. A casa."

"Niña!"

"No, me voy."

The dark crescents under her eyes appeared to have darkened. And around the pupils, before the great expanse of white, her eyes were grey and yellow.

"Maybe you should. Sit down in front of a fire. You'll come for dinner though? I'll ring you."

Her face slipped into resigned sadness. She dipped her eyes and rubbed her hands.

"We'll have coffee in Candelario," Ian said. "Las Vegas. And something to eat. We'll get Irish coffee."

We had Irish coffees and toasted sandwiches in Bar Las Vegas in Candelario. We were the only ones in the bar. Las Vegas was a very basic bar with a television and a pool table. It had maple trees outside and in summer they were a good shade against the sun. There was a tiny disco at the back of the bar. Felipe, the owner, who had a permanent worried look on his face, said we were mad to go out on the sierra. He said it was dangerous. We should wait. After three Irish coffees, we were not inclined to listen. Ian left the car outside Las Vegas and we walked the rest of the way up the sierra, Liam and Ian holding the big tray, about another kilometre along the winding road.

I stood in the snow, watching the two of them get on his tray, Liam behind Ian, at the top of a steep slope. Snow was still falling, the flakes smaller and less dense than earlier. I'd already gone down twice and nearly killed myself bringing the tray back up the second time. In the freezing air of the sierra, my lungs ached with the effort. And my feet were wet. A slow numbing there was developing into a painful coldness. I jumped up and down on the spot and moved my arms around, but the cold was winning the battle. Liam put his hand up and waved to me and Ian took away the stone he had keeping the tray from moving. It began to slide, slowly at first, so that I thought they'd stop, then faster, until they disappeared into the mist and the falling snow.

I cleared some snow off a rock and sat down. Long grass still poked through the deep snow. The rock was freezing and I could only sit on it for a few minutes at a time. I sang to myself and wished they'd hurry and get back up. I'd had my fun. I was cold now. I wanted to go. Better indoors, warm.

They hadn't come back when the snow stopped falling and the cloud on the sierra began to lift. I made my way down the slope, through thick snow which got deeper the further I went. I tried to keep to the route I'd followed coming back up with the tray the first time. I fell twice and then sank into a deep drift up to my waist. It was comical, me trying to get out of the drift, and when I managed it I lay down in the snow and laughed out loud, hoping that would attract Liam and Ian and save me from having to go any further to find them. Perhaps they'd gone on further. It was possible, if you pushed again. If they'd done that, they could have gone all the way to the forest below us. Then they'd take ages getting back up. They might take the road. It would be easier. Longer but easier. I considered going back up and then along the road to meet them. I started back up and then stopped.

There could have been an accident. Ian was a terrible messer. No. They would have called out to

me, and I hadn't heard anything. I should have heard
something. I moved on down, going around the drift
and moving slower. I was going to call out, to see if
they were okay. They'd only think I was stupid if I
came down all worried about them. I hated when
people worried about me. I once threw a cup at Liam
when he'd said he'd been worried about me. There
was another possibility but I was pressing that down
so that even the suggestion of it couldn't form in my
consciousness. My hands were cold now, they were
throbbing like my feet. I blew hard into them and
thrust them into my pockets. But my pockets were
wet and my hands got colder. My nose was running
and I pulled a sodden handkerchief from one of my
pockets and wiped my nose and blew it. As soon as
I'd returned the handkerchief, the nose was running
again. There was no wind and the silence in the snow
was sublime. Suddenly I felt vulnerable. It would be
easy to disappear, to vanish without trace. Felipe was
right. I listened and all I could hear was my breathing,
fast and wet and heavy, struggling, like when you
make love. I sank back into the snow and I was warm
for a while, until the wet seeped through my jeans
and I had to stand again. I went further, cursing the
two of them for making me do this, wondering if
when I got there, they'd be back at the top, calling to
me and getting ready to go. I could taste the fondue

and the mulled wine, and imagined myself beside
the fire or covered by the rug around the brasero,
drinking, full, and only bed before me. And Liam.
Tired eyes looking at each other in expectation,
waiting to see when our desire to go to bed would
overcome our comfort.

They were on the ground when I saw them. My
heart raced. Jesus, I thought, something's wrong. I
went to run but I fell in the snow. They were still a
good distance off. I picked myself up and was going
to yell. Then Ian stood up and Liam dived at him and
they rolled in the snow. Ian got up again and Liam
lay in the snow. They held their positions for a couple
of minutes. It was like they were frozen stiff. Then
Ian went down on his knees beside Liam. He held his
arms up, kneeling there. Liam pulled himself up and
Ian hit him dead square in the face and then held his
arms up again. Liam stood up, holding his face, and
backed away. Ian just knelt with his arms up.

I stood, watching, hoping they would see. They
didn't. I hesitated. Then I turned around and climbed
back up, scrambling to be there, sitting on the rock
when they came up. I had to be there, waiting. They
couldn't know I'd seen them. As if their not knowing
would make it not have happened.

At the top, on the wall, wet and freezing, I sobbed.
It was quiet lonely sobbing, not for anyone to hear.

They came back up, throwing snow at each other and shouting at me. I dried my face. Liam ran at me, throwing snowballs and yelling.

"Hi, there," he said. "That was fantastic. We crashed. I got smashed up a bit. Want to go down with me?"

There was bruising on his cheek and a small cut above his eyes, at the temple.

Ian was clearing snow off the tray. He had a cigarette in his mouth.

CHAPTER SEVENTEEN

I thought if we went to Madrid for a weekend, it would help things. In the way that a different environment can if you're willing to let it. Neither of them was aware I knew what was going on, and they were very friendly around me. But it was there, under the surface, tension you could touch. And I didn't want to bring it up, not if I could get rid of it. Anyway, Ian wouldn't come. After saying he would. It was a last-minute thing. He suddenly didn't want to come. Perhaps he wanted it to come out. To give Liam and me some time together so it would come out. If that was it, I don't know what he expected would happen after. I knew it was pretty certain Liam would bring it up when we were alone in Madrid. I could sense he'd been straining to do it. And I was prepared for it even though I'd have kept it down if there'd been any way I could. I suppose I should have been disappointed at Ian not going with us, and not gone myself, but I wasn't.

Madrid was freezing. We booked into a hostal on Delicias, near the Estación Sur, the terminus of the bus from Béjar. It had been about three and a half hours with a stop in Ávila. I'd wanted to try hitching but the cold and Liam's arguing against it persuaded me that the bus was a better idea. There had been a train service to Béjar at one time but that had stopped. It was really eerie if you sat at the old station, down the road south going to Cáceres and Seville, watching the sun drop below the peaks going into Portugal, and the half-light of dusk playing tricks with the shadows.

The elegant woman who ran the hostal referred to me as Liam's wife and we didn't correct her. There were crucifixes on the walls of all the rooms she showed us. We had a choice of three rooms. I chose. I played up to the woman, kissing Liam every time we were in her presence, picking up her children and kissing them, and saying how lovely they were. He kicked me any time he got the chance.

"This is much better than being at home," I said to him. "We can be anyone we like here. We're free."

We had dinner in a Chinese restaurant across from the Sur and a coffee in a bar up the street from our hostal. We rang Ian, to see how he was, but there was no answer. I wasn't concerned. He seemed an age away. There was a soccer match on television in the bar, and some right lads were cheering for Real Madrid at one of the tables, making a terrible noise whenever

Real did anything remotely good or bad. They were drinking beer from bottles and eating tortilla on little saucers. They were smoking, too, heavily.

Liam got worked up about the smoking and the noise but wouldn't do anything about it. So when Real put one in the net, and they were slapping each other and banging their table with their bottles, I elbowed a jug of water on the bar counter all over the floor. The water swamped their shoes and they had to stand up and move back till it was mopped up.

"Shit, Chrissie," Liam said.

I winked.

"Hooligans."

I apologised and they accepted my apology because men like that always think they've got a chance with you no matter how obnoxious they are. Fuckwits. I didn't mind shitting on fuckwits. They deserved it.

Later, we walked up the Paseo del Prado and across to the Parco del Retiro. Liam put his arm around me and that was nice. Warm too. It was truly freezing. We walked around and around the park, like we were building up to something but were afraid of what it was, and after an hour I thought we were going to leave without having said anything more than how nice it was and how cold the weather was. We both knew exactly what we were circling, and I wanted to start things, but I knew I should leave it to him. It got to a point where it was too cold to stay any longer without good reason and that crystallised everything. It was then that he spoke about Ian.

"We had a fight, Chrissie."

"I know."

"You didn't say—it wasn't much. He could have creased me if he'd wanted. He could have creased me, you know. He's—"

"I know."

"He says he loves you and you're in love with him."

"He's tried to kill himself. He's not well."

"Is it true?"

"I've been trying to help him."

"What the fuck did you ask me down here for?"

"He's a nice guy. He really is, you know. I met him at the side of a road. Did he tell you that? Weird."

"Why the hell did you ask me down?"

"I love you. I want you."

"Sure! Terrific. Do you love him?"

"Don't know."

"What's that mean?"

"I don't love him like I love you. If I do, it's different."

"That makes me feel good."

"I didn't mean this to happen."

"What did you mean? You ring me up, tell me you

love me, keep saying I should come down, how wonderful it is, keep telling me that, and I'm falling apart missing you, not able to do any work—what did you mean?"

"I don't know. He's sick. He needs me."

"And I don't?"

"Not like that."

"You want me to be sick?"

"Don't be a bastard."

"What are you doing—playing Florence Nightingale?"

"He's tried to kill himself."

I started to cry, not because I was feeling so hurt, just to disarm him.

"Don't cry."

"I can't help it if you're going to be like this."

"I suppose you slept with him?"

"No, there wasn't anything like that."

"Come on, Chrissie."

There was a long pause. He looked right through me.

"I was drunk. I got drunk. And I had some dope. Just once. I don't remember much of it. It wasn't—"

"What are you going to say? It wasn't good."

"I don't remember. I told you."

"Was this to get me back?"

"No!"

"Sure?"

"You weren't there."

"So it's my fault."

"It's no one's fault. It happened. That's all. I never came at you for screwing Clare, did I?"

"What?"

"Don't tell me you didn't. She wanted to bed you. I know she did."

"You know that's not true. Sure, I'd a chance when it could have happened, but you know what? I didn't press it. And you know why? Because of you. That's why. Because I loved you."

"Fuck off. Mister fucking wonderful. How gallant. They should give you a medal. Where the fuck were you when I had my insides taken out? Where?"

"I didn't want you to."

"Didn't you?"

"I asked you not to."

"Fine! Another great gesture. You never screwed anybody but me?"

"No."

"More fool you."

He turned and walked away from me. I hadn't meant that. I wanted to tell him but I couldn't.

In bed I tried to make love to him but he pushed me off and said he was tired.

The next day we went to the Prado to see

"Guernica." There was a crowd in there with us and I told Liam to hang back till they'd all gone and we could get some time alone with it. It's better to see it alone. The comic strip crudity of life and death. No Goyan nobility, no sublime realsim. Picasso stood Goya on his head and then turned him inside out, laughing at him. We got a couple of minutes with the thing and Liam stood back, searching, yes, that's what it was, searching, and he was alone in whatever he was looking for in it. Whatever it was. He didn't speak much all day. And all I could do was watch him being eaten up by whatever was going on in his mind.

"I feel let down, Chrissie," he said to me in bed that night.

While the traffic roared outside.

"I love you," I said.

"Do you?"

"Yes. Isn't it enough?"

"I don't know. I just feel let down."

"Are you going to be able to deal with it?"

"I don't know."

"Oh! There's nothing I can do. That's the way it is, Liam. I wish I could do something. I do."

"Do you?"

"Please."

"What?"

"Please. I love you."

"The same?"

Again I pushed closer to him and made an attempt to kiss him which he pulled away from. He didn't speak after that.

At dawn we moved closer to each other for warmth, and I put my hand between his legs and he responded. But when he tried to penetrate, I was tight, and he couldn't get in. I tried to relax but I wasn't able. He rolled off me and sighed. I can't say how useless I felt, how completely useless.

"I'm sorry, Liam."

"It doesn't matter."

"I think I'm afraid."

We slept again.

When I woke the covers were off and Liam was kissing my vagina. His prick was hard and erect. I tensed. I never liked him doing that. And he knew it. He knew it.

"Liam!"

"I love you, Chrissie."

I could either stop him and endure whatever would happen, or consent. There was no choice, was there? It wasn't easy. I had to stop thinking and try and enjoy what he was doing. To let go to him. Completely. I arched to help him. He was using his tongue and I could feel it inside me. I kissed his body and took his prick and put my mouth over it. He unconsciously thrust at me when I took it in my mouth. It nearly choked me. It's humiliating when you don't see him, I think. Like he's just using your body as an instrument. Completely dominating. But there's pleasure too and the pleasure takes over, which I suppose humiliates more, because you've given in and allowed yourself lie back and be treated like an object. I could have said no, pushed him off, but he was going deeper with his tongue and using his lips, and I was so excited having his prick in my mouth, sucking him while he sighed and thrust at me, that I felt I couldn't say no, not now, not there in bed, when I owed him and wanted him, so we carried on to the point when you can't say no, when yes is all there is, and yes is a god and you are at worship.

We lay under the crucifix in our room. I stared at it while I stroked him. I felt that terrible need for him, and an ugliness. And I didn't want to feel ugly, not with Liam.

"Do you believe in reincarnation?" I asked him.

"You're always asking that. Why?"

"Because I do. If you get it wrong you'll get it right next time. I'll be a bird in my next life, or a whale. Just floating on my own."

"I believe in the resurrection of the body and life everlasting. Amen."

"Crap. Imagine going on with the same life forever. Boring. I want loads of lives."

"One's more than enough for me."

"Are you going?"

"Want me to?"

"It's up to you."

"Is it?"

"What do you want to do?"

"Whither thou goest."

"Shut up, you're going sludgy."

"I got that from a film or something. Do you want me to stay?"

"Of course I do. But you must do what's best for you."

"You mean you don't want me?"

"That's not what I said."

"That's what you meant."

"No, it's not."

"Why'd you ask me out here?"

"I love you. I didn't make you come. It was your choice. You decided to come."

"What about getting away from me?"

"Do we have to get into all this? It's done. Let it be. And don't get angry with me. You want everything labelled and pigeonholed. You're so bloody suburban, Connolly. Let's go camping next weekend. We can use Ian's tent. The three of us can go to Extremadura.

You haven't been down there yet."

"Have you?"

"Once."

"When?"

"Before you came."

"With Ian?"

"He knows everywhere."

We had hot chocolate for breakfast but the café owner didn't have any almond slices.

On the bus to Béjar, as we passed the giant cross in the Valle de los Caídos, I wished we didn't have to go back and I imagined us just passing by, carrying on perhaps to Africa. To Africa and the desert, and disappear. It was a big place to get lost in, the desert. Liam slept and I wanted to get inside his mind, to understand what he was thinking, the truth, whatever that was. I put my head on his shoulder. I hated doing that, being female, being dependent. But it was so nice, to have him there. Even if he didn't forgive me. As if I deserved to be forgiven, as if forgiveness came into it. Why did I believe I needed forgiveness from him?

Ian was in the piso when we got back. He still had a key. He had the table set and a meal ready for us. He stood at the door, dressed in black tie, with a flower in his lapel.

"Sir! Madam! Welcome to this humble eating

house. Dinner is served. And may I say madam and sir look as if they've had a fabulous time in the great city of Madrid. Madam looks particularly jolly. What!"

I threw him my jacket and played along.

"Thank you, Lester," I said. "Champagne on ice?"

"Rioja eighty-seven, mam. A fine vintage."

He took Liam's coat from him.

"May I say, sir's looking very distinguished."

Liam didn't play along. He went straight into the bathroom. Ian carried on. He was upset by Liam's coldness but he carried on. I tried to get Liam to join in when we were alone in the living room, waiting for Ian to serve dinner. He wasn't having anything of it. I wanted to press a button and make him disappear.

If Ian wanted to be in control, he had already lost it. After dinner, when we sat back with the fire burning and the brasero on, and drank Rioja, he reclined on some cushions from the couch beside the fire and smoked dope with his wine. He put a tape of Verdi in his ghetto blaster and put the ghetto blaster on a small wooden table beside the window. Liam and I sat at the table with the brasero and a couple of bottles of Rioja. I flicked through a copy of *Time*. We had scores of books and magazines. All Ian's. He had so many books that they fell out of presses in his place if you opened them without asking him first. He had about fifty cassette tapes too, in a cardboard box.

"Want a smoke?" he asked Liam.

"No."

"It's a drug, like alcohol or nicotine."

"That's nothing to do with it."

"I'll have some," I said.

Ian needed that.

I dropped *Time* on the floor and got down beside him. He took the joint from his mouth and placed it in mine. I tried to look as if it was second nature to me but I couldn't disguise my inexperience. I drew on it, timidly—I remembered before—and Ian winked at Liam.

"Harder," he said.

I did. I gave it back to him and coughed a bit.

"Nothing," I said.

My brain was drunk on the wine and I couldn't feel anything else.

"Are you sure it's real? It's not real. You're having me on."

"It's real all right. It doesn't always work. It's not heroin or anything."

I sat back and put my legs into a lotus.

"We should sleep here tonight," I said. "It'll be freezing in the bedroom. Madrid was like a fridge."

"I was in my woollies last night," Ian said.

The dope was starting to sing to me.

"We could all get in bed together, though," I said.

"Fabulous!" Ian said.

"Don't be stupid," Liam barked.

"Don't fancy me love?" Ian said in an effeminate voice.

"No, I fucking don't."

Ian's face changed. He drank a whole glass of wine and then poured another and drank that.

"I was joking, Liam. You two can have your bed. I'll have my sleeping bag."

"Don't be like that, Liam," I said.

"Like what?"

Ian flicked wine at him and I picked up a near-empty glass of wine and threw the wine at him. It missed and went all over the wall.

"What'd you do that for?" Liam said.

I had no answer.

"Get a cloth."

He got up.

"I want to dance," I said.

I grabbed him as he was going to the kitchen. He pulled away from me.

"Screw you," I said.

I sat down on the floor again. It was cold. I knew it was cold but I couldn't feel the cold.

Liam got a cloth from the sink and wiped the wall. The wine had run down it in two long lines.

"I'll dance with you, Chrissie," Ian said.

He pulled me up. I was semi-comatose, floating in and out of myself.

We started to slow dance by the table. My head sloped against his chest. He was still smoking and the fumes were adding to my high. Liam plonked himself back at the table and picked up *Time*.

"You don't mind me snogging your bird?" Ian said.

"No."

He was pretending to read *Time* and watching our every move. I could have stopped what I was doing but it was easier to stay there, being propped up by Ian, and anyway, my sense of judgement was arseways. I shouldn't have taken that stuff.

Ian moved his hand around my back, stopping at several places to rub it, finally resting it at my bottom. Tell the truth, I was enjoying it, but not because it was Ian. I did nothing to stop him. We hung out of each other, close in, for a few minutes, moving in a small circle. Liam was still pretending to read.

There was a battle going on, and I was the spoils. Jesus, fuck them, I thought, fuck them both. How dare they fight over me. I jerked suddenly and pulled back from Ian, unbalancing him. Then I shoved him and he fell back helplessly against the table, hitting his head and dropping the dope from his mouth. A bottle of Rioja fell over on the table and the wine in it spilled out on to the table and down on to the floor. I watched all this in a kind of weightless timelessness. Liam's mouth dropped. He went to get up, didn't and then did. I couldn't stand any longer. I sat down on the floor where the wine was spilling from the table.

"Shit, Chrissie," Ian said.

I laughed at him, a hard false laugh. He had a look of urgent distress on his face. His eyes were weakening.

"Get the cloth, Liam. I'm all wet," I said.

"You've drunk too much."

"I can't take it."

"You shouldn't drink so much. You get pissed too easy."

He got the cloth again.

Ian stood up, rubbing his head.

"Are you okay?" I asked him.

"You gave me a hell of a crack."

"Sorry. I'm sorry. You looked funny."

He sat down on a chair and poured himself what was left of the wine.

"Fuck you for that, Chrissie."

"Fuck you too. Go on, fuck off."

"You cracked my head, you know?"

"I'm sorry. Chrissie's sorry. Hurting everyone. Chrissie's legless."

"Yes, you are," Liam said.

"I love dominant men."

"It was an accident, Liam," Ian said. "Don't get worked up about it, mate."

"I'm not."

"No, it wasn't," I said. "I did it deliberately."

"Sit up and dry yourself off."

"Fuck off, Liam, telling me what to do."

I threw my hand out in a forced dramatic gesture.

"Passion! You say something passionate, Liam. He can be pretty passionate when he likes, our Liam. Know that, Ian?"

"Shut up, Chrissie, you're pissed."

"Fuckwit."

"I'll get her to bed, Ian. Stop smoking that shit. That's what has her like this. You shouldn't have given her any."

"Rubbish, mate. She's pissed."

"Giving her dope's like putting a match to petrol."

"I didn't make her. She asked for it. You think she has to be made?"

"Piss off."

I threw up on the bathroom floor. I was bent over the toilet bowl but at the moment of paroxysm I fell forward on to the wet tiles. Liam had to hold me while I retched. He kept warning me about choking on my vomit. More chance of me choking on his prick, I thought. I was out of it, semi-conscious, talking to myself, singing, even reciting a few words of Browning.

"You really did yourself tonight," he said.

"Shut up. I feel awful. Put me to bed, Liam."

"When you're clear. I don't want you puking over me in bed."

"If you loved me you wouldn't mind."

"You'll get your reward tomorrow, so I won't argue with you now."

"Bastard."

"You hurt Ian."

"Yeah. That's me. That's me all over. That's Chrissie."

"His head was cut."

"I'm sorry."

"Tell that to him."

"He's screwing—guess who he's screwing?"

I felt Liam weaken, like all the strength had been whipped from him in that instant. What the hell was I saying?

"He's screwing—"

I threw up again.

"Shut up, Chrissie."

"Do you love me?"

"Yes."

"Through everything?"

"How do you feel?"

"Little bit better. I think I'm finished. He's screwing Paoli."

"Fuck off."

"She told me. Tom doesn't know. At least, I think he doesn't. You're not to say anything."

"I wish you hadn't told me."

"I wanted to share a confidence with you. Will you marry me?"

"You're drunk. Ask me when you're sober."

"No."

"Let's get you cleaned and into bed. I'm frozen. So are you."

"He's had heaps of women."

"Who?"

"Ian."

"I don't want to hear any more, Chrissie. Please."

Screws everyone, I said to myself.

"Can you get up?"

"Get me water. I want a drink of water. I'm parched."

I turned on the shower and stuck my head under the nozzle. The cold water burned through to my brain. It was as if someone had attacked me with a million pins all at once. I roared. Bits of puke were falling from my face into the bath, getting stuck in the plughole. I wanted to die, I'd have given anything to be dead then, for the peace of it, to stop it, and the whole bathroom was spinning so much I thought I was going to fall off, right off, and go sprawling into space. It was frightening. The water ran over my head and down my clothes into my jeans, freezing winter water from the sierra, and I didn't care.

"Damn you, Ian, for giving me that shit!" I yelled. "Do you hear me?"

Then there was the sound of running on the tiles. Scared.

"Jesus, Chrissie, he's got a knife in the living room. Chrissie! He's got a knife and he's cutting himself. Jesus, Chrissie, he's cutting himself. He's going to fucking do himself, Chrissie."

Liam had me by the shoulders. He was shaking me. What he was saying was getting through, and I wanted to do something but I couldn't. My body wouldn't respond. I damned it and fell on the floor. Liam pulled me to my feet and slapped me across the face. It hurt, I know it hurt, it's just that the hurt got caught up with a load of other feelings.

"He's cutting himself, Chrissie!"

I followed him into the living room, falling down except that he was holding me up. I wanted to puke again and then pass out. Oh, Christ, you fucking bastard, Ian, why now?

Ian was sitting at the open window. His face was dirty from crying. He had a carving knife. The point of it was at his stomach and there was blood trickling from a wound at the point.

"Hara-kiri," he said, smiling. "If I cut right across, which one of you will finish me off with a sword blow? Which one of you is friend enough? Now let me see. I don't think either of you are. Either of you. Chrissie, will you do it for me? As one friend to another. Mates. It feels easy now."

"For God's sake, Ian," Liam said.

"God? What the fuck has God got to do with this? God? There's no God any more. God was an Englishman, did you know that? But he got pissed off with England and gave up. Thatcher wanted to privatise him. That's funny. Buy shares in God—No, it's not, is it? It's not funny. Nothing's funny today. You didn't even think my Jeeves bit was funny, Liam. Nothing funny. Funny, funny, funny. Funny ha ha. Funny peculiar. I'm funny."

"Give me the knife, Ian," I said.

"You Henry from Hill Street? Talk me down. Talk down the crazy. Go for the Howard solution. Just fucking waste me. Like the shit I am. That's what you think. Just fucking waste me."

He drove the knife in a little more. Only a little more.

"Look, Ian, I'm near collapsing," I said. "Get back from the window and give me the knife. My fucking head's killing me. Stop pissing around."

"Oh, I'm pissing around, am I? Ian shouldn't piss around. Buster shouldn't piss around. What? Deserves to be belted. Belt Buster."

"This is ridiculous," Liam said. "I don't believe this."

"Would you believe this?"

Ian smashed his head off the wall.

"See! There's other ways."

Then he did it again. The stonewash tore the flesh from his forehead.

"Oh, Christ!"

Liam made a move towards him.

I pulled him back.

"Don't."

"The fucker's mad."

"Raving. That's what they say."

"Stop feeling sorry for yourself, Ian," I said.

"Sorry! Who's feeling sorry?"

I kept thinking about something Liam had told me about New York when he was there: a photograph of a man falling from a bridge. A big photo, on the front page of a tabloid, close up so you could see the man's face. He'd climbed out and threatened to jump. I suppose when he'd climbed out he'd intended to do it. A policeman came along and, after a while, talked him into coming back. Only when he tried to come back, he found he couldn't, and he was slipping. The photo showed the moment he finally fell. When he faced up to what he'd done.

"Ian, I don't want you to do this."

"Why'd you hurt me, then?"

"I didn't mean to."

"You did. You said you did."

"I was out of my head—was? Am out of my head. I shouldn't have that stuff. With the booze. It—"

"Yeah, you can't take it, love. Ever seen a man killed, Liam? Dead?"

"No."

"You haven't? You should. Quite a sight. Seen one seen 'em all: that's what I say. I have. Lots."

Liam sat down in the chair nearest Ian.

"You don't like me, do you?" Ian said to him.

"I do."

"No, you don't."

"Look, I'm sorry if—"

"No, you're right. You're right. I'm in the wrong. I'm always in the wrong. Kiss Me Kate used to say that. In between the other things. You're always doing the wrong things, Ian."

"I don't want you to get hurt, Ian. Nothing's worth that."

"It's okay, then, is it?"

"What?"

"Loving her."

"That's up to you."

"Yeah, sure."

"I'm a free soul, Ian," I said. "Free. Liam knows that."

"Are you?"

"Look, I don't want this, Ian," Liam said. "I just don't want this. Listen, if you want to talk to someone, you can talk to me."

"Can I?"

"Yes."

"That's a laugh."

"What's the matter, Ian?" I said.

"What's the matter? The matter? The matter is—I'm—you're—all—it's all the matter. The big matter. And—"

He looked down behind him at the blackness. Three floors.

"Maybe I can fly. Chrissie, you'd like to be a bird. Join me? Let's fly off together."

"Maybe you've had too much to drink."

"Far too much. Far too much."

Liam stood up. Ian made a pretence at pushing the knife in further. His eyes fixed on Liam.

"Kiss me," he said.

"What?"

"You heard. Kiss me. Show me you care. Love me."

"Listen—"

"I said, kiss me—on the fucking lips."

Liam looked over at me in distress. I nodded.

He walked up to Ian, very deliberately, one careful step at a time, and time seemed to disappear in what was happening. He stood in front of Ian, and they looked into each other's eyes, almost like lovers, wondering. Ian's grip on the knife loosened. His whole body loosened. He might have fallen over. But he was held, by Liam's stare. Liam put his hand on Ian's shoulder, barely touching, and held it there several minutes. I was too sick to be part of this, too tired of Ian, and somewhere within me a small piece of me wanted him out of the way. But then I was sick. So sick. Liam moved his hand to Ian's face and caressed it.

"It's cold, Ian. Shut the window," he said.

We waited.

Ian shifted in some.

"I'm tired," he said.

"I know."

Liam put his two hands on Ian's face and kissed him, on his torn bloodied forehead, on each eye and on the lips.

CHAPTER EIGHTEEN

Liam might have gone if Paoli hadn't offered him a job. He ran out of money pretty quickly and we were struggling on what I was getting. So I suppose he had to take it. There was a kind of truce with Ian. If truce is the right word. Liam wanted to care, I think. But with me, he was different. Not so much in action as tone. I couldn't put my finger on it and if I didn't know better I could have thought I was imagining it. But it was there and it was deliberate. Designed to hurt. Some of it must have been his book. He went back to it for a while. Only a while. Then it died and I think that injured him even more, especially if someone asked him how it was going. I stopped asking. But, in a small town, once it got around that he was writing a book, people mentioned it now and then when they'd nothing more to talk about, not knowing he'd stopped. Paoli and Tom were big offenders. Ian did it a couple of times, too. It wasn't their fault they didn't understand and at another time and in another place it wouldn't have mattered. Whatever about the others, Paoli meant well. She needn't have given Liam the job, we weren't pushed or anything. Liam was reluctant to take it: he must have been tempted to run. I was. The job took care of the money problem, and my portrait took care of Ian for a while. It was Tom's idea I do an oil portrait on canvas. I'd never done one before. And Ian was perfect for it. Anyway, Ian insisted it should be him. Tom hated the idea but couldn't find a reason against it being Ian. He came up with the idea in the Otre Casita, a small more plush bar down from Bar Sol, drunk and ordering beers for everyone they didn't want. Chris Rea was coming through on the PA. We were sitting at a corner table under posters of James Dean and Marlon Brando, Paoli sulking because her husband wouldn't talk to her. She tried to corner Liam but she made the mistake of asking him about his book, and after he shut up, Tom stole him from her.

"What d'you think of Chrissie painting this degenerate, Liam?"

"Yeah!"

Ian raised his beer.

"Here's to fascists. Voted Reagan, he did, you know? Voted Reagan."

Tom shoved his face up at Liam's.

"It's a wonder we all haven't been busted by the cops. This guy's the profit margin for every petty dealer from here to Tangiers. God!"

He shook his head.

Liam wanted no more part in their argument than he wanted to talk about his book with Paoli. But his Irish politeness was holding him back from just leaving—politeness or obsequiousness, I'm not sure which actually. The Irish walk a borderline. Perhaps just plain duplicity.

Ian pulled at Tom's moustache.

Tom brushed his hand away.

Ian did it again and Tom slapped his hand away.

Ian smiled.

Paoli flushed and then sighed.

I turned to her.

"What do you think, niña?"

"Good. It is good."

"Fabulous," Ian said. "I've good features. Chrissie, you have to get my aristocratic lines. True stiff upper lip lines. Land of hope and glory."

He raised his glass again.

"Piss," he said.

Piss indeed.

My restlessness came with the spring and the first warm winds which licked at the ermine mantle coating the sierra. And Elena. Elena was fourteen and covered in puppy fat. She had a pretty cabbage patch face and was one of the better students I had. Over the months, I had developed a sort of big sister affection for Elena and I always enjoyed class with her and the four other teenage girls she came with. They were full of fun, and we spent most of our time talking about pop stars. Michael Jackson was all over Elena's folder.

One Sunday evening, after siesta, I met Elena on Calle Mayor, outside an underground bar called Cafeteria Béjar, with her first boyfriend. They were arm in arm, looking slightly uneasy together, maybe made more so by meeting me. His name was Santiago and he had no English, so we spoke in Spanish. It was quite normal to meet students and their families and friends on the street in Béjar. Sometimes you could be delayed ages, meeting every member of someone's family. It was a shock meeting Elena, though, something I wasn't prepared for. I had never before thought of her as anything more than a kid, and seeing her there, hanging out of this awkward youth, made me sad. It had started for her. I imagined her in years to come: bloated, wrinkled, bent over from working or illness, sagging from childbirth, a withered flower with nothing left but to decay and return to where she'd come from, to make way for something new. Born to die, to wither and die. I hated life for that: for holding out such promise and then whipping it away. I hated the illusion of beauty, the seductiveness of youth, ever hopeful. There had to be more. Than illusion. She had to have more than that before her. More than impregnation and redundancy; discarded once the next generation was secure. Spirit betrayed by flesh. Was that what it was? Disappointed spirit in endless pursuit of a dream through disappointing flesh. I wanted to tell her. To warn her. But there was no point. There was nothing I could do for her. We exchanged pleasantries about the day, and I shook hands with Santiago. Then we parted.

After that, I had to get out of town. To breathe, to be free. I headed off up a dusty track, to a small farm which overlooked the town and the road to Cáceres and Seville. The farmhouse was squat and white-washed and capped with a broken terracotta roof. I sat on the hard ground in one of the fields beside an old bath the farmer, José, used as a trough for his cattle. There was an oak between me and the farmhouse. José was a stooped old man, missing three teeth, and he coughed and spat a lot. He'd inherited the farm from his father, and his brother'd had to go away to work. His brother was now wealthy and he was still struggling. At the time he'd inherited the farm, it seemed he'd had the better deal. I think he felt cheated. He had a wife he didn't love and children who'd gone off and never visited. He treated his animals like children and made acid comments about his wife.

I knew he would come over to me if he was around. And I wanted that. He was a friend, my friend, and when I wanted to get away, I came and talked to him. I think I made him feel young again, less wasted. And he made me feel safe. It was a few minutes before I heard him coming behind me. He slapped his hands when he walked, a sort of nervous gesture. He sat down beside me. There were no greetings. No need. We simply talked. The EC was going to make things better for him, he said. Felipe Gonzalez was too good-looking to be a politician and much too good-looking to be a prime minister, especially a socialist prime minister. He was a socialist. He asked me if I was. I said I would be except I didn't believe much in ideologies. He said I was right, that he didn't really either. The land was his ideology. If he wanted to believe in anything, he just had to come to the land and the sierra behind him. He laughed and clapped his hands and spat in the dusty soil.

We had been there an hour, talking, when he asked me if I'd like a drink. I said I would, that I'd nothing much else to be doing and I'd like to see the sun go down. He went back to the farmhouse and brought out a bota. The wine in it was rough and harsh, and it burned the back of my throat. And I thought the bota resembled his skin in texture. We passed it back and forth until the sun went down. He said I was lucky I could travel and work where I liked. That I could speak English. I said it wasn't all choice. That things weren't good at home. He spat again. That's what it was like on the fringe, he said. He regretted not having travelled. His brother had travelled. Worked in Germany and France. A lot of Spaniards from places like Béjar worked abroad. Many came home in summer and the population of Béjar jumped from about seventeen to twenty-three thousand. There were students too and rich people from Madrid who came to the chestnut woods and the sierra to escape the stifling heat of the capital, but the workers were the ones people wanted to see. José said it was funny me coming to Béjar to work when people from Béjar were having to go to France and Germany. I said it was and I didn't understand it. The rich getting richer, he said. He asked me if I'd ever marry. I said I didn't think so. Would I take many lovers? That would be nice, but I didn't think so either. He laughed and spat again. It would be nice, but I wasn't a man, and unless you're a man, taking lovers is considered wrong. It was too bad I wasn't a man. I agreed.

And so it went with me, from spring to summer, as I worked on Ian's portrait. And my restlessness brought depression to me, depression I could not easily explain, depression that was as black as the blackest pit you can imagine. I would cry for no reason and shout and scream if anyone disturbed me and I didn't want to see them. The kind of thing people blame on the time of the month, only this wasn't time of the month stuff, this was Chrissie stuff, Chrissie crisis, despair on a grand scale, despair and uselessness I was becoming smothered in. And that made me angry, not just annoyed, angry, savage fury, harsh cruel anger, a friend to no one. I could still act friendly, if it pleased me, if there was a good reason, but inside I was angry.

Liam fuelled it with his campaign of low-intensity resentment. I could feel it. Close. It was clear that there was a large chunk of him soured towards me, that didn't much want to be with me any more. Not if there was a choice. And he wanted me to know that. I guess I'd destroyed some sort of illusion he'd had about me. And he resented that. If I'd been in a better state, I might have been able to ride it out. Big if. Instead, I just got pissed off with him and the way he was.

Each day I woke, I would look at Liam and try to hold on to my feelings of tenderness for him. But they were slipping. Some days, I used to wish he'd disappear, get out of my bed, fuck off. Why had I needed him so much? His touch? When now I sometimes couldn't stand to be touched, stand to be loved, stand to be entered, to hear his voice, to feel him in me. God, I wanted to be able to talk to him, to have him tell me it was okay, but I couldn't, not even that. And Ian, posing for me and my canvas, thinking I was admiring him, maybe loving him, and all I could do was see the hell in him, coming out at me from the painting, every day. And all this blackness made me hate myself, simply for being me, for not being able to cope with them and their needs, or satisfy my own. When you're growing up, they tell you to fulfil your potential. Well, what about those who don't know their potential, who don't know anything about themselves, who can't be summed up in a nice neat equation, what about them? About us? When there's a demon you don't want, a demon you didn't ask for; when everything you do, no matter how good, does nothing for you; when everyone you love, no matter how much, does nothing for you. That is a black time, when the spirit has left and the body floats alone.

There was a break in the friction when Sean Kelly won the Vuelta d'España and Ireland did well in the European Championship. The Vuelta came through Béjar early on, with a local boy, Lale Cubino, in the lead. The town went mad, and Ian had a chat with Kelly in the foyer of the Hotel Colón. He was on cloud nine over that for days after. It was probably why we all went to Madrid for the end. To see Kelly win. Ian won a load of money from Tom in a bet. That didn't help things between them. Liam won it all from Ian a few weeks later when Ireland beat England. Jesus, it was great. I never thought I could get so excited over soccer. So bloody patriotic. And it was wonderful between Liam and me that night. Wonderful. We made real love. Because we weren't thinking. It was just instinctive. The way it had been at the beginning. The beginning. It seemed a million years away. But that night we were back at the beginning.

Then, suddenly, it was over, and we were doing summer morning-only classes and looking at the end of the year.

The weather was unbearably hot then. In August. I remember that. Mad weather.

Will I ever forget those days?

I remember when it really began to crack with Liam. Staring at him across the dinner table, trying to reason with myself about him. Would he be there all my life? Across the table? And if he went, or I went again, or whoever went, would I feel the emptiness of before? The emptiness that brought me to him, or him to me? Was that how he felt? Jesus, why can't you get into people's minds when you want, to be sure. He couldn't feel the way he had, not Liam, not after what had happened. Not dear sweet Liam, lovely Liam, who never hurt anyone, who never cheated, or killed or anything like that.

"Will you love me forever, Liam?" I asked him.

"What?"

"Forever. No matter what?"

He didn't answer.

"Well?"

"Come on, Chrissie."

"Well?"

"Yes."

"Not sure?"

"Forever's pretty long."

"You used to say it so easy. You never say things like that now. Why don't you say things like that now?"

"I will."

"No, you won't. You don't now, do you?"

"I do."

"You don't. I can feel it. You're not interested. Cold."

"Cold! You can fucking talk about cold! When's the last time you felt anything in bed with me, Chrissie? When? When we beat England? Weeks ago. Jesus, we were both so out of it then I think we'd have done it with anyone. Need booze now, Chrissie? Can't without it? Don't talk to me about cold. You make me feel like a rapist, you know that? Dirty. Cheap and dirty."

"I—"

"What, Chrissie? Tired of me again? Go off and pick someone new up. Go on. Hitch your way on to a new stage. This performance's getting stale. I don't know what the hell it is you want. I really don't. I used to think it was only a matter of you getting some of the crazy shit out of yourself, then you'd be normal, like, settle down. Because that's what I want. And I feel strange wanting it around you. Wanting what's normal. Wanting to—"

"Semi, wife, kids. Who's the suburban dream? Mr writer all washed up chasing rainbows. Not as easy as they say in the books, is it? I don't know what the hell you came here for, Connolly. I don't."

"You wouldn't, Chrissie, not in a million years. I don't think you're capable."

"Fuck you."

"I won't bother replying."

I wanted to say sorry to him. I'd gone way too far. But I couldn't say it. I was held back.

He got up and walked out. I heard the front door slam but I didn't go after him. He might have wanted me to go after him but I didn't.

I went down to the school because it was late and there would be no one there to disturb me. I told

myself I was going down to prepare classes for the
morning but I was going down to be alone, to lock
myself in and be alone. I took a long route down
through little side-streets, kind of wandering where I
felt like it, dulling my mind by singing to myself in
my head. All I want is a room somewhere—somewhere
over the rainbow. I met a couple of students out
walking with their baby, two bankers who wanted to
help themselves on with a bit of English. They'd been
at it two years and still couldn't get much of it
together. It hurt seeing them happy together even if
they were struggling with their English.

I was going to turn on the light in the reception
area when I heard the noise. At first I thought it was
coming from out back. There were pisos behind the
school and there was always noise coming from them:
kids screaming, parents screaming, everyone
screaming. Screaming was big in Spain. But this wasn't
screaming. It was guttural, low, from the depths of
somewhere, struggling noise, jerked, violent. I stopped
and listened. It was coming from the class on my
right, the one Ian used, and it was getting louder. I
walked on, wishing the rotten splintered floorboards
not to creak, holding my breath, hearing my heart
pound in my chest. I think I already knew what it
was. I needed to be sure. I was sweating, cold sweat,
dry mouth, parched lips. I eased along the wall to the

door. It was wide open.

Neither Paoli nor Ian saw me. I just wanted to run away, not to see, but I couldn't.

They were on the table, naked. She was on her hands and knees. He had her by the hair, pulling her head back, forcing her to arch her back so much it looked like it would snap, kissing her from behind. And he was thrusting himself into her arse. I wasn't sure at first, I didn't want to be sure, I suppose, but there were lights from the streets and the pisos and the moon and the stars, shafts of light in the classroom, and he was doing that. Violent dagger thrusts, sharp, and wincing every time he did it. There was pain on his face. It was taut, at the very limit, like he wanted it to tear.

"Fuck!" he cried. "Fuck, fuck!"

And she cried back, saying something I couldn't understand. And the noise grew louder. I'm sure anyone nearby, outside on the street, must have heard it. It got that loud. It got loud enough to frighten me, the sheer violence of it. And I couldn't do a thing. Except watch, fascinated, the way people are fascinated by the grotesque, the horrible; the way people can watch others die and make an outing of it; the way people can watch a bull be ritually slaughtered and cheer.

"Ven, Ian!"

"More!"

"Ven!"

"Harder. Fuck, harder. Christ!"

"Oh, no!"

"More!"

"Ven, Ian!"

There were more periphral noises, moaning and gasping. He sat on her and wrapped his legs around her.

"Now!"

"Fuck, fuck!"

"Jesus!"

They were rocking so hard I thought the table would break under them, and their moans and gasps had become screams. Run, Chrissie, run, I said to myself. Get away. Hide yourself from this. This is not your world, you don't want this. Not this.

But I didn't run. I watched them come together.

"Ian!"

"Now!"

"Please!"

"Shit!"

"Ian!"

"Fuck, oh fuck!"

They rocked on the table. Lumps of her hair came out in his hand. She reached back between her legs and grabbed his balls—the way—oh, shit—and

grabbed his balls and squeezed him, and he urged
her to squeeze him more, tighter, swearing until he
roared like he was dying, and she hit him, swiping at
him with her hand, anywhere she could strike him,
tearing his flesh with her nails, and he roared more
with every blow, and they shook each other off the
table and they crashed to the splintered wooden floor.

Silence followed the way silence follows a great
explosion. Then I could hear outside again, and my
heart, and the two of them panting on the floor,
struggling to get up. I moved back. They couldn't see
me. I couldn't let them know I'd seen it. Not that. All
that twisted torture. How could you do anything for
that? How could you hope to help that? Had I been
a part of that? Had he forced me to be a part of that?
I wanted to be sick. I could hear them talking, simple
things, about classes. I slipped into another classroom
and sat on the floor and put my head in my hands
and cried.

At the front door, they talked affectionately. I
peered out at them. He had his arm around her
shoulder. She kissed him on the cheek. They giggled.

"I must go," she said, touching his face. "I must
go."

"He won't be there."

"I must go anyway."

"We could have coffee. In the Sol."

"No."

"If you came home with me, he wouldn't even notice."

"I must live here."

"Leave him."

"For you?"

"Leave him."

"For what?"

"Must there be a what?"

"Yes, there always must be a what."

They stepped out on to the street and slammed the door shut.

After midnight, I was in Bar Sol, alone, sitting at the counter, reading *El Pais*, drinking a con leche and dunking a churro in it. Pablo was clearing away with two of his barmen at the other end of the bar.

"Hello!"

I didn't have to look up.

Ian took a stool and sat beside me.

"I thought I saw you when I was passing. No Liam?"

"No."

"Fine. Anything in that?"

"No."

"It's hot."

"Yes."

"Am I just going to get monosyllabic answers?"

"No."

"There you go again."

"Sorry."

"Qué pasa?"

"Nada."

"Sure?"

"Nada."

"Qué quieres?"

"This coffee's fine. Get yourself something."

"I'll have a lemon juice. Want a lemon juice?"

"I told you, the coffee's okay."

"Yeah, you did."

I turned back to *El Pais*. I hadn't the slightest interest in the article I was reading. *El Pais* was too intellectual for me on a hot evening sitting with someone I didn't want to be sitting with.

"What's the matter?" he asked.

"Nada."

"Come on, Chrissie."

"I was reading."

"Thanks."

"I was."

"Well, screw you, miss shit."

He got real agitated and started to point at me.

"I just want to read, Ian."

"Has he been at you?"

"Who?"

"Liam. And don't tell me he doesn't because I

know he does. I watch him. And you."

"Do you?"

"Yeah."

His eyes were blinking rapidly.

"No, there's nothing wrong with Liam. Nothing big anyway."

I wanted to say I saw him. It wouldn't come out though. This had nothing to do with Liam. I don't know why we were talking about Liam. Only Ian could make something big out of Liam.

"Pablo!" he called. "Limón!"

Pablo came over with a Schweppes and a load of ice.

"Where were you tonight?" Ian asked. "I called around after dinner. You weren't there. Either of you."

"I was out."

"Where?"

"What is this, twenty questions?"

"Don't want to tell me?"

"No."

"Fine, just fine. Fucking fine."

"Please, Ian."

"Don't create a scene, Ian, is that it?"

"I'm tired."

"Then go to bed. I'm sure he's waiting for you. Waiting for your warmth. Nice to have warmth at night. Maybe not tonight though. Bit hot. But in winter. It gets cold in winter. Without anyone beside you. Know that?"

"Ian!"

"Of course, sorry!"

I ate my churro and finished my coffee and called Pablo back to pay him. Ian cut me out and shoved money at Pablo.

"I'll pay," I said.

I was going to make an issue of it.

"Let me," he said.

"No."

"Let me, Chrissie."

"No."

Pablo stood confused and embarrassed while we pulled at each other's arms. I was building a fury inside I was afraid I wouldn't be able to control. Not just for Ian. But he was there and he was the one I'd been disgusted with, the one I couldn't stand talking to then.

He pushed me aside and gave Pablo the money for the coffee, the churro and the lemon. I guess I flipped.

"Piss off, Ian!"

I threw two one-hundred pieces at him and rushed to the door. He followed me, pulling at my shoulder. I kept going till I was outside the bar.

"Jesus, I'm sorry, Chrissie. I'm sorry," he said.

"Fuck off, Ian. I'm going home. See you tomorrow."

"Come on. Chrissie. I'm sorry. I said I was sorry."

"Go home, Ian."

He pulled at me again.

I lashed at him with my hand and missed.

He looked at me, astonished.

"I was in the school tonight!" I yelled. "In the fucking school."

"Christ! Christ."

"Get away from me."

"Chrissie!"

"I said, get away."

I pushed him and rushed over to a taxi waiting at the rank at the edge of the Plaza de España.

"And you're so special," he yelled at me. "What about judge not and all that? Let him who is without cast the first. Have a good look at yourself."

I was getting in the taxi. I stopped, told the driver to wait and crossed the road to Ian.

"What do you mean?"

"Nothing."

"You do."

"I—I—I feel, you know. Her. You. I didn't—with you—why'd you have to see?"

"I'm sorry. I shouldn't have."

"No."

"Ian!"

CHAPTER NINETEEN

I finished his painting two days later, after lunch, during siesta. It was good, I know it was good, and Tom said it was good, said it had a character of its own, a character that was like a signature, that I could be better if I stuck at it—If I stuck at it! I wanted to tear the damn painting apart, wreck it so it wouldn't be there any more, as if its not being there any more would somehow release me from something. Liam knew what I was trying to do and said I should wreck it or leave it or whatever else on my own because even if he did give an opinion I wouldn't listen to it. I slapped him for that because I knew what he meant. And perhaps I didn't like the idea of his knowing me so well. I'd always thought no one would ever know me that well. That I could always surprise. But I could no longer surprise Liam. And I knew he would put up with me less and less, until finally he could break free and he would go. I knew that. And I feared it because, by then, I couldn't do a thing to influence him. Only sit back and watch, and mourn for what might, or should, have been.

In a sense, finishing Ian's painting finished Ian with me except for a certain residual affection that would always remain. In the end, perhaps that was all he was to me, a series of brush strokes, intense brush strokes, colours in oil on canvas, an image formed to be forgotten. There was never the same bond with Ian as there was with Liam. Something at the base was missing. Empathy perhaps. We could know one another only up to a point. Too many differences. Not on the surface. You had to dig to find them. But they were there. And that's where it ended with us. Where we could go no further. We had managed to submerge them for as long as neither of us wanted to make an issue of them. A pact. And I broke the pact. For my own reasons. If I'd been stronger, I could have helped him, should have helped him. That was what he wanted from me, what he expected. If only people would stop expecting. I failed him. And when I failed him I failed myself and slipped a little more into the shade, afraid to come out.

We were all ticking over at the end of the summer, waiting for the whole thing to end, to release us. None of us was coming back, each of us knew it. We never talked about the future, only the past where it was a happy past. My anger subsided because anger is a hard emotion to maintain, and anyway, I could see light at the end of the tunnel, and an escape, a chance to get out, go somewhere else.

When he saw it, Ian went overboard with compliments about the painting. Ian hadn't a clue about painting, so his compliments were worthless except as compliments. He insisted on celebrating with champagne. I didn't want to have to go over to his place, so I said we'd cook dinner for everyone in our place, and Liam agreed to help even though I could see he didn't want to help. Poor Liam, the things he had to do for me: poor me, the things I had to put up with for him. I'd say we were even. Anyway, I cooked chicken though I hate meat and didn't eat any of it myself. And I made a kind of a yoghurt and ice cream sponge with strawberries. I'm not a great cook. And I don't like cooking meat. Not for anyone.

The night was very humid, dead still. Paoli looked tired, worn out. I hadn't been talking to her all day. I couldn't bring myself to. Smiling at her was about all I could manage. I wasn't doing much talking to anyone. I wanted to be in the kitchen alone, cooking, to be on my own for that at least, but they wouldn't let me. It was a bad night for all of us to be together.

Tom was in one of his moods and drank a whole bottle of champagne before the meal, on his own. Paoli kept going in to him, in between annoying me, asking if there was anything she could help with when there wasn't. She'd come back more upset each time. I toyed with the idea of Tom knowing what was going on with Ian. The thought of all that still made me want to puke. Our friendship was dying in my disgust and I couldn't understand why. I'd known it was going on before I saw it. I'd been part of it. Perhaps if I hadn't been part of it, I could have let it go. And I was looking for an excuse to distance myself from her.

We drank two more bottles of champagne, and four bottles of wine, and then Ian and Paoli started smoking dope. Tom was going to say something but there was too much champagne in his veins, so he just turned his head away as if that would make it not happen. Liam wasn't too pleased with it either. What the fuck were they getting so worked up about? They'd been pouring champagne into themselves. It was then Ian said we should all go climbing the next day to the lagunas in the sierra. Each of us looked at the others, trying to think of a reason to say no. None of us could. So we agreed in a way you agree when you want to kill something. But we agreed. Paoli stopped it going any further by saying we should all go to Napoli, a disco, after coffee. Now none of us wanted to go there either, probably not even Paoli, but the alternative was sitting in that living room, drinking and smoking, waiting for the inevitable.

The disco was filling when we arrived. We had to

wade through a throng of bodies and a stinging blanket of smoke to get to the bar. Paoli and Liam went off to dance on their own. Ian said he'd get the drinks, and Tom and I went to find a seat. I tried to talk with Tom about painting but he wasn't in a listening mood. I suppose—at his worst—Tom was the rudest man I ever met. Plain rude, I mean. Not caring a damn for anyone else. He could ask you for a drink and then get up and leave before you'd finished, or walk off to the other side of the bar and leave you alone. And drunk, he was at his worst. Ian said Tom didn't care about anything he didn't own or want to own. I gave up trying to get through to him when he started to focus on Paoli and Liam, dancing together. God knows what he was thinking. I said I was going to help Ian with the drinks. He wasn't listening by that stage.

When I finally found him, Ian was outside, sitting on a window ledge, talking to a girl. One of his students. They were both drinking from bottles. The girl was good-looking. And she wore her clothes well. Ian's hair had dark streaks of sweat running through it, and his shirt was unbuttoned.

"I was wondering when you'd come out," he said. "Got sick of him, did you?"

"He's not paying attention."

"Is he ever?"

"What are you up to? I thought you were getting drinks."

"I'm drinking with my bird. Beatriz. Know her?"

"Don't think so."

"Particular class. Don't worry, she can barely put two words of English together. I've been teaching her for the last year. Like some tumble weed?"

"No thanks. You've been smoking too much."

"Climbing high, Chrissie. You narked?"

"Yeah."

"Liam in a fury? Why aren't you dancing with him?"

"Leave it, Ian, it's not your concern."

"It is. You're my concern. You have my mark."

"I could tell you to fuck off."

"Do you want to?"

"Give me a drink."

He passed me his bottle.

"Is she legal?"

"Fringe benefits."

"You're a bestial bastard."

"Got to get it somewhere. You know?"

"That all it is to you?"

"Is it any more to you?"

"Paoli not providing?"

His face firmed. His grip on the bottle tightened.

"Bitch!"

"I'm sorry. I shouldn't have said that."

"No, you shouldn't. You've no right."

He took out some crumpled five hundreds and unfolded them carefully.

"Beatriz, go get us all beer, will you love," he said to the girl.

She looked puzzled. He repeated himself in Spanish. She took the money and went inside.

"Beautiful fringe benefit," Ian said.

I sat beside him.

"You must think I'm a prick," he said.

"Why?"

"The way you treat me. Sorry you came here?"

"We're friends."

"Are we? I still want you."

"Ian!"

"I have erections when I see you. You're the one I think of when I'm wanking. I wank even when I'm not dreaming. Do you know that? You've no need."

"You're gone. You're trying to provoke me."

"Could be. I don't know. Where'll you go?"

"What do you mean?"

"After."

"Don't know."

"You're not coming back."

"No."

"What'll you do?"

"India. That's where I was going."

"Boyfriend?"

"I don't know. You?"

"Maybe I'll start walking trips in Andalucía. I'd be good at that. I'd like you two to visit."

"Thanks."

Beatriz came out, dripping sweat, and handed me my beer. She sat on Ian's knee and they started kissing. Trying to prove a point.

"I'm going in," I said.

"Hasta," Ian said, still kissing Beatriz.

Paco, the DJ, wearing a singlet with a picture of Status Quo on it, grinned at me and raised his thumb to me and winked as I passed his box in Napoli. I smiled back. I pushed over to the bar and leaned on it. An overweight man next to me stank heavily of sweat and aftershave. His belly was pouring out over his leather belt, and his pink shirt was open to below his chest. His face was pockmarked. I tried not to breathe in his direction. His eyes followed me. I hate that. "No Woman, No Cry" filled the disco. Liam and Paoli were in their own world on the dance floor. I could see their hands above their heads.

"No Woman, No Cry" changed to "Gimme Hope Jo'anna." Liam was talking to a pick of a girl. Trying to get her to dance with him. She looked around before saying yes. I didn't feel anything. He was too tall for her. Paoli vanished behind three girls.

I stood at the bar, watching it all, distanced from it all, distanced by the alcohol in me, distanced by my want to be somewhere else, someone else. That big slob still had his eyes on me. Fat fucking slob. I wanted to scratch those fucking eyes of his out. Was Liam ditching me? I was waiting for it. For him to come and tell me he was ditching me. I was leaving it to him. To tell me. I was giving him the time and the space.

A hand touched my shoulder. Ian. He was ruddy and breathing heavily, a drop of sweat running down his body between the open halves of his shirt.

"I thought you were on the make," I said to him.

"Plenty of time. I'd rather—"

"It's stuffy here, don't they have air conditioning?"

"You should be here when it breaks down. We might get fireworks tonight—thunder and lightning. Air's thick enough outside. There's a great view from Everest if there is."

Everest was a bar up at El Castañar, a picnicing area in the shade of chestnut trees above Béjar. The small stone bullring at El Castañar was said by locals to be the oldest in the world. It was surrounded by barbeque pits and open-air bars and there was some disagreement as to whether it was the oldest bullring in the world since a lot of other places around Spain—

particularly in the south—claimed they had the oldest bullrings in the world. The El Castañar ring had a church beside it. It was a place of pilgrimage because of its virgin. The black-wigged statue was paraded through the streets on feast-days. All pretty weird. Bar Everest had a balcony and looked right down on Béjar and the surrounding country.

Ian put his arm around me.

"Listen, Chrissie. Let's get out of here. Together."

"I don't want to, Ian. I'm fine here."

"Are you? Why don't you go and dance with Liam?"

"Why don't you?"

"He's busy. Seen that?"

"He can dance with whoever he likes."

"Very understanding. Is he that way?"

I didn't answer.

"I'm going to have dinner," he said.

"You had dinner in our place."

"Dessert then. Beatriz."

"Does Paoli know?"

"Shut up. It's a short life."

"Yes."

He gripped my arm tight.

"You're hurting me, Ian."

"Never. I'm not like you."

He let go.

"No, I suppose you're not."

I stared deep into his eyes, to let him know how I felt. It didn't work. He wasn't seeing.

Beatriz squeezed between two men. She smiled at me, frowned, kissed Ian, whispered in his ear and pulled him towards the dance floor.

"Bye bye, Chrissie, dear."

"Bye, Ian."

The heat and the acrid smell made me want to get out again. I thought about walking back to the piso. No one'd miss me. People were shoving up against me, calling the barmen, passing money, spilling drinks on the counter, and on each other, talking about the heat and the records being played. Big male mouths, sometimes covered in hair, and small female mouths, with good teeth and love on their lips. One woman pushed up against me. She leaned over my shoulder and took three drinks from the bar. I moved left to avoid the drinks but she got me with her cigarette ash on the shoulder.

Liam was pushing his way over.

"Hello."

"It's hot."

"I'm drenched. Paoli's still going. And she's supposed to be sickly. Want to go out for a while?"

"Want something to drink?"

"Small tinto."

We sat down outside beside a water fountain on the turn off for El Castañar. Liam drank his tinto and put the glass down.

"Could be thunder and lightning," I said.

"It's thick enough to cut."

"Ian thinks there'll be lightning."

"I saw him with one of his girls. How are you? Haven't had a chance to talk to you."

"I'm fine. Bit tired."

"Going home?"

"Might."

"Okay."

I brushed my brow. My hand was wet. Small beads of sweat on the fingers and a streak of sweat across the palm. I pushed it to his face. He kissed the palm and licked it.

"Salty," he said.

"Good for my weight."

"You look nice. Not dancing?"

"I love a bop. On my own. Thanks for the compliment. You haven't said that for a long time."

"No."

"Are you happy?"

"Should I be?"

"No."

I touched his face and scraped some of the sweat with my nails.

"Hating me?" I asked.

"No."

"Some of the time?"

He didn't want to argue. I could tell.

"Think you'll be able to get anything when you get home?"

"Doubt it. They're giving out leaflets on how to emigrate."

"I love you."

"You used to tell me to shut up when I said that."

"I know. Maybe I'm changing. People do, Liam. I think you want everything to be the same. I've changed. I think I'll go home too. Would you mind?"

"Up to you. Home to what? I might go to London."

"You don't want me along?"

"I didn't say that."

"I know what you're thinking. I can feel it. Last night I felt it. You hurt me."

"Sorry. But you can talk. You're so cold, Chrissie. Cold. It—here we go again."

"Make love to me, or beat me up. You used to be kind to me."

"So did you."

"You hurt me here."

I touched the side of my breast.

"I'm sorry. I didn't mean to."

"Why do you make love if you only want to hurt?"

"I don't."

"I'd have preferred if you'd hit me, beaten me up, or walked out. You won't forget, will you? You're like a garotte. One twist at a time. You're really good at it. You enjoy it."

"You really think I do? I thought you knew me. If I could for one moment show you what's going on inside me, maybe you'd understand. It isn't just you and Ian. It's me, it's everything."

"You're a real one for self-pity, Liam. I always knew it but now I'm really seeing it. I snogged another guy once, had a fling, and you're reliving the passion of Jesus. No one gives a shit. It doesn't mean anything. I love you. For God's sake, I don't know why."

"You love him."

"I've decided not to."

"You don't decide not to love someone."

"Okay. I still love him. A bit. But I love you more. Fuck it, why do I have to excuse myself? So you're not my exclusive lover."

"No."

"I let you down, didn't I?"

"Give me a hug."

We embraced.

"I want it to be fine, Liam. I want it to stop hurting you."

I licked his face.

"Want to walk?"

"Where to?"

"Anywhere."

He took me by the hand and we started strolling up the road to El Castañar. We passed a brothel and a small bar in the chestnut trees where the teenagers gathered. Two of them were sitting on some steps below the bar, kissing. U2 filtered down from the bar. "I Still Haven't Found What I'm Looking For." Liam pulled me closer to him and put his arm over my shoulder. Away to the west, through the trees, the jagged mountains stretching into Portugal silhouetted in the night. The road to El Castañar wasn't lit, and where the trees were heavy, it was hard to see. The darkness was pregnant with tension and the air got heavier. The smell of the trees and the grass was strong in the moist night air. It was a rich smell and it filled the night. It seemed like forever as we walked in the darkness. Like forever. If there is eternity, maybe this is what it's like: walking arm in arm at night, I thought.

We were kicking stones in the driveway of Bar Everest when the first bolt of lightning ripped open the sky, over to the west, directly above the jagged mountains. It made them fierce-looking, like the teeth of some preying animal. Liam jumped and spun around. I threw myself back. We watched for another.

The balcony in Everest gave a view all the way to

Portugal. Liam ordered a bottle of wine and two glasses, and we sat and watched the lightning approach. Trunks of it tore great gashes in the darkness, lighting up the whole area as if it were day. And after it came the thunder. Angry claps that made us excited in our seats. I leaned over the balcony, and Liam sat back and stretched out.

The lightning danced its way across from Portugal.

"I want to go to India, Liam," I said. "Will you come? I don't want to go home. Let's go to India. We can live cheap there. And teach English. If we need money, we can teach English. Let's go. Will you come?"

I finished off my glass of wine and poured another. It was becoming so easy to drink that stuff.

"You don't want to go, do you? Going to London? You'd hate London."

"Just watch the show, Chrissie."

"Why do you have to be like that?"

"Like what?"

A group of teenagers were playing table soccer in the bar. They let out a roar and began to shout at one another.

"Want something to eat?"

"Hungry again? Wasn't dinner enough?"

"I'd like chips."

"Cochon."

"I'm a growing lad."

"Why don't you eat chorizo?"

"Okay."

"Do and I'll brain you."

"You suggested it. Now you don't want me to."

"I want you to do what you want."

"And if I do, I get brained by you."

"I can't pretend I don't care."

"Okay, I won't have anything. I've lost my appetite. It's too heavy."

"Are you going to hold it against me? You hold everything, you do. Do you forgive me?"

"For what?"

"You know."

"No."

"Fuck off."

"What about Ian?"

"He wants to marry me."

"Are you going to?"

"He thinks we're going off without him."

"And aren't we?"

"Melt. You and him. I wish you'd both ease off a bit."

"We just see things different. Smell that? The rain's coming on."

"Do you want to marry me?"

"I asked you once."

"Yeah, but do you really want to marry me? If I said, yes, what would you do?"

"Is this a proposal?"

"God, no. I just want to know what you're thinking. You say all these grand things so easily. I just want to know if you mean any of it. I always have the feeling that if I tested you, you'd run a mile. All this I love you stuff. It just rolls off your tongue. You've a sweet tongue. It kills me to say it. It really hits home. I feel it. Shit, I'm coming out with it now."

"Do you think I lie?"

"Do you? You say you love me but you don't act it. You act hate."

"Can't I feel both?"

"Not if I can't love two people at the same time."

"It's not the same."

"Why not?"

"My emotion's all concerned with you. Opposite sides of the same coin. Yours is split, debased, watered down."

"Hail, Liam. I think I'd prefer to be loved with someone else than to be hated by the person who loves me."

"You take up all my feelings. Everything's invested in you. The bad feelings are—"

"Are what?"

"I don't know. Hate, pain. I'm trying to cope. I

told you."

"With what? See. I don't fully believe you. I want to. If you love me, forgive me. It should be as simple as that. No conditions. Love me and forgive me. And forgive me again."

"That's the theory. Would you if you were me?"

"I don't know. I'd try."

"I'm trying."

"For how long?"

"There should be a time limit?"

"I don't know. But I think there's a kind of invisible wedge between us. I want things to be fine, Liam."

As if right on cue, Ian's 2CV came along the road beneath us, horn blaring, and turned into Everest. We stopped talking. Ian came into the bar with Beatriz on his arm and Tom and Paoli trailing.

"If it isn't the two lovers," Ian said. "I thought you'd gone home for some torrid sex."

"Shut up, Ian," I said.

"Yes, mam. I'm out of it again. The lightning's fantastic, isn't it? I've promised Beatriz here that a leg over with me's the same."

He looked about for a response.

"Sit down," Liam said.

"I should get my camera and try and shoot this," Tom said. "I don't think I've the right film."

Paoli sighed and reached over for my bottle of

wine.

"Things still going strong down in Napoli?" I asked her.

"I wanted to stay," Tom said. "She wants to vamos."

Paoli drank from the bottle and didn't even look at him.

"More drink?" Ian asked.

No one answered.

"Well, I'm getting some."

He went into the bar and came back with more wine.

"Here's to love," he said.

"Shut up, Ian, you're being a pain."

He put his finger to his mouth.

"Won't say a dicky bird."

Beatriz put her arms around him.

He leaned over to Liam and whispered in his ear. I could hear him.

"She's aching for it. Keeps asking me to go home."

"Would you fuck up and watch the weather," Liam said.

"Sorry for being alive. Have we interrupted a Chrissie-Liam love tiff? Can't have that. Jesus, you two think you're so special. I'm your fucking friend, Liam. You don't treat your friends like that. At least, I don't. And you, miss proper tights. Fuck both of you."

"No," Liam said. "We know how you treat your fucking friends."

"What the fuck's that supposed to mean, mate?"

"You fucking know."

"No, I don't. Tell me."

He put a bottle to his lips and drank it until it ran down his front.

"Chrissie, what the fuck does lover boy mean?"

"Shut up, both of you, just shut up."

"Screw you, bitch."

Liam slammed his hand down on the table.

"Just fuck off out of it, Ian. Just fuck off. What the fuck did you come up here for? Do you never know when to lay off?"

I'd had about as much as I could take. I got up and went into the bar. I sat down on one of the stools.

Liam followed me.

"Don't let him get to you," he said.

"Him! Him! What about you, Liam? My own personal inquisitor. At least Ian's honest. Are you honest?"

"What are you like this for all of a sudden?"

"All of a sudden! Jesus! I've been like this for months only you've been too caught up in yourself to pay the slightest bit of notice. Liam—"

"Why didn't you say?"

"Shit, I don't believe this."

"But you should have said."

"To who? To you?"

Ian came in to us, holding a bottle of wine and wearing a straw hat. He looked ridiculous. So ridiculous I forgot that I was angry for a moment and laughed. It wasn't much of a laugh but it was a laugh.

"I didn't mean anything, Chrissie," he said. "It's started pissing outside. Come on out. I'm going. I didn't mean anything. Listen, I'll make it up. Why don't I cook you both dinner?"

"Leave us, Ian," Liam said.

"No, don't, I'm coming out, Ian. Do what you like, Liam."

We all filed out after Ian. Liam sat at the bar and had a coffee. There was a film on television.

Outside, the rain was torrential, and the sky was furious with lightning and the sound of thunder. Ian started dancing in the rain. He grabbed me by the hands and swung me around in the rain, splashing both of us through deep puddles in the muddy ground.

"Dance!" he roared. "I could have danced all night."

I joined in the song with him until my head seemed to be floating in the night air.

He must have felt me letting go.

"Hang on, Chrissie," he said. "We're going to take off."

But I couldn't. I let go and fell into the mud, rolling over with the force of our action. When I got my bearings again, Ian was sitting naked on a wooden fence in the car park, his straw hat bent up at the brim, holding his shirt in his hands.

"Toro!" he was yelling. "Toro!"

I rubbed the mud from my face. There was a black cow in the long grass at the other side of the car park, barely visible. Tom stood against the wall of the bar with his hands stuffed deep in his pockets, laughing, an empty wine bottle under his arm. Paoli stood beside me in the rain, hesitating. Then she knelt down beside me, slowly. It was surreal.

Ian got off the fence and approached the cow.

"I'm going to do this poor defenceless animal to death," he said. "It's been sentenced, so it must die. For being a bull."

"It's a cow," I said.

"Ian, look what you have done to Chrissie," Paoli said.

"Sorry, didn't mean to. Everyone gets hurt. Even Buster. Hurt Buster."

I looked at Tom. He stopped laughing.

"It's okay, you didn't hurt me," I said to Ian. "Get your clothes on."

"But this way you see me as I am, dear. Naked so to speak. Warts and all. I've no warts, by the way."

He went right up to the cow.

"Chrissie doesn't like killing defenceless animals, do you, my love?" he said.

"Ian, you're drunk," Tom said. "You'll catch a cold. You look stupid."

"I've a good body. Ask Paoli what she thinks. Eh, Paoli, fucky, fucky, fucky, wow!"

He thrust his pelvis forward three or four times.

"Ian!" I cried.

Paoli looked at me. She was crying. Her face was bleeding, where she had scratched it with her nails, and the rain was running down her face and mixing with the blood.

"What the hell's he saying?" Tom asked, coming at Ian.

"Fucky, fucky, fucky, Tom," Ian said.

"You fucking bastard, Ian," I said.

He was standing at the cow, stroking its nose.

"I didn't mean it, did I, Chrissie? It came out."

Tom walked over to him, rain streaming into his eyes. He turned to me as if to let me know what he was going to do. Ian raised his hands like in surrender. Tom hit him hard in the solar plexus, a single blow. Ian cried out and buckled up and sank into the mud, wheezing. Tom kicked him twice and pulled him up and hit him again in the plexus.

"What are you doing?" I screamed at him.

I rushed at him but he shoved me out of the way. I almost fell over. He punched Ian on the face and when Ian hit the ground he kicked him again, and again. I was picking myself up when Liam caught Tom from behind and dragged him off Ian. He got a locking grip on Tom's arms and jammed his leg into Tom's knee.

"Jesus, man, you'll kill him!" he said.

"Yeah. Bastard!"

He wrestled Tom away.

Ian was huddled up in the mud, like a baby.

"I love you, Chrissie," he said.

"I know, love," I replied.

I rocked him in my arms and sang.

CHAPTER TWENTY

I n the morning, I was woken by Concha banging on our front door. My head spun the moment I lifted it from the pillow and my throat felt raw and swollen. I struggled across the tiled floor, stepping in three puddles which had formed from leaking during the lightning storm. Water was still dripping from the ceiling, although the sun was pouring in through the windows. Concha had our mail in her hand. I considered mentioning the flooding but my head was too sore and my stomach too sick to really want to talk to her. She gave me two letters and a rolled-up *Irish Times* addressed to Liam. She wanted to be asked in for a chat but I just thanked her and shut the door before she even had a chance to turn away. I almost fell in one of the puddles in the hallway, getting back to the bedroom.

A large lump of phlegm was fixed at the back of my throat. I brought it up and it almost made me throw up. I rushed into the bathroom and found myself in more water. I spat the phlegm into the toilet bowl and gave into a urge in my bowels. My feet were in dirty water as I sat on the cold seat. I had my eyes shut. My throat was burning. The removal of the phlegm left a dryness at the back of my throat. I sucked hard to make saliva. It worked a bit, smoothing out the lining, easing the rawness.

Lying in bed again, under the newspaper, I called on anyone who could to ease my sickness. Then it hit me: classes! No. No classes. Saturday. No bloody classes. And the night before?—the night before came into focus with a clarity I didn't need. I swore at all of them and wished there was some way I could sleep them all off. Stay in bed until it was all over. I dozed off again and woke up with a shock half an hour later. The sunlight was stronger, in great beams, illuminating particles of dust floating in the room.

I had four cups of coffee and three yoghurts. The coffee was for my head, the yoghurts for my stomach. The coffee didn't do much except make my throat feel a bit better. I sat in one of Liam's shirts and read the paper. Outside, swallows were flying among the roofs. *The Irish Times* was a Saturday paper. Liam had been asking his mother to send out a paper since January, and this was the first she'd sent. She always said there was no news, not realising that everything is news when you're not there.

Concha was screaming at someone below me. I could hear her clearly through the open window. It could have been her son. She was always screaming at him. Whether she was angry or happy with him. An odour of frying fish in olive oil came in through the window on a breath of wind. It turned my stomach.

After a shower, I put on a t-shirt and shorts and went for a walk up Calle Mayor. I hadn't wanted to go out and I couldn't remember making the decision to go out. I just went, as if under the instructions of some unseen director, acting on some kind of instinctive autopilot, not knowing why or where I was going. And it was boiling. Some children were playing by a fountain, splashing water at each other. A black cat lay in the shade near them, one eye open. It was cut under the eye. The blood had coagulated. Liam had cut himself, shaving, and there had been blood in the washbasin, in the foamy scum full of his fine facial hairs. Where the hell was he? Off sulking again. I'd been too hung over to worry about him. Hung over saps your strength. The sun was too hot for me. I shifted my course into the shade and tried to jumpstart my brain.

I must have had my head bowed, because, suddenly, the 2CV was coming at me down Calle Mayor, filling up the street, blaring its horn. Ian was waving from the driver's seat. Liam was flopped back in the passenger seat. There was no expression on his face.

"Buenos días, Chrissie!"

Shit, I thought to myself. This is one of his crazy dreams. I'm in one of his crazy dreams. Perhaps that was it. It was all one of his nightmares. And we were back in Paris.

"Hi."

I leaned in the window.

"We were going to get you. You ready?"

"What for? I thought you'd—"

"Climbing," Liam said.

He gave me a look that was as good as a speech. There was going to be no choice in the matter. He'd had no choice and I'd have no choice.

"Remember? He wants to go."

"Shit, no."

"Don't tell me you don't want to go either?"

"The lagunas. Shit, Ian, I feel shit. Don't you feel shit? I mean—"

"Me? I never feel shit. Soldier of the Queen, you know. Iron."

He touched his biceps.

"We'll never get another chance. You'll love it. Get away from here. Last night—well, I don't know—"

"Don't."

Liam's eyes pleaded with me, like he was trying to convey a secret to me. I couldn't think of anything

I wanted to do less than climbing. I thought after what had happened, Ian would have been quiet. Perhaps off on his own. That was all a blur again. A bad dream. He was smiling his bloody butter-blond smile.

"We've packed food, Chrissie. Liam and I'll carry everything. All you have to do is walk. It'll do you the world of good."

"Ah, no, Ian."

"Please. I—"

"Ah, Ian. Liam?"

Liam shook his head, resigned.

Ian lowered his voice.

"Listen, I could do with being out of here today. Please, Chrissie. Will you come?"

Liam nodded his head quickly, scowled and made a gesture both of us understood.

I couldn't say no.

We drove up to the second platform, a kind of car park on the sierra and the furthest you could bring a car up. Ian sang all the way and had the sun roof open and his stereo playing the *Messiah*. Liam and I said nothing. I watched the great wall of the sierra come closer. Ian drove fast and a couple of times I thought we'd sail right off the road. Not that I cared that much. We took a load of photographs before we left the car. Ian insisted on it.

We had been climbing for over an hour, and the strong dry wind of the sierra had taken all the moisture from our lips, so that the sun had an easy job of making them sore and chapped. My throat was dry again, and full of dust, and my legs had a thick layer of black topsoil stuck to them. Ian was wearing culottes, and they were black around the bottoms. He had a vest on too, exposing his shoulders, and they were red and dry. Liam wore no top and didn't seem to notice he was getting red. He was about as miserable as I'd ever seen him. Below us, Béjar had vanished into the haze and the dust of the sierra.

We stopped on some flat broken rocks where one track ended and another began. All the rocks had flat tops from the wind, and the vegetation was long grass and thick scrub. The farmers had brought their cattle up to the higher pastures, and there were black cattle with bells around their necks feeding on the tall grass. Liam took his rucksack from his back and opened it and searched for a bottle of water. It was at the bottom, below the barras he'd prepared, and the fruit. The plastic coke bottle was wrapped in a towel to keep it cool. He drank some, held it in his mouth and spat it out.

"Don't swallow," he said.

He passed the bottle to me.

I drank and let it run to my throat, but I didn't

swallow. I washed my mouth and my throat with the water and then spat it out. It mixed in with the black stony soil, some of it sinking, the rest running down in a tiny channel. I licked my lips. They were rough and sore, and they itched at the sides. The sun was strong at that height.

"All chapped," I said.

I passed the bottle to Ian.

"Your face's filthy," he said. "Don't worry, it'll help protect it from the sun. I'm putting something on."

He took out a sweatshirt with a Southern Comfort logo and pulled it over him. His lips looked like mine felt. We should have brought cream, I thought. Now we'd come back like lobsters. We should have brought cream. When he'd cleaned out his mouth with the water, and poured some on his face, Ian gave the bottle to Liam who put it back in his rucksack and pulled the rucksack on again. I looked down to where I'd spat. It was all gone. I brushed some of the black soil from my legs and let the wind take it from my hand. God, I felt shit. The wind and the cow bells played the lonely tune of the sierra.

"We'll really need a bloody swim after this," Ian said.

"Point the way," Liam said.

I ran my hand through my hair, to brush it back

from my face. It was knotted and thick with dust, and it felt like a wire brush. I had to push to get it back. Ian's had dark streaks of dirt in it.

I led on. Why me? My legs felt like lead weights. We zigzagged across the sierra, along tracks marked with stones piled one on the other. It made climbing longer, but easier. Sometimes we stopped for a minute or two, to catch our breath. Breathing was hard and it took getting used to. We aimed for a big disc of a rock at the top of one ridge. There'd be others beyond, but we could take each of them in turn.

On the big disc of a rock, Ian took a block of cheese from his rucksack and sliced three pieces from it with his Swiss army knife. He handed one to me. I had no taste. I spat it out.

"I could do with a steak now," he said.

"Oh, yeah, brilliant," Liam said.

"The whole way up I've been thinking about it. Maybe we could do one of these cows. Fry up steaks. Would you mind, Chrissie?"

I didn't give a fuck.

"It'd be a bit difficult."

"Just bleed one of the smaller ones. I know where to cut."

I thought about pursuing it and stopped. He was slicing into the cheese with obvious skill.

"I used to kill lobsters," Liam said.

"Where?"

"New York. I had to kill them by splitting them from the mouth to the tail, and then pulling their stomachs out."

"Is this macho man hour?" I said. "Do you have to talk about this?"

"There's a serious side to this, Chrissie."

"What?"

"Listen. You put a jagged knife in their mouths and cut down and pull out the stomach. Then chop the claws and feelers off. At first, I hesitated. I wondered what they were thinking. Stupid really. I was going to disembowel them with my knife, drinking a cup of coffee and chatting, about thirty of them. The first was a seven or eight-pounder with claws that could take the top of your finger off. I had a feeling of power—and cruelty—both at the same time."

"It's all in the mind," Ian said.

He passed Liam more cheese and put the knife and block of cheese away.

"Yeah," Liam said. "When you have to do thirty, and thirty more after that. We did dozens of them every day. One of them had a go at my nose the second or third day, and that was it. In the end, we used to play around with them, cutting bits off them, slowly, for fun. It was a boring job."

"That's disgusting," I said. "What's so fucking serious about it?"

"It's obvious. Brutality. How you can become brutal."

"I think it's disgusting."

About mid-afternoon we reached the top. Oh, Jesus, how happy I was to reach the top. My lungs were near collapsing, and my legs were almost lifeless.

It was flat, and the ground was arid and stony, with small pieces of vegetation clinging to the soil. On the other side, we could see the Laguna Grande, where we were headed, and the rocky slopes which surrounded its icy blue waters. To our right, the smaller lagunas, higher up, were half hidden by ledges. The climb down to the Laguna Grande was over boulders and across grassy shelves uncovered by the receding snow and protected by the mountains and the cliff wall. There were cattle on these shelves, sitting by little streams which flowed from the sierra to the lagunas. Cold water, cold like steel.

Ian ran some of the way, after which he could not run because there was a succession of sheer drops to the different grassy shelves. It was slow work, getting down from one to another, but we could stop and pour water from the streams over us when we wanted, and the soft soil under the grass made it easier going than the hard rocky tracks on the way up. The further down we went, the less the wind was, until eventually there was no wind and we felt the full heat of the sun like a hot iron on our necks. On one of the boulders, Liam jumped badly and fell. His rucksack came off his back and rolled over the edge. He managed to stop himself before he followed it. I did nothing. Ian rushed after him and had to stop himself falling over by hanging on to a small rock embedded in a deep fissure in the boulder. He smiled while he hung, almost tempting something to make him slip. We laughed, and I climbed down to where the rucksack was and picked it up. Liam cleaned a cut on his leg with some water from one of the streams.

The Laguna Grande was still, and you could see clear through to the soft mud bottom. The sight of it made me feel better. Not great, but better. Ian got there first, rushing to it like it was a treasure trove, and stood at the edge of a rock, looking in. I watched him as Liam and I came behind him, across the stones and the long grass immediately around the shore. He stood to attention and took off his sweatshirt and shoes.

"Don't get in yet," I said. "Wait a bit. Till you've cooled down."

"Let's see if I get cramp."

"Don't be silly."

"But it's inviting. Look, it's sort of calling."

I sat down behind him.

Liam pulled out a bottle of water and took a swig. He swallowed this time and then passed it to me.

"Just put your foot in. See what it's like," he said to Ian.

"It'll be ice."

Ian dipped his foot in the water.

"Give me an orange."

"How is it?"

"Freezing."

Liam gave him an orange, and he took out his knife and sliced into it and peeled off the skin in segments. He handed me a piece, then Liam.

"This'll help," he said. "Ever been to Pamplona, Liam?"

"No, why?"

"Courage. Man must be courageous. That is his destiny. My father says that. Courage, Buster. But courage like the rest of this dear little world can be deceptive. Take Pamplona. I've run with the bulls. A courageous man, you might say. Eight in the morning, the gun goes and the crowd goes and the bulls run. But most of us run way ahead of the bulls. Only the locals, who know what they're doing, and the tourists who are too drunk to know better, run with the bulls. No matter what you think, you'll run off as far as you can. They're huge fucking beasts. Seven hundred and fifty kilos. Toss you like a rag doll. Two of them got one chap between them one morning. They pulped him. I don't know if he was brave or drunk. I wasn't running then. I was watching. Best to watch. Doesn't take much courage to watch. And when the crowd's in the ring, they send in some little chaps. And their horns are taped up. It looks dangerous, and you can play brave, teasing the little bastards, wrestling them to the ground. They start by letting one little fellow in. And the crowd jeers and teases him. He can give a bit of a bruising if he hits home. Things are better for him when they give him a partner. It's not nice being alone. Maybe they should let a fighting bull into the ring. Let's see how many stay in with one of them. The lidia, that's the real thing. Thing is, for all his bravery, even the matador has the deck stacked in his favour. But the mob want courage and they're prepared to overlook that. Maybe they feel courageous through him. That place runs with piss, you know. All week. Great party except for the piss. You're walking in it. Courage."

He put half the orange in his mouth and bit down. The juice poured in rivulets from his mouth and down his chin. He coughed a choking cough and laughed and spat juice, and the knife dropped from his hand. It stabbed his shin and stayed there a fraction of a second before falling out and into the water. The blood followed, first a globule, deep red, then a neat flow, down his leg, over his bare foot, to the rock. He watched and spat out some pips. I reached for Liam's handkerchief and held it up for him. He pushed it aside.

"Let it go. If it keeps going—"

"It won't. It'll congeal."

"It might."

I reached into the water and picked up the knife from the soft mud where it lay, half buried.

"Clean it up," I said.

He put his finger in the blood and then licked his finger.

"I am going," he said.

"What?"

"Going."

"Look, clean that up, it could get infected."

"Would you like me gone?"

"No."

"Liam?"

"What?"

"It doesn't matter."

He showed me his wrist scar.

"I made a muck of that."

Suddenly, I felt scared with him. He wanted to talk. I could either listen or shut him up. I put the handkerchief in the water and then on his wound.

"Why'd I mess it up?"

I shouldn't have answered. I knew after, I shouldn't have answered.

"Maybe you didn't want to."

He sighed.

"Perhaps. Or I hadn't the courage. Lack of moral fibre. Do you think that?"

"No. Don't talk like that."

"You must think I'm peculiar. Is that it? Don't upset Ian too much. Is that what she says, Liam? He might top himself. It's only a cry for help. That what she says?"

I couldn't believe what Liam said.

"I knew someone whose neighbour hung himself because he didn't get a good Leaving. That's the final exam in school at home. He hung himself."

"Poor bastard."

"Was yours a cry for help?"

"No."

I thought it was over then. He just stared at the water. I left the wet handkerchief on his wound.

"I think I'll get in. I want to float," he said.

He stripped down to his togs.

Then he turned to me.

"You two going to marry, Chrissie?" he asked.

I was totally up-ended. I fidgeted and looked at Liam. He sighed and looked up to heaven.

"It's not so simple," I said.

"No, it never is."

Liam spat out some pips.

Ian dived into the water and floated along the bottom. The bottom was fractionally disturbed. I followed him as he floated. He broke the surface about twenty yards out.

"It's magnificent," he said. "Come in."

I was content where I was. The attraction of the water had worn off. I put my feet in as a half measure.

"That's enough for me," I said.

"Chicken."

I raised a finger to him.

"Liam!" he roared.

"It's freezing. Maybe later," Liam said.

Ian lay back and floated spreadeagle.

"It's bloody cold," I said.

"At first—like cutting your wrist. I was scared shitless at first. Then, when the blood came out, I got really peaceful. Like now. I'd given up then. I sat down and bled and felt really peaceful. Then I sort of panicked. And I felt the pain. But when I'd given up, I felt peace. It's great when you give up. It took months for me to give up on Kate. I cut the wrong way. I should have cut with the artery instead of across it. Across, you hit tendon."

I was going to reply but I left him to talk. He was

talking to himself, really.

"He's getting strange again," Liam said. "Get him out of the water, Chrissie, I don't like this."

"I'll go in with him. He wants someone in with him."

"Get him out."

"I'll go in."

I stood up and walked around to a higher rock and stood at the edge and looked down to make sure I had the depth in which to jump. I jumped, and the water broke under me, and I descended into a cloud of disturbed sediment and bubbles. It was a feeling of acute contrast. The heat of my body draining away into the cold of the water, the water cleansing me, washing away the sweat and muck which had caked on me through the morning. I wanted to stay under and feel safe and let the water do more to me. It was not like I was drowning. I was not struggling. I came to the surface reluctantly, broke it, threw my head around, took deep breaths, laughed and slapped the surface of the water with my hands.

"It's terrific," I said.

"Lie back and look at the sky," Ian said.

My shorts and t-shirt had blown out in the water and I looked like a jellyfish.

Ian rolled over and swam to a submerged rock near me.

"I'm going, Chrissie," he said.

"Where?"

"Away."

"Mysterious."

"No."

"You fucked things up between Tom and Paoli."

"I'm sorry. They were fucked up already. I could have torn him apart last night."

"I don't like him."

"You don't have to say that. You don't. I got what I deserved. I wanted it. I knew what I was doing. I think I needed it. It took a hell of a lot to get him like that. Last night was only the end result."

"Why?"

"Exactly. Liam hit me—once. Then he wouldn't any more. No matter what I said or did. He wouldn't."

I wanted to reach out for him.

"Understand?" he asked.

I didn't, not fully, but I nodded.

On shore, we ate barras filled with tomato and cheese, and drank water and apple juice.

Ian lay out and put his sunglasses on. Liam sat with his feet in the water. I wanted to go. To get up and go. Start running. But I couldn't. I wasn't in control of this.

"Are you glad you're here, Liam?" Ian asked.

"Are you?"

"What do you think?"

"I think you'd rather I wasn't."

"Do you?"

"Yes."

"Think I'm a cunt?"

"No."

"Yes, you do. I know you do. You don't have to be nice because she says so."

"I'm not."

"No, you aren't."

"Jesus, there's no pleasing you."

"Yes, there is."

I think Liam realised what was happening.

"Listen, mate, forget it."

"Forget it? Forget what?"

"Look, just forget it."

Then I said it.

"He doesn't mind, Ian."

He sat up.

"Fuck off! Hear what she said?"

"Yeah."

"Of course he fucking minds. Anyone would. Anyone would beat the fucking shit out of me. Fucking kill me. I'd fucking kill—"

"Who?"

He looked at both of us, quickly.

"Only once. It happened only once. And she was

out of it, weren't you? You know how she gets drunk.
I was out of it too. I feel like shit for it, Liam. I like
you, you know? I feel like shit for it. She threw me,
you know? Didn't you? Threw me for you. It was
only once. We were pissed. I don't even remember
much about it. We were pissed. You must think I'm
a cunt. I remember when I saw my wife with this
bloke of hers. I wanted to stick him. You must feel
like that with me."

I wanted to shout. He was talking about me like I
wasn't there. But I was empty. There was a minute
pain in some distant corner of me, but essentially I
was empty. That night slipped in and out of my mind.

"Listen, Liam, I shouldn't have said anything,"
Ian said. "I feel like shit. If you wanted to stick me,
I'd understand. I'd understand."

Liam tried to calm him.

"I don't want to do anything to you, Ian. I like
you. We're friends, okay."

"No."

"Look, Ian," I said, "there's no reason to go into
all this. Liam understands."

Ian kept running his hand through his hair. His
mouth was wide open and his colour had receded.
He had a terrible wasted look. I wanted to put my
hand on him. He needed to be touched by someone,
anyone. To feel human warmth. But I couldn't. I

looked at Liam for support.

"Do I?" he said.

What the fuck did he say that for?

"I've ruined something, haven't I?" Ian said. "That's all I'm bloody good for. Oh fuck!"

He slammed his hand down on the rock several times, hard, so that the first time he lifted it, it was marked, and little stones were jammed in the palm and the fingers, and the second time, it was cut and scraped.

"Here, stick me," he said.

He put the Swiss army knife down beside Liam.

"Don't be stupid," Liam said.

Ian slammed his hand down again.

"Stick me, fuck you!"

"Ian!"

He picked up the knife and turned away from us. I realised what he was doing and grabbed his arm before he could cut the skin.

"For fuck sake, Ian. Liam!"

Liam dived for him and helped me get the knife from him.

Ian stared at me. I felt only sorrow for him. He was fighting to get out. His eyes were terrified. Any thinking I'd been doing was eradicated by the fear he shot through my body.

"I love you," he said.

I didn't answer.

"I love her, you know," he said to Liam.

"Come on, mate, it doesn't matter."

"I couldn't even top myself."

He was talking but he was slipping away. And we were trying desperately to stop it.

I put the knife in Liam's rucksack.

"She'll brain me for talking about it, won't you, Chrissie?" he said to Liam.

"No, she won't."

"She will. I know she will. I love her, you know. She'll brain me."

I slapped him across the face.

"Ian! It's over. Past. Give it up. Please. I care. Liam cares. We care."

"Sure! I need care."

"We do, mate," Liam said.

"I do too."

He moved over to the water's edge and dipped his feet in.

"I'm hot. I'm going to swim."

He was in before we could reply. He stayed under water again, this time for longer, and he wasn't moving, just lying on the mud bottom. I had a bad feeling running through me but I didn't want to believe it. If I jumped in and I was wrong there'd be more scenes. Liam too. I could tell. He hated being

emotional with other men. It drained him doing it.
A failing on his part. He knew it enough to admit it.
Men don't cry. Take your punishment like a man. A
load of bollocks. But bollocks has a way of getting
hold of you and strangling normality. Ian wasn't
coming up. Bubbles had stopped rising around him.
Everything was still. Even the disturbed mud around
his body had settled.

"Ian!" I screamed.

I don't know whether I expected him to hear me.
A bird flew low over the water where he was. His
arms slowly swung out and his legs parted. The bird
flew back again. Liam was already in.

"Chrissie!" he yelled.

I swore to myself and jumped in after him.

It seemed like an age before we got to him. When
we did, I hesitated before diving under. It would be
easy to let him be, I thought. A complication removed.
Ian would be a memory. Out of the way. Liam was
way ahead of me. He took Ian's legs and pulled hard
to get them up and then moved his head, dragging
it to the surface. The sight of his face, passive,
accepting, made me shake, and my shaking made
helping get him up more difficult. We got him to the
surface and Liam hit him three times on the back and
twice on the face. As much in anger as in an effort to
resuscitate him. Ian was jerking, and water came from

his mouth, and he began to cough in spasms. I held his head out of the water, and we dragged him along the water to the shore and hit him some more.

On the rocks, Liam just went ape and hit him between the shoulder blades and on the face. Ian made a swipe at him and then fell around in uncontrollable coughing.

"You fucking cunt," Liam yelled. "You're not going to do this. Selfish cunt."

He punched him in the back and slapped him all over.

"Fuck off," Ian said, choking. "Just fuck off."

I jumped on Liam to try and hold him back.

He was kicking Ian. Ian screamed and rolled over. I thought he'd been hurt badly.

"Get off him, Liam," I cried.

"Fucking fucker," Liam said.

"Why don't you fuck off, Liam. I was okay," Ian said.

"Fucking fucker. You were drowning yourself. Fucking drowning yourself. Who the fuck do you think you are?"

Liam was out of control. The anger in him seemed to make him want to hit Ian more, to really hit him.

"You big pisser. What did you do that for? Why?"

He knelt down and punched Ian on the face. Ian was still coughing, trying to say something and coughing, and spitting water. Blood poured from his nose when Liam hit him. He fell over and huddled up, putting his hands over his head.

"Stop!" I said.

"Stop what? This? You really want to die, Ian? I'll fucking give you death. Let's see if you really want to die. You cunt. You scared the shit out of me. Let's see you face it now. I'll carve your balls off. Give me that knife."

"Don't. No," I said.

He wasn't listening. He hit him again and again on the head, and gradually the blows got lighter and less accurate until he missed him and was only swinging his hands around above Ian's head. Finally, exhausted, he fell over him.

"I love you," Ian said. "I really fucking love you, Chrissie."

"So what? What do you want for it?" Liam asked.

"I'm sorry."

"You've said that before," I said.

"I'm sorry about now."

"I'm still fucking shaking," I said. "You're fucking dangerous. I think I'm going to be sick. I feel bloody rotten. Christ, Ian, Christ."

"Where'd you meet her, Liam?" Ian asked.

"College. You know."

"Yeah, but the very first time."

"I don't remember. It doesn't matter."

"I do. Side of the road outside Avignon. See?"

"Brilliant," I said.

"You'd have preferred if I'd died."

"Fuck off. Selfish bastard. For Christ's sake, Ian, you need fucking help. You're screwed up, boy."

"Yeah, I told you, I am a pisser."

"Come on, Ian. No analysis," Liam said. "We're not ready for soul-baring. I could do with a bloody big drink. Enough to send me into limbo for a month. You know when you plan things?"

"Life's what happens when you plan things," I said.

I tried to laugh.

"Too bloody right," Liam said. "Too fucking true. We could stay here and just stop living. That'd be up your street, wouldn't it, Ian?"

"I'm a fucking wanker to you, aren't I? A big wanker."

"Yeah, you are, Ian. You're a prize fucking wanker. I don't know if I'm not up there with you though."

Ian pulled his head back and looked up at the sky.

"Buster—come on, Buster—come here. Let—let me—touch—touch there. Don't. Don't. That hurts. Ouch. No. I didn't—I don't want to. I didn't—don't—please—please don't."

Liam touched him on the shoulder.

"Ian."

Ian looked at him again.

"Thanks," he said.

"For what?"

"For—"

"For what, Ian?"

"Helping me."

"Did I? I didn't know I did. I want a drink. I want a drink. So I don't have to think. I don't want to think. I'm afraid to think. That's why I want a drink, before I start. I'm still sick with fright. The minute that wears off, I'll start to think. Jesus, I don't want to fucking think."

"Thanks anyway," Ian said.

He picked himself up and went, very slowly, over to his rucksack. He reached in.

"See this?"

"Fuck!" Liam roared.

"Ian!"

It was a revolver, dark and menacing.

He spun the chamber.

"Ian!"

He put the gun to his head and pulled the trigger.

"Ian!"

The revolver clicked.

"Ha!" he laughed. "You thought I'd—didn't you?"

"Please, please don't," I said. "Give it to me. Please."

"Please," Liam said.

"It's his," Ian said. "My father's. He was in—I can't remember where. But somewhere courageous."

He spun the chamber again.

"Here we go, here we go, here we go."

"Please, please, Ian," I said.

"Ah, Jesus, Ian," Liam said.

"You helped me, you did."

"Please."

"Please."

He put the gun to his mouth.

"Cocksucker!" he roared.

He shoved it in.

"Ian!"

He smiled and pulled the trigger. I can still hear that noise. I will always hear it. The back of his head exploded and he fell back into the water in a shower of blood and brains. He lay, floating there, on his side. I looked at Liam. I was frozen. I couldn't speak. Neither could he. He was covered in blood. I touched my face. There was blood on it too. I scraped some of the blood from my face with my hand and stared at it. The water in the laguna was staining red.

The bird which had been flying over the water settled on the shoreline and dipped its beak in the water.

PART III

A WHIMPER

CHAPTER TWENTY-ONE

Liam Connolly's brother, Cormac, lived in Thornton Heath, the 124-125 grid of the London A-Z, over a car showroom. Like most London suburbs, like most suburbs anywhere, a fairly forgettable place. Liam went to London because he felt there was no point in going home. There was no work there. And no matter how much he wanted there to be work there and things to be okay again, there wasn't and they weren't. He was running too, for shelter, for someone to lean on. And Cormac came good for him. A brother when Liam needed a brother. Changed for the better, Liam thought. At home, before, they couldn't exchange two words without a row. In London, they were comrades. And Liam needed a comrade. Cormac said he could stay as long as he liked. That kind of no strings attached acceptance was what he needed. It was good to have Cormac on his side, he felt. He got all nostalgic about Cormac. His little brother. Twice the size of him. His opponent in a hundred fights. Sometimes to tears, sometimes to blood. And always friends again fifteen minutes later. Once, in Lahinch, where they'd gone on holidays every year, religiously, because of their father's passion for golf, Liam had thrown Cormac over his shoulder. Nothing to do with his skill. Cormac just came at him, charging like a bull, and Liam ducked and threw him. He landed on his head, and there was an ugly moment when Liam thought his brother was badly hurt. They'd been fighting in the rain, at night, in a muddy patch of someone's garden. Neither of them could even remember what it was about. Cormac lay there in the mud, motionless, and Liam dived down beside him, scared. Cormac was laughing. There was mud in his mouth and he was laughing. He shoved Liam's head in the mud and Liam let him hit him a couple of times and the fight was over.

Cormac accepted Liam partly because he was his brother and needed someone to rely on and partly because it made him feel good, having his older brother beholden to him. After being second, it was nice to be first. He didn't say it like that to Liam. Liam figured Cormac just liked having his big brother there with him in London. As a kind of protection. That was foolish. Cormac was older now. Older than Liam in a way. And he wasn't running. He wanted to be where he was. He was having a good time. All his friends were there. Liam thought everyone felt the way he did. He laid into his mother's rationalisation of Cormac's going to London. As if Cormac cared a toss or needed Liam to fight his corner. He knew what he wanted from where he was.

"Cormac's in the City," their mother would say. "Doing well. Got a job in three weeks. Plenty of jobs over there. We didn't want him to go, but it's good experience. He can come back experienced."

The great experience.

Yes, the mothers. Sitting down to tea and biscuits, and cards, in the golf club, bleached hair and faces fighting to stay middle-aged: I'll open with two sons doing well in New York. I'll see your two sons and raise you a daughter in commercial banking in Hong Kong. Is that Eilish? No, Eilish is in Paris. She was posted there in October. She's buying a flat. As an investment. Garret's in Saudi, but they meet in Rome when they can. Isn't it great for them? I'll raise you a son who's a qualified accountant in Sydney. And the bidding rises.

The great experience.

Liam wanted to wipe Spain from his mind. Chrissie. Ian. The horror. The endless questions: cut; take two. And he desperately needed to succeed. To make up for the failures. The failures: Ian stuck in his brain like a tumour, swelling. He knew it was there but he could ignore it until the pain came: Ian floating, bobbing in the waters of the Laguna Grande.

On his first night in London, Ben Johnson was stripped of his Olympic hundred metres gold medal. Cormac and Michael, the fellow Cormac shared with, said it served Johnson right and started making racist jokes about monkeys the way Irish people do when they're alone among their own. Liam was feeling sorry for himself and felt sorry for Johnson, and more sorry for the people who'd believed in him. Michael had a load of beer in the fridge, and they drank it into the small hours, watching the games. Michael had a languid look and big ears which appeared bigger because he'd shaved his head at the sides and only had a thin carpet on top. He was into body building and T-Rex, and he'd a whole pile of weights in his room and a juke box in the main hall which only played T-Rex. He'd done law at Trinity and worked for an insurance company. He hated the work and was thinking of jacking it in and going somewhere else. Hong Kong or somewhere.

Liam had a kind of list for London. To keep him occupied. And the first thing he had to do was ring Tony Bruton. He dreaded that. But he wanted to get away from everything in Spain and not have any time to sit and think about it. Tony could help him find work and maybe they'd make up for the way they'd parted. It was going to be humiliating, but it had to be done. And the way Liam was, humiliation wasn't such a big thing with him.

Tony was working for a controlled circulation business magazine. Liam hadn't told him he was coming. He hadn't told anyone. He'd just assumed Tony'd be there able to help. He would have, if he'd been able. Only when Liam rang him, he'd quit his magazine and was getting ready to fly out to Boston the next day. He said he was writing Liam a letter about it. It was more embarrassing for Liam than it should have been. They were able to get out for one drink before Tony left, and Tony gave Liam advice on what to do and said that if it didn't work, Liam could follow him when things were going okay for him. It was all very up in the air. He said he was applying for a visa for the States, one of the Donnelly things, and that it would be good if he got one. He figured the States would be better to him in the long term than London. Liam felt left out. Tony told him some old gossip and that felt good.

"Charlie's shacked up with Lisa."

"You're kidding."

"No. About three months. I don't see them much. They're going to Australia, I think. Clare'd tell you. Haven't seen much of her either. You don't see much of anyone here. It's a shit lonely place, Liam. That's why I'm getting out. You only fucking exist here.

There's no life. And you've young lads coming over here looking for nirvana with a fiver in their pockets."

They sat in Soho Square after and talked about Dublin. Tony kept looking at his watch.

He told Liam to get a job quick, any job. Then he could worry about getting into journalism. So Liam got a job in the accounts office of a printing company, through an employment agency. It was crappy, but the money wasn't bad, and it meant he could go looking for somewhere to live by himself. Cormac had got used to having him around and wanted him to stay in their place—a mutual affection had grown—but Liam said no. Now he felt he had to stand alone if he was going to salvage himself. And he was trying to salvage himself. Trying to show he was tough enough. Tougher than he was. Taking the hard road when there was no need. Getting a place by himself was part of it. Part of standing by himself. It was a very important part. He bought a *UK Press Gazette* and started writing to everyone looking for journalists, and he went along to the NUJ on Gray's Inn Road and got some advice on where he might find some work around London. They asked him if he'd done any subbing because it was easier to get work as a sub-editor than a reporter. He hadn't, and he wasn't keen on being a sub anyway.

He bought the *Standard* every day and rang everything

he thought he could afford. But there was always someone who'd beaten him to it. Cormac said he should get on to an agency for a flat. Liam preferred to look for himself. And the more he did things for himself the more he found himself wanting to do everything alone. Not rely on anyone. Another closet. He was getting more and more uncomfortable even living with Cormac. Better him than anyone else, though, he thought. And Clare was on his mind. She was on his list too. She'd been on his mind since Barajas Airport, since he'd stepped on the Iberia Airbus. Her face appeared in his mind and came back repeatedly, like it was trying to tell him something. He should ring her. He said he would when he got a job, but he didn't. Then he said he would when he got a flat. He was going through the *Standard* again, still looking, when she rang. He was going to ring her. When he'd gotten settled. He was going to ring. She was on his list.

"Why didn't you ring, Liam? I heard it from Charlie Shaw. He rang and told me."

"Charlie!"

"If you don't want to see me, I'll understand. Just say if you don't want. Chrissie's not with you?"

"I'm sorry, Clare. I'm trying to get settled. We can meet. I would like to see you, if it's okay. And don't tell Charlie. I don't want to meet him. How the hell does he know?"

"Course it's okay. Tomorrow, after work. How about the Lamb and Flag? Rose Street. Near Covent Garden. You're working?"

"Yeah. Off Tottenham Court Road."

"Good. Go down to Leicester Square tube station, then left and find Garrick St. It's off there. Upstairs. I'm down in Fulham. It's on my way home. I can't believe you're in London. What's the job?"

"Printing company—accounts department. Dad'd be proud. I'm trying to get into newspapers."

"It's a start. Are you staying with Cormac for good?"

"No. I'm looking for something for myself. I've got the *Standard* now."

"I'll help, if there's anything you need, I'll help. We'll have a great chat tomorrow. About eight. I don't get out till seven most nights."

"Okay."

Liam returned to his *Standard* and came up with three more places to ring. They were all taken.

He got to the pub early because he was nervous as shit, and ordered a lager. He'd had Guinness in London years before and decided it wasn't on.

He sat on a stool, looking in a mirror. Eight came and went, and Clare hadn't arrived. He went downstairs to check if she was there. She wasn't. A plain girl followed his eyes for a few moments and then went back to her clear drink. She had fat legs and fishnet tights. He was walking back to his stool when he heard Clare's voice and his name.

"I thought you weren't coming."

He kissed her on the cheek, and then they kissed on the lips.

"You look healthy. Spain agrees with you."

"Some."

They went over to where Liam was sitting.

"What'll you have?" he asked her.

"Spritzer."

"Yuppie."

"Naturally."

"Spritzer it is then. I suppose it's better than meths."

He bought her a spritzer. While the barman was pouring it, he had a chance to look at her. Her hair was back to where it had been; she wore a suit and a long coat, and a chequered scarf tied loosely around her neck. Her face looked fresh, and her figure was still fabulous.

"I see you wore my tie," she said.

"Do you like it on me?"

"Yes."

"Good."

"How's Chrissie?"

He didn't need that.

"Fine."

"Don't want to talk?"

"Not really. I came here to meet you."

"Did you?"

"Annoyed at me?"

"Not any more. I was. I got over it. I was going to write a couple of times. I couldn't think of what to say."

"No. Me neither."

"So you're over here as well."

"Yeah."

"And you want to get back to scribbling?"

"If I can."

"You're full of information."

"Sorry."

"Lisa's living with Charlie. Can you believe it?"

"All that seems like ages ago."

"They're thinking of getting married. Those two getting married. It's not so bourgeois now. He's working for a law firm. They've a flat in Croyden. Lisa's as bouncy as ever. She'll want to see you."

"Not with him."

"He's affecting an accent now. Pain in the neck. Every time we meet he asks me to a party somewhere. I've never gone. I don't know what she sees in him. Maybe she just needs someone. You've got more serious. Did I tell you that? It suits you, I think. Your skin's better. And your mouth's harder."

"Now I'll go around looking at my mouth and skin all the time."

"I haven't seen you since—"

"No. How's your dad?"

"Not the best."

"No."

"If you're interested, there's a third room at our place. If you're interested."

"I'd like to see if I could get something like a bedsit. It's not that I wouldn't like to. That sounds trite. I thought you'd tell me to get lost."

"No!"

"Okay. And if I can't get somewhere, I'll take you up on your offer. How about that? And I'd like to buy you dinner for offering."

"Is this a date?"

"Yeah, why not?"

"Where?"

"What about Chinese?"

"Lovely."

"We'll have to arrange a time. I'll ring you."

They had dinner on Gerrard Street and then went drinking in a wine bar near Covent Garden. They got a taxi back to Fulham and sat up talking till dawn. Both afraid. Clare told him about a fellow named Peter, who was a doctor. It had lasted six months and she still wasn't sure what she felt for him. She wasn't sure what she felt about anything. And she was browned off with London. He couldn't know how happy she was to see him. To be with him. He could never know. She knew that. But it was lovely having him there anyway.

"I was never big on the Irish thing, Liam. You know. And I don't mind the odd joke. It's when it's told for the third time I put the foot down. There's a couple of real Tory types in our place. Pricks."

"Up the rebels."

"You know I'm not like that. But there's still something about being here. Under the surface."

"Nigger complex?"

"Yeah."

It was a studied conversation, thought out in glasses of white wine. And at breakfast, over bacon and eggs and toast, she was happier. Peter was in Edinburgh, and she was glad. He wrote every week. She showed Liam a box of letters she kept under her bed. Some of his were there too.

"I didn't know you kept my letters," he said.

"I keep everything," she said.

She let him read Peter's letters. He didn't much want to. There was a kind of jealousy in him. He read two of the letters. Peter sounded fine. Distant maybe. The letters were distant. Respectful and caring, but

CHRISSIE 355

distant. When Clare was about to put the box away,
she pulled out a letter from under a small pile in the
corner of the box. It was from Chrissie. An old letter,
from when they were at college. When Clare had
gone to Germany. Liam read it. There was one
reference to him: "Heard anything from Connolly?"
The rest was about Geneva and how wonderful it
was. And there were several lines about Charlie and
what a pain he was.

"She was interested," Clare said.

"Not really."

He stayed the weekend. Clare's flatmate was in
Manchester, and Liam took the spare room. The
Saturday was a dry day, gloomy and dry, and they
walked in Hyde Park, along paths full of dried leaves.
At the Serpentine, they sat on a bench. The dull
autumn day made Clare's beauty stand out, and she
turned a few heads in the park. Neither of them could
recall when they held hands first, but by the time
they sat down, they were holding hands, and neither
of them was uncomfortable with it.

They went to the midnight show at the Comedy
Store in Leicester Square and got drunk and heckled
from the shadows at the back. Ian—Liam couldn't
think about him without seeing the blood and feeling
the pain—had once tried out at the Comedy Store.
He'd wanted to be a script writer. It hadn't worked.

He'd spent a year on the dole getting nowhere. Ian. Statements. He'd told no one. No one could know. No one could share that. Except Chrissie. He brushed Chrissie away.

They didn't go back to Fulham immediately after the Comedy Store. Maybe because they both knew what would happen. They strolled through the London night, streets dappled with light-drenched puddles, black cabs everywhere. Liam put his arm around Clare, and she leaned her head against him and put her hand in his coat pocket.

In her flat, they sat for an hour, looking at one another. The talk was inconsequential, hiding what they were feeling. It was a thin veil, and Liam tore it finally, to relieve the pressure from her.

"Breakfast at noon?" he said.

"That's nice. Okay."

"I want to sleep with you."

"Yes."

"It's just—"

"I'm not Chrissie."

"No. I'm not sure why I want to."

"Do you have to be?"

"I don't know. Are you?"

"It would be nice."

"Very nice."

"You can have the spare room again."

"I think that'd be best. You annoyed?"

"No, I'm having a lovely time."

"You're very—very unselfish."

"I'm not."

He kissed her. Their lips barely touched.

"There's no rush, Liam."

"No."

"If you liked, we could maybe just sleep together. Nothing else. In my bed. I'd like to have you next to me."

"It would happen."

"And if it did?"

"You're very beautiful."

"Something should have happened."

"Before?"

"Yes."

"Circumstances."

"Chrissie."

"Perhaps."

"Are you thinking of her?"

"Now? No."

"But you do. You were thinking of her this afternoon. When we were in Selfridges. I could see it. I didn't want to ask. It was written all over you. You were, weren't you? You don't have to be scared to say it. I won't bite your head off. It takes two to tango and two not to."

Beside Clare, in bed, he looked at her while she slept. Naked. Her shoulders showed from under the sheets. Her hair was spread out on the pillow. One of her hands touched his chest, the barest of touches, and if he had stirred from where he lay, it would not have touched him any more. He should love this girl, he thought, with everything. But he didn't. She was beautiful and kind and thoughtful, and he didn't love her. He felt everything else up to that but not love. And he felt bad, for letting her down. As if he wasn't worthy of what she was offering. Maybe he could make an effort. Over months. It could happen. If he tried.

He was thinking in snapshots. Chrissie was in some of them, and Clare vanished for instances when Chrissie was there. He was a bloody hypocrite. Being with Clare. He had no right. Why hadn't she thrown him out? He'd made his choice. He'd no right to be with her. And yet, he was comfortable. Not like with Chrissie. It was safe. Clare was sure and safe. They stayed in bed until lunchtime. He brought her lunch in bed, and they played Trivial Pursuit all afternoon.

He got a job in a small local newspaper in north London, filling in for someone over the Christmas holidays. The pay wasn't great and there was no promise he'd go beyond the holiday period, but he dived at it. It meant he couldn't go home for

Christmas. His folks sounded pleased enough when he told them about the job even though he knew they probably weren't. He didn't mention that it was only temporary. He sent a load of stuff from Fortnum and Mason home with Cormac, to make up for his not being home for Christmas again. Christmas had assumed an enormous importance at home. Everyone ran their lives around trying to be home for Christmas. Clare wanted to stay in London for Christmas too but he persuaded her there'd be no point since he'd be working all the time. They were seeing a lot of each other but it hadn't gone any further than it had that night in her bed. Tony couldn't go home for Christmas either. He didn't want to take the risk.

It had taken Liam a month to find a flat—in Wimbledon. It was really a bedsit but Liam called it a flat. He had Clare around to dinner in it a couple of times. The second time she stayed the night, but again they just slept together. He was still waiting for something inside him to say it was all right. Something to say Chrissie was over. It was strange the way Chrissie would crop up. A word, a movement, and he would drift back to Spain and think of something they'd done, and feel happy or sad according to the occasion.

Chrissie slipped a bit further away from him when he got made permanent at the paper. They were going to let him go, but the fellow he was covering for handed in his notice when he came back. Clare moved from the Japanese firm she was working for to another Japanese firm. Lisa got pregnant, and they met her just before she and Charlie were due to go off to Australia. Without Charlie. Liam had been dreading meeting Charlie. Conveniently, something cropped up and he couldn't come out with them. Maybe he'd acquired a bit of tact, Liam thought. Maybe. He'd a job lined up in Perth. Lisa was heavy, real pregnant. She was kind of standoffish. Different. Liam decided he expected too much of people, expected them to stand still for him. That Chrissie was right. When they'd had a few drinks, things got a bit better. When Clare and Lisa talked about Chrissie and the house in Ballinteer. And for a moment, time vanished. For a moment. Lisa said to give her love to Chrissie if Liam saw her. He said he would if he saw her. They all looked at each other and giggled.

Chrissie.

"Does she still think she's a movie star?" Lisa asked.

"What do you think?"

"I vant to be alone."

"Exactly."

"It's a hell of a movie."

They all smiled.

Clare gave Lisa and Charlie five years. Liam said

she was being bitchy. She agreed.

It took the cynicism of the Tiananmen Square massacre to shake things into happening between Liam and Clare. She took it very badly because she'd been on a holiday to China and had a pen friend there. She rang Liam at work the day after, crying. They went to a couple of meetings, but in the end they were forced to recognise, like everyone else, how small individual human beings really were: shrunk from the glory of being made in a divine image to the banality of being just another chemical reaction to gravity, Liam said, quoting from somewhere he couldn't remember. A cold feeling.

And all this affected them both more than they realised. After one meeting, they got a train on the Circle Line and rode around for two hours and then went on a binge around Soho. Liam thought he told the taxi driver in Soho to go to Clare's place, but they ended up at his. It wasn't how he'd wanted it, and he was sure she felt the same, though she didn't say. He didn't know she didn't care too much. She was beyond that. He didn't remember much about it, except that it was fast, far too fast, and he didn't do anything right. In the morning, he was sick and had to rush to the toilet. Clare stayed in bed all day, and he went out to clear his head and get away. He got the tube to Charing Cross and sat in Trafalgar Square, watching people protest outside the South African Embassy. He would have liked to join in, but his stomach felt awful. He rang in sick for Clare and then for himself. The fellow who answered the phone in Clare's office had an American accent. He paused before replying when Liam told him she was sick, like he was someone important. Maybe he was. Liam didn't care. He told him to fuck off in his mind.

CHAPTER TWENTY-TWO

Chrissie Halloran stayed on in Spain as much to show she wouldn't run from whispers as for anything else. She enjoyed that. Even wore black. Ian's half-sister, whom he'd never mentioned and looked nothing like him, came down for the body, alone. Ian left a pile of diaries. Black, soulless diaries. Chrissie read them and then burned them. She met his sister for a day, decided she didn't like her and that the sister didn't like Chrissie either, left her to herself and headed south to Andalucía, to Ian's small farm. The hundred vines. He'd given her a key and an open invite, so she took him up on it. She'd wanted Liam to be there. She'd wanted that. She'd wanted so many things. Ian's death didn't change her. No more than anything else changed Chrissie. She'd wanted it to change her like she'd wanted other things she'd done to change her, but there was no chance. And staying in his house didn't help more than to put fond memories of him in her head and make her cry for him. She never wished he wasn't dead. Never that. It was like she'd expected it all along. For him to die. Like that was his role. His part. Exit Ian, stage right. She didn't feel it was being harsh on him. It was the way it was supposed to be. She could only stay a few weeks on Ian's farm. His sister followed her down and slapped a for sale sign on it. She told Chrissie she could stay till it was sold.

After that, Chrissie drifted home and spent six months in Dundalk, sitting in front of a television set, before she went to London. Sitting in front of a television set, watching old videos, flicking from channel to channel, speaking the lines. Her mother and grandfather tried to get her to see a doctor, but Chrissie wouldn't go. She knew there was nothing a doctor could do for her. Her grandfather had a mild stroke out campaigning during the 1989 election in Dundalk. An old Fine Gael hack, he couldn't resist the door to door: Chrissie didn't get her personality from the stones. When he came home from hospital, she played nurse to his patient and that brought her out of herself. She thought a lot then, about everything, about whether she'd done the right things. Over the old arguments. She came to the conclusion she had, the only conclusion she could, any doubts swamped by the sheer force of her character. Or characters.

It was already past autumn when she finally came out of hiding and made her move. She decided it in

a second. Just like that. Or that was how she wanted
to believe she decided it. It was a slow disguised
process, really, but she liked the instantaneous feeling
of it all. It felt like someone had given her the last
page of a script, a missing last page, and now she
knew what to do. Her mother didn't want her to go.
She'd spent six months asking Chrissie what she was
going to do, telling her she had to do something,
then when Chrissie had made up her mind, she didn't
want her to do it. Chrissie covered her in kisses and
promised to write every hour on the hour. Her mother
could do nothing but give in.

Liam was making an omelette and trying to watch
the Nine O'Clock News on the BBC—they were on
the streets in Berlin, hacking at the wall—when the
bell rang. He figured it was Clare. They'd settled into
something. What, he wasn't sure, but something.
More her than him. He couldn't bridge that gap. Too
much of his past resurfacing when he didn't want it
to. So much for erasing it. She called around a lot.
Bringing things. And they went places as a couple.
Clare and Liam, people said. He hadn't gotten used
to that. Should he move in with her? Like the others.
So fucking ordinary, living together. That was why
he didn't want to. Not one of them would have done
it at home. When they went home, they took separate
rooms and pretended. It was okay to pretend. So long

as the cause was good. And there was an emptiness. He couldn't explain it—or didn't want to—but it was there.

So he was reluctant to get up. The bell rang again. He'd have to get up. He went over to the intercom. There was no answer. He swore. The bell rang again. He went down the darkened staircase to the hall, cursing. He tried to find the light switch at the door. It was a timed light, but he couldn't find it. He pulled the front door open and a gust of wind entered, causing him to tense.

"Hello."

Only a dim lamp across the road threw light on the porch. Liam came closer to be sure it was really Chrissie. It was one of those times when saying or doing anything was a complete waste of time. He was not in control. So he gestured to her to come in and led her upstairs through the darkness to his flat, as if he'd been expecting her. And when they were inside, facing each other, in clear light, he looked her over a couple of times, just to be absolutely sure. Combat jacket, jeans, torn runners, hair combed to one side. She made a face and let her duffle bag fall to the hard worn carpet that scraped your knees if you knelt on it.

"Aren't you going to say anything?"

"I don't know what to say. When did you get

here?"

"Today. I rang your office. They said you weren't in. I thought you were sick. I bought some Lemsips and Anadins. I thought you might have flu. It's freezing. I thought you might have flu. And I have cake. Mum baked it. And almond slices. I thought you'd be in bed. It was hard to find this place. Like Rathmines. Bigger. Do you want me to leave?"

"No."

He held her hands.

"You're cold."

"I was wandering about. I didn't know—well, you know. Will you give me a hug?"

He put his arms around her, and they hugged each other tight, trying to press themselves into each other. Liam was shaking inside. She was there, in his arms. He couldn't quite fathom it. He sat down on his bed. The emptiness: he knew what it was now. Looking at her move around the room. Watching her smile. She sat down at the veneer table next to the cooker, under a poster of Steve MacQueen on the wall beside the cooker. Left behind by whoever'd had the place before Liam. Along with a whole pile of James Herbert books. She opened her bag and took out a packet of crisps and offered them to him. He got up, walked over and took a handful.

"Are you surprised?"

"I don't know."

"Your mum gave me your address. She was all bubbly about you."

"What have you been doing?"

"I went to Ronda. I was there a while."

"You didn't stay on?"

"No."

"Go home?"

"Yeah. Lick the wounds."

"I wasn't home for Christmas."

"No. I'd have written. I didn't know how you felt. I still don't. I'm going to Paris, then India."

"I didn't expect to see you."

"You can tell me to get out."

"I don't want to. Have you eaten?"

"I have the cake and almond slices."

"There's a chipper around the corner. Would you like to get some chips?"

"And something to drink—hot chocolate."

"I have some."

"Good."

"I've got this job—you know that, don't you? Mum tell you everything?"

She sat on the floor.

"How are you?"

"Fine. You?"

"Okay."

The chipper was empty. There was a radio blaring, so Liam had to shout his order. Chrissie sat down at one of the tables and leaned on her elbow. She threw smiles at Liam every time he glanced at her. He looked more competent. She didn't tell him that. She didn't want to boost his ego.

"What are you doing?" he asked.

"Seeing if you're different."

"Am I?"

She lied.

"Don't know yet."

He lied.

"You're not."

She was. She was sadder. Beneath the surface. He'd noticed it immediately.

"No?"

"No."

She tossed her hair.

"Think I look like Meryl Streep?"

"Shut up."

She grinned.

"I want salt and vinegar."

"Okay."

"Why were you out today?"

"Story. Out meeting someone."

"You look a bit pale. So where were you?"

"In town. No one special."

"All day?"

"Yes. Want French fried onions?"

"Yes, please. Can we get chocolate?"

"Sure."

"And last night?"

"What?"

"Where were you?"

"What do you mean?"

"I watched your place. I slept in a porch across the road. You weren't in at three."

"Bitch."

"Yes. Where were you?"

"Fell among thieves."

"Who?"

"Clare. Some others."

"You friends?"

"Of course."

He steered her away from that subject.

"Know Lisa and Charlie Shaw are married?"

"You're joking?"

"I got a card from Australia. They're there. They went in June. She's had a baby."

"I should have written."

"Yes. She sends her love."

"Jesus, Lisa. Charlie Shaw."

They called into a corner shop on the way home, and Liam bought three stale cakes for no reason.

Chrissie said he shouldn't. There was enough in what she had. He bought them all the same.

In the flat, they sat on the bed and ate.

"Will you come to India?" she asked.

He was biting into a chip covered in tomato sauce. The sauce was dripping on to the bedclothes.

"Still want to go there? What do you want to go there for?"

"It's there. Paris first."

"What about here?"

He did not mean that as an invitation. At least, he didn't think he did.

"You don't want to come," she said. "I didn't think you would. Is the job so important?"

She was only teasing him with it, she told herself. Only teasing him. But there with him, it was all so exciting. There, with him. With Liam.

"We could have fun in India. And Paris. London's boring. I used to live here. They speak English. I'm sure there'd be something you could do in Paris. Maybe write again—you don't like me, do you? I'd like to get into translation. Ian said if you're good enough, you could make a fortune. Remember that? Do you miss him? I have his painting rolled up at home."

"Don't do that, Chrissie."

"No. He'll have another life though. A better one.

Won't he?"

"Maybe."

They sat staring and thinking for a while. Together.

"Think we could have helped more?" Liam asked.

Chrissie shrugged.

"Do you like being a hack for some old rag here?" she said. "Is it good, your paper?"

"It's a borough thing. It's fun. Very small. But I like it that way. And I do like you."

"Yeah. When you left, I wanted to belt you. I thought you'd stay with me. Come to his place. And you didn't. You left, just like that. Packed before I could say anything. That was rotten, Liam."

"I know. All that. I had to—"

"Some of them thought we did it."

"Maybe we did."

"No. Concha's fixed the roof. The leaks damaged the wiring in her place. Come to Paris."

"I had to get out, Chrissie. How long are you here?"

"Few days. Where's Clare? I'd like to see her."

"Fulham."

"You are pals, aren't you? I don't mind. She's lovely. I love you."

"I thought you didn't like all that."

"I wanted to say it. Do you?"

"What?"

She elbowed him.

"You're going to make me squirm again, you bastard, Connolly. Do you love me?"

C hrissie stayed two weeks with him. He took the
second week off work for her and cancelled a
weekend trip to Devon with Clare. He didn't tell Clare
why. Chrissie changed her mind about seeing Clare.
Liam didn't say anything. The two weeks went quick,
and at the end of them they were lovers again. On
her last day, Chrissie made Liam run around London
with her. She was directing. Both of them knew it.
On the corner of Shaftesbury Avenue and Piccadilly
Circus, they had their caricatures done by a street
artist. Liam thought his was fine but Chrissie didn't
like hers. She told the artist she could do better. He
laughed, and she smiled, and he accepted her
challenge. She did a brilliant caricature of herself and
then one of him. He was really impressed. She took
a bow for a couple of Finnish tourists who were
watching. The artist didn't charge for the caricatures.
Later, on Curzon Street, Chrissie wanted Liam to take
her picture at MI5's door. He wouldn't. Journalist's
paranoia. She said he was being stupid. He thought
perhaps he was. He shot a whole roll of her posing as

Liza Minelli playing Sally Bowles on Half Moon Street. She sang songs from *Cabaret*.

Liam was able to go with her to the station before work. Chrissie was happy, making jokes about Charlie and Lisa. They held each other, him saying he'd try and get over to Paris for a visit, her saying she'd look around for something for him. She cried a single tear from each eye, and Liam was doing his best not to cry because he was self-conscious about crying in public. He dried her eyes with his scarf and tucked a St Christopher into her top pocket. He told her to leave it there till she got to Paris.

She waved and shouted at him as she was passing the ticket checkpoint.

"I love you."

It made him go red. He couldn't help laughing inside.

Outside the station, it was raining, hard heavy rain, and Liam pulled his coat collar up and shoved his hands in his pockets and walked towards the river. At the river, he stood on Westminster Bridge and stared at the rain hitting the surface of the water. Water on water. He stood there until it was time to go to work. Then he concentrated on the story he had to do.